PRAISE F

"Sensational . . . Masterful . . . Brilliant."—*New York Post*

"Riveting . . . [A] chilling tale of obsessive love from Thriller Award–winner Zandri."—*Publishers Weekly*

"The action never wanes."—*Fort Lauderdale Sun-Sentinel*

"Gritty, fast-paced, lyrical, and haunting."—Harlan Coben, bestselling author of *Six Years*

"Tough, stylish, heartbreaking."—Don Winslow, bestselling author of *Savages*

"Non-stop action."—*I Love a Mystery*

"Vincent Zandri nails readers' attention."—*Boston Herald*

"[Zandri] demonstrates an uncanny knack for exposition, introducing new characters and narrative possibilities with the confidence of an old pro . . . Zandri does a superb job interlocking puzzle pieces."—*San Diego Union-Tribune*

"Well worth every minute . . ."—*Suspense Magazine*

WHEN

SHADOWS COME

OTHER NOVELS BY VINCENT ZANDRI

The Remains
The Concrete Pearl
Permanence
Scream Catcher
Everything Burns
Orchard Grove

THE CHASE BAKER SERIES

The Shroud Key
Chase Baker and the Golden Condor
Chase Baker and the God Boy
Chase Baker and the Lincoln Curse

THE JACK MARCONI PI NOVELS

The Innocent
Godchild
The Guilty

THE DICK MOONLIGHT PI NOVELS

Moonlight Falls
Moonlight Mafia
Moonlight Rises
Blue Moonlight
Murder by Moonlight
Moonlight Sonata
Full Moonlight
Moonlight Breaks Bad
Moonlight Weeps

WHEN

SHADOWS COME

VINCENT ZANDRI

THOMAS & MERCER

Published by Thomas & Mercer, Seattle

www.apub.com

Amazon, the Amazon logo, and Thomas & Mercer are trademarks of Amazon.com, Inc., or its affiliates.

ISBN-13: 9781503934238
ISBN-10: 1503934233

Cover design by Stewart Williams

Printed in the United States of America

For Laura, because I found you again.

"They lay together now and did not speak and the Colonel felt her heart beat."

—Ernest Hemingway, *Across the River and into the Trees*

"The important aspect of the mind's extreme dissociation is that each ego state is totally without knowledge of the other. Because of this, the researchers believed they could take a personality, train him or her to be a killer and no other ego states would be aware of the violence that was taking place. The personality running the body would be genuinely unaware of the deaths another personality was causing. Even torture could not expose the truth, because the personality experiencing the torture would have no awareness of the information being sought."

—Lynn Hersha, *Secret Weapons: How Two Sisters Were Brainwashed to Kill for Their Country*

Chapter 1

Venice, Italy
Fall, 2012

A stranger is watching us.

Has been for ten minutes now.

Or maybe I should say, I'm convinced he's been watching us. I feel his eyes, like you'd feel two lasers burning holes into your skin. A pair of obsidian dark irises set inside deep sockets on the face of a man standing stone-still, barely twenty feet away from the table I share with my fiancée.

The man who is eyeing me . . . eyeing Grace . . . is maybe forty years old. He's tall. Taller than my five feet ten inches. He's got short, dark, almost-black hair and a matching black beard that's cropped close. He wears a long overcoat that, at present, is getting soaked in a rain that's been falling on and off since we arrived a week ago.

But here's the catch: I'm blind.

I can't actually see him.

Can't physically see him right now, anyway, which is why I have no choice but to rely on Grace. My affliction, if you want to call it that, is intermittent, what the specialists term a temporary "hysterical" blindness brought on by the effects of the war. A byproduct of post-traumatic stress disorder, or what we old grunts refer to as the dreaded PTS fucking D.

In other words, the darkness comes and goes. Sometimes it occurs in just one eye, but more often in both. On other occasions, the loss of vision is partial. It can last a while, as in days. Or it can last an hour here, an hour there. There are times when the blindness isn't even blindness, but the abrupt appearance of spots that block my field of vision like a thousand miniature white bats flying at my face.

Today I'm not seeing squat.

Not so much as my own hand in front of my own face. Certainly not the creep who's been staring at us. But the blindness has taught me one thing: you don't need a working pair of eyes to actually see something, especially when that something might be a threat.

The threat?

Am I being paranoid? Is Grace overreacting?

I can't see him, but I know he's still there. Standing not twenty feet away, gazing at us, watching us, surveying us. I'm a professional soldier. A lifer. I'm trained to sense these things even when the night vision goes out. It helps that Grace has nervously described him to me with the exact detail and nuance of one of her *Paris Review* poems.

"Should we stay or should we run now?" I sing, somewhat under my breath.

"Or maybe we should sit tight and ignore him," Grace asserts. "We've got every right to enjoy ourselves."

"You got a point, Gracie. Maybe he's not really looking at us, but something else entirely. Something over our heads. Or maybe he's spacing out, looking at something inside his own head. Happens all the time, right?"

But just how long we can hold out . . . *I* can hold out . . . is anybody's guess. I'm a dog of war. The blood speeds through my veins at the first sign of trouble, and the battlefield fury rages inside my brain. There's no reaching for your sidearm or your eight-inch fighting knife in Venice, and I'd rather Grace never know the fury firsthand.

————

For now, we occupy ourselves with playing one of Grace's "get better fast" healing games. A game, incidentally, that never ceases to drive me batty, no matter how much I'm learning to love this woman all over again.

"Now feel this, Captain." Her voice is hardly more than a whisper, but her tone is insistent. Strong. I hear the movement of her hands on the metal caffè table. The rain is steady and loud as it sprays against the canopy above us, yet quiet and soothing when it showers the cobblestones in the piazza.

I hear more since I began sliding in and out of blindness six weeks ago. I hear the sounds of wineglasses clinking, plates shifting across circular tabletops, knives and forks meeting ceramic. I hear the birds, the barking of dogs, the purring of cats. I hear voices. The steady murmur of voices. Inside and outside my head. But right now . . . right this very second . . . I listen only to Grace.

My Grace.

"Come on, Nick. Clear your brain and concentrate. Do it for me. Do it for *us*." Her hand curves against my cheek, softly, for just a second.

The eyes of a stranger on me . . . on us . . .

I want to put my hands on him, wrap them around his neck, thumb pressed against his carotid artery, his overstressed pulse pumping faster and faster until, *boom*, his heart seizes up. Or perhaps a full nelson will do, both my arms shoved under his, hands locked against the back of his head, bending his neck until it breaks. Lately, my imagination scares me.

Cupping my hands, I set them palm up on the table. It comes as a slight surprise when Grace touches my fingertips. I feel the ticklish drag of her fingernails against my palms and the cool damp of the metal table against the backs of my hands. Hands that have reached an age when a soldier like me, well versed in bringing death, should have put the wars behind him.

"Look at me," she says, and that's when I begin to laugh. But she tells me to keep my head straight and it suddenly comes to me: my eyes are drifting again. When the blindness comes (once for two full days), my eyes are not a part of me anymore. They are no longer in my control. They become rudderless brown boats drifting in pools of tears.

"Get ready, Captain Nick." She grabs hold of my hand, sets a small object in it, folds my fingers into a loose fist. "Okay, what, pray tell, do you feel?"

This one is simple. A small metallic band to which a jagged stone is attached. The engagement ring I bought for her fourteen months ago, before I shipped out on what I promised would be my last Afghan tour . . . a forty-six-year-old career captain brought to his knees by a younger woman.

What I'm experiencing is not so simple. Gracie makes me feel like a child learning to speak, learning to crawl. Maybe I should remind her that of course I'm able to recognize something obvious like a ring made of platinum. Or maybe I should explain that being blind is not so much having lost my vision as it is learning to see things in other ways. I must rely on touching, smelling, listening. Remembering. I have to learn how to feel all over again.

But I have not lost my memory, which means I can recall the simple shape and cold metal touch of a ring almost as well as I recall Grace's radiant green eyes, smooth, tan face, and shoulder-length dark brown hair.

"FYI for Grace Blunt," I say. "I'm ready for something more challenging than engagement rings."

I listen for the light tone of Grace's voice. But it doesn't come. Her silence might be as cold and hard as her diamond, but it also means I'm *not* ready for something more challenging yet. It means that, in her eyes anyway, I need to make more progress before she'll push me too hard.

———

Here's what I do in the name of progress: I open my fingers, allow Grace's engagement ring to slip from my grasp, like the pin on a hand grenade. When the ring drops through the humid air, it makes not a sound. But that single half second of silence is followed by the metallic jingle of the ring landing and spinning on the cobblestones.

The table tilts against my hard belly. Even if I can't see her, I know Grace is reacting to the dropped engagement ring like a mother to a wayward child. She's jumped up from her chair with blinding speed.

"Please sit, Grace," I say, now feeling like a jerk for having dropped the ring on purpose. "I'll find it. I promise I will find it."

"Wow, never mind the eyes," she grouses under her breath. "What we have here, ladies and gentlemen, is the same old Nick Angel. As always, I have no idea who the hell you really are."

But I think what she's really trying to say is this: she doesn't know what I'm capable of, now that the war is over for me but has only just begun for us.

I lean hard to one side and nearly fall over, but manage to regain my balance by grasping the metal table. I search with my fingers in the linear spaces between the cobbles, through the chunks of wet, sandy dirt, rotting food, and spent cigarette butts.

Grace inhales, exhales, clearly trying to rein in her anger. Nobody wants to be pissed off in Venice.

"Forget that creepo in the overcoat," she says. "Everybody is staring now, screw you very much." The leather on her coat rubs audibly against the table when she slides back into her seat. "God, the whole joint is looking at us."

"I'm making a scene. My Lord, say it ain't so. Maybe you should call Andrew. Ask him what he would do."

She falls silent for a beat. Then, "Something you want to discuss with me, Nick, that we haven't already discussed one thousand times already? Some things you just have to learn to forget."

I go into lockjaw mode. Because who am I to reveal my true feelings? I'm a rawhide-tough soldier of fortune. A man who can take the torture without cracking. "I think it's nice you and the ex are getting on swimmingly again after so much time. Tell me, Gracie, does the English professor still wear bright red socks with his loafers?"

I laugh like something's hilarious. Without needing to see them, I can tell the entire crowd is once again eyeing us.

"Sorry for picking on Andrew," I say, picturing the ring I have yet to recover. "And I don't mean to keep attracting unnecessary attention, especially with Mr. Creepo over there."

"It doesn't matter to you, does it?" Skin glides against skin as she rubs her empty finger. "You can't see anyone."

"Oh, now, that hurts."

Here's the way I look at it, if you'll pardon the pun: Grace is right. What other people see doesn't matter. It's not like I'm about to get naked in front of them. But being sightless definitely has its perks. It makes me feel superhero-invisible.

On the other hand, that stranger in the overcoat is not something I can so easily ignore, no matter how many times I tell myself I'm imagining his gaze, that the telltale hair-raising tickle at the base of my neck is wrong.

"This is silly," says Grace. "Why don't I pick the ring up for you?"

"Patience, Grace. Patience."

I continue probing, feeling. I try to see with my fingers, like I'm reaching for the extra ammo clip I set out on the ground before the shooting started. I discover the ring wedged between two cobblestones. My gut instinct is to toss it away. Toss it out of the square and into the canal. Toss it away for good, like a man who knows how to take control. A man who is whole. A man who is in command of his senses.

I can't help imagining it flying above the tables, above the heads of the seeing people, above the head of Mr. Creepo. So here's what I do instead: I raise the ring up and hold it above the table like a magician who's pulled off a fantastic illusion. The hand quicker than the eye. The hand better than the eye.

Out of nowhere comes the feeling of another hand against mine as Grace snatches her diamond away from my now-filthy fingers.

"Can we please stop horsing around?" she asks.

I press my lips together and whinny.

"Not funny, Mr. Ed. Everyone thinks we're fighting."

"Aren't we?"

"We're talking. Just like the old days. I reveal a little bit about myself here, a little there. And you just clam up or better yet, say stupid shit to avoid reality." She giggles. "Maybe that's why you like running away to war so much. Tell me, Captain, when exactly are you planning on shipping out again? Or were you going to wait until your eyes recovered before laying that one on me?"

"You know what, Gracie?" I say. "How's this for the truth: I love you more than myself, and you know that. You are my state of

Grace. But what you need right now is another drink. Kill that bug up your perfectly shaped P90X behind."

Maybe she's smiling.

"It's not funny, Nick. You can't see them. You can't feel their eyes."

But she's wrong. I feel them all right. The same way you feel the ceasing heart of a man you've just shot from two hundred feet away. The same way you feel a bad dream hours after you wake up, even if the dream is already forgotten. The same way I feel the stranger's eyes aimed at me.

"You really should have spent some time in the Peace Corps before art school, Grace. A little blood, guts, and shit on your boots makes you pretty indifferent to people who like to *stare*."

I shout the word "Stare!" and the whole joint goes quiet. I can't help but laugh. Sometimes you have to look on the bright side, even when all you see is darkness.

If Grace's embarrassment were a flamethrower, my face would be burned away. Why the hell am I being so tough on her? Maybe I'm projecting my anger. My disappointment. My sadness. My profound sorrow for the loss of the man I was before I cut out my heart and left it on the brown hills of Afghanistan to be ravaged by the crows and the wolves and the relentless, dust-filled wind. Or perhaps that's not quite right. Maybe I managed to rip my heart out long before the Afghan war.

Back when they fished my first wife out of the Hudson River.

Get your act together, soldier, and stop being an ass. Stop lamenting a past that, for the most part, seems like a blur . . .

I reach out for Grace's hand, but instead, manage only to tip over my beer.

"Nick!" she cries, sliding back her chair to avoid the tsunami.

Feeling for the tipped glass, I drown my fingers in the beer that's pooled on the table. At the same time I feel the rainy mist blowing under the canopy, coating my blushing salt-and-pepper-stubbled face. Christ almighty, I'm helpless. The fearless leader, finally put down.

The waiter approaches.

"Non è un problema," he insists. I know he's wiping up the beer because I hear the cloth against the tabletop. *"Un' altra birra per voi signore."* It's a question.

"Uno birra," I say. *"Due birra. Tre birra* . . . and a fucking shot of Jäger."

"Most certainly," he follows up in his perfect King's English.

While he retrieves the beer, the tourists gradually resume their conversations. Grace sits, stewing. I would never tell her this, but I like it when Grace stews. Gives me time to think. Probably if we were back in America, back in upstate New York, she'd have stormed away by now to the apartment we rented together in Troy not long after we met five years ago. Maybe she'd secretly place a call to her ex-husband. But she isn't going anywhere and she's not making any calls.

Not in Venice, where we're four-sided by water, and only one out of two sets of eyes are in working condition.

⌣

After a time, Grace lights what for her is a rare cigarette, slaps the lighter down on the now-clean table. The waiter is back.

"Uno birra," he states. "And one *fucking* shot of Jägermeister."

Grace and I both burst out laughing. That's exactly what the doc ordered. A waiter with a sense of humor. As he sets the drinks down onto the table, Grace reaches into her purse.

"Remember," I say, running both hands over my military-short hair. "Tip's included in the bill."

"Grazie," she says politely. Tyler School of Art, undergrad. Vermont College, master of fine arts in poetry. A dual artist is my Grace. Funny, I didn't meet a soul in Afghanistan, my side or theirs, who went to Tyler or did an MFA in writing school. But I did have a guy in my squad who made it through one year of juco where he studied construction management. Stepped too close to an IED, got "blowed up," as the army grunts like to say, and lost both his legs all the way up to the business part of his groin. Now he's a spokesman for the Wounded Warrior Project.

Grace smokes for a while.

I think about asking for one. But then I'll want to smoke the crap out of a whole pack and I'll want to drink more Jaeger and more beer and my dark mood will darken further. Getting hammered in Venice without the use of my eyes is not my idea of a good time. Not now. Not when Grace and I are supposed to be getting reacquainted after my year-long tour in Indian country.

The initial tour was supposed to last six months, but the army has a way of persuading you to overstay your welcome, especially when you've traded in your dreams of becoming a great American novelist for a career in ambushes, night watches, and enemy eradication—a job I happened to be pretty damn good at. Maybe too good.

So then, getting drunk is most definitely not a smart idea. Not when we're supposed to be forgetting the mistakes and missteps that occurred during those twelve months when we were so very far apart. Not when so many questions remain. Questions about fidelity, about fault. About forgetting. About letting go.

Drinking down my shot of Jaeger, I set the empty shot glass back onto the table. I feel the slow burn in my chest and throat. Grace stamps out her cigarette, exhales the last hit of ash and nicotine so that I catch a good strong whiff of it.

"What exactly is it you've been trying to tell me, my lovely wife-to-be? Or, put another way, what is the nature of the message you are trying to convey with your object identification game?"

I sense a big fat sigh. Because there's a voice speaking inside her pretty little head. It says, *Maybe now's a good time to tell him. Tell him exactly what happened with Andrew. If there was more than that one night.* Or maybe the old soldier is just trying to size the enemy up. The enemy being the unknown and the overimagined. Is it possible there's nothing to tell other than what she's already confessed?

What about you, Captain? You gonna open up for once, reveal all the juicy tidbits you carry around? Tell her about the head shots you've perfected, the way a knife feels when you plunge it between the ribs and puncture a lung or, if you're really lucky, sever the pulmonary artery? Tell her what happens when your eyes get better—about that plane ride back to Kabul?

"I'm trying to help you heal," she says. "But did you have to drop the ring like that?"

"Is this about losing the ring, Grace Blunt? Or is this about my embarrassing you?"

She's shifting uncomfortably in her chair. If only I could see inside her mind, get the true scoop on her thoughts.

"Well, have I?" I push.

"Maybe a little, but . . ."

"Uh-oh," I say. "One of those dreaded improvised explosive dangling buts. Very dangerous. But *what* exactly?"

"I'm not trying to insult you, Nick. It's just difficult for me. We haven't been this close in a long time. Physically close. Give me a chance to understand. You're a different man now, but the same too. You're that closed-in man. A protected shell of yourself. It's only gotten worse with every deployment."

"You trying to say I'm emotionless and so bottled up I might spontaneously explode? Or better yet, maybe I'm the Manchurian

Candidate and all it will take is a specific word or two spoken over the phone to persuade me to climb a tower, start shooting people?"

"Not . . . at . . . all."

"Well, you are aware that in the old days, a man like me would have been referred to as the strong and silent type."

"Yes, you're strong," she says. "But who the hell are you? It's impossible for me to know what you're feeling. I know you see things inside your head, in your dreams, because you say things in your sleep." She exhales. "I don't know what you're seeing inside your head when you're awake. Whether it's me right now, right here. Or the made-up, pretty picture of me you carry around in your back pocket next to your pistol. You can't see the real me, Nick, we're doomed. If you go back to that never-ending war, we are so absolutely doomed."

What I see is nothing. The nothing I see is not cold, absolute black. The nothing I see is dark gray and lifeless.

But here's what I imagine: Grace's fingers fiddling with her engagement ring. A nervous habit of hers I recall from long ago. From before six weeks ago, when I ordered the airstrike on a small Taliban stronghold situated on the top of a mountain with a name I can no longer recall. Mountain 346.1/B or some such army fugazi nonsense. Just a hill, really. Not a fortress but a village made of stones fitted together without mortar, and thatched roofs and dirt floors. A village surrounded by terraced gardens, dogs, horses, chickens, and the occasional cow grazing the property. And one more thing.

A small boy.

When it was all over, and I found myself the victim of an inexplicable temporary blindness, the army doctors and shrinks thought a nice relaxing stateside vacation might do me some good. They promptly shipped me back to New York. But I had barely stepped off the plane when I began hitting up every officer I knew from West Point to DC to pull some strings. The US was the last place

I wanted to be to heal. Too many memories there. Too much hurt from a first marriage that ended in a suicide, and brand-new injuries from a fiancée I hadn't seen in over a year.

I'd had hours to think it over on the plane from Germany to JFK and for some reason all I could picture in my head was Venice. I'd traveled there fresh out of college, and it had been a time of hope for my future. I was going to follow in the steps of Ernest Hemingway, who came to the water city to write one of his greatest war novels while serenading a beautiful Italian countess in Harry's Bar, just footsteps from Piazza San Marco.

I would go to Venice to heal. But I couldn't do it alone. Not in my condition. Didn't matter how badly Grace and I were feeling about our bruised and battered, forever put-on-hold relationship. I needed her as much as she needed me. But if we needed fixing, we would do so far away from familiar places. We would do it in a place where the only people who knew us were ourselves.

Just as it had been twenty-five years earlier, during my first visit to Venice, the future was uncertain. Now, like then, I was entirely blinded to what it had in store for me.

For us.

"Close your eyes, Grace. See for yourself what your memory drags up from out of the past. What do you see first? Who do you see? Me or somebody else?"

Once more comes the sound of her hands tap-tapping the table. She's playing with the diamond and growing agitated. I sense the voices in her head, whispering, warning, scaring the daylights out of her. Who does she see exactly?

"Close your eyes," I press. "Stop looking back at the stranger in the overcoat and tell me what you *see*."

Her table tapping stops. She begins to speak slowly, softly, almost whispering, and I know she has closed her eyes. "Okay, wise guy," she says. "Here's what I see. I see that man standing by the fountain.

I see him even with my eyes closed. It's pretty damned frightening, Nick. He's scaring me with his black eyes."

I down the last of my beer. The sitrep is getting serious. Defensive position officially compromised.

"Black eyes are impossible."

"They feel black to me, Nick."

I turn and try to get a look at him. But, of course, all I see is darkness. Still, you can't stop more than twenty years of military instinct on a dime.

"Well, like the song says, you got to know when to fold 'em. I think it's time we retreated . . . Hastily, me lady." My insides are beginning to do a slow burn. I feel like a helpless new recruit who doesn't know diddly about defending himself, much less his brothers and sisters in arms. I should take action, but the most I'm capable of is waving my arms at the stranger and making a fool of myself.

Grace takes hold of my hand. This time there is no object to push into my palm. No engagement rings, no drinking glass. Nothing. There's only Grace's touch.

But what surprises me is this: her hands aren't trembling.

They are the hands of a calm, secure woman. A woman who, at this very moment anyway, is secure in her love for her future husband and so very sorry for what happened when I was away. The hands are thin and warm and smell of rose petals and they beg forgiveness. The hands are the way I remember them when I asked Grace to marry me, and I want never to let go of them again, the way I did Karen's.

"Just promise me one thing," she says. "That you won't go back. Do you promise me? I mean, who keeps going back to war again and again unless you're programed to go back. Like a robot. Please tell me you won't go. Won't . . . fucking . . . go."

"You're my state of Grace," I say, feeling a pressure behind my eyeballs and my throat constricting. "I want you to be happy."

The pressure builds until something inside my head goes *click*, like a light switch that's been turned on, and for the briefest of moments, I'm in a windowless room, a bright white light shining in my eyes. I feel a tickle on the back of my neck as my hairs rise up and the vague beginnings of a headache settle in. The image fades—but then so does my blindness. A gradual undimming while the shades covering my eyes are slowly drawn open. Shapes begin to appear. A head and a body. Arms and hands. Tables and faceless people sitting at them. Pigeons walking along the cobbles and taking flight inside the square.

I let go of Grace's hands, shift in my chair, and turn toward the fountain. The blurry image of a man is standing there. He's the only person standing still in the rain. He's wearing a long overcoat. He can't be more than twenty feet away.

Turning back to Grace, I begin to lift myself from the table. The alcohol kicks in, making me unsteady and off-balance. I reach out with my hands, try to take hold of the table, but the table isn't there. Grace catches my arm as I'm about to fall over.

I peer into her face.

A somewhat obscure face that is only now taking shape.

I'm beginning to see her eyes. She steadies me, holds me tight, as if to assure me, *Don't worry, I've got you now.*

"What is it, Nick? What's happening?"

I want to tell her I'm in the early stages of sight again. That my blindness is receding. That I can even see the stranger in the overcoat. But I have no idea how long this will last. One minute or one day or one year. Telling Grace that I can see right now will be a cruel joke if, just a few seconds later, I'm once again blind as a bat.

"Let's just go," Grace insists. She slips her left arm around my right arm, begins to guide me out from under the caffè awning, past the tables of tourists who can't help but notice the blind man and his lover.

Stumbling away from the caffè in the direction of the apartment we're staying in, I see the birds and the stone fountain inside the square. Through blurred vision I make out the overcoat man as he follows us with eyes so impossibly dark, they look like two round black holes set inside a gray, featureless face. Just like Grace described them. His gaze makes me feel weak and cold and exposed.

The cool rain touches my face and I sense the hard, unevenly placed cobbles against the bottoms of my boot soles, my heart pounding in my chest, and I suddenly feel the need to be away from this piazza. Away from my memories. Away from the stranger with black eyes.

I've been crippled by combat and bid my farewell to arms. For the moment anyway. But one thing is for certain. The war wages on inside my head, the true extent of its many casualties only now beginning to reveal themselves.

Chapter 2

The last thing I saw was death.

I ordered an airstrike.

The last thing I've truly seen with these eyes is the death that came about because of that airstrike.

For a few brief moments, the blindness has gone away. But I do not see anything like I did on the morning I requested the services of an A-10 Thunderbolt "Warthog" to blow a hot village to kingdom come. I see that moment all the more vividly as my eyes again fill with darkness. See things my Grace could never imagine. Brilliant colors and vivid shapes. Blue skies, brown rock, and running brooks with water so green you would swear it was liquid jade. I see an old village with a stone well in the center. I see it during a time of peace and tranquility. I see women tending to children, and men seated on the ground, finger-combing their thick beards and engaged in heated discussion.

My mind sees something else, too. Something not so tranquil.

The gentle layer of white dust that covers the arms and legs of a boy. The black object strapped to his chest. His little hands laid out palms up over his head. His bare feet.

My mind sees his face. His eyes.

I am haunted by his eyes.

What's left of them.

Chapter 3

You learn to sense the dangers all around you while in-country. You use your built-in shit detector like it's a warning beacon. I'm using it now. For me and Grace.

"Stop," Grace says, as we come to the far edge of a piazza. "Stop, Nick," she pleads, gripping my arm and digging her heels into the cobblestones.

Leaving the caffè, my eyesight already dimming to shadows, I was certain I could make out a pair of footsteps that were different from the others. Footsteps that for a brief second or two seemed rapid, but that slowed as we slowed, stopped as we stopped.

The stranger. Following us? I'm not about to lead the enemy . . . any enemy . . . back to our temporary home, so I stop again and listen. "Is he there, Grace?"

"I don't see him," she says. "Now you're the one who's scaring me."

For the past few minutes I've insisted on taking a circuitous route past the Grand Canal, the water taxis, the barges, the water busses, the sleek black gondolas creating a confusion of swells and ripples in the dark green water. Through three different passages, all of them narrow, all of them going to a different place inside the heart of the water city. A route that will confuse a man trying to tail us.

I can almost feel the fear radiating off Grace, as if it were a vapor. Her arm wrapped around my own, I'm pressed up against her beating heart.

"You're sure he's not still behind us?" I whisper. "Don't turn right away. Just do it gradually."

"Nick. There's no one there."

"He was following us," I say. "I could hear him. Feel him. See him in my head. We should go to the police."

"We don't know for certain that he was. Maybe he was just taking the same route. Or maybe he wasn't behind us at all."

"Do you really believe that?"

"Maybe . . . A little. We've had a lot to drink today. We should just go home."

But I know the truth. It's because of us that the stranger was staring. Grace *and* me. My condition. My secrets. My wars.

The pain returns to my head. Is it because of the booze?

Click . . . A scream coming from a man's open mouth . . . It's my face, frightened, wide-eyed. I'm a ghost looking down on my own body . . .

Dizziness sets in.

I reach out for Grace, balance myself by holding on to her shoulder.

"What's the matter?" she says, urgency in her voice. "Are you feeling sick?"

I shake my head slowly. "Something's happening. But I don't know what."

"If he shows up again," she says, "we'll call the cops. Okay?"

Grace takes hold of my hand, and leads me home.

I set my hands on the thick wooden door of what used to be a shop that housed rare books. So I've been told. Grace already has the keys in her hand. She is always thinking ahead now that she has been forced into the role of seeing-eye human. She pushes the big silver key into the dead bolt lockset and twists. Metal clacks against metal as the bolt releases and the green-painted door pops open. She grips my sleeve and guides me through the opening.

"Watch your step, love," she warns. Already, we have forgotten about the stranger in the overcoat. But then, that's not right. Not by a long shot. Let's just say we choose not to mention him for the time being. We've also forgotten about our little, let's call it, spirited spat. Put it behind us for the moment anyway.

I'm helpless without my Grace. And she knows it.

I lift my right foot and step over the wood saddle, enter into the long, stone interior of the building. Here's where things begin to get tricky. My eyesight is nearly gone. The eyesight is a tease. It comes and goes when it wants to. It plagues me like a demon. Maybe because I am a demon. Just ask the people of that village.

Grace takes my hand, leads me through the dark interior of the building. Like every building in Venice, the place smells of must and mold and decaying mortar. If Venice doesn't sink into the ocean one day, it will simply disintegrate.

We come to the staircase leading to our top-floor studio apartment. How do I know this? When you can't see, you learn to count footsteps. Ten steps to the staircase. Twenty steps up to the apartment. Another two steps to get inside the door, another four to reach the toilet inside the bathroom. Eleven steps to the kitchenette refrigerator and beer. Twelve steps across the living area to the place Grace and I refer to as "the bedroom."

At the top of the stairs, Grace unlocks the door and opens it for me.

"I'll get something going on the stove," she says, but I know what she really wants to do.

"Paint, Grace," I tell her, as I remove my leather coat, feel for the hook on the back of the door, then hang the damp coat up. "You've hardly touched your work since we got here. It's Venice, for God's sake. Home of the Biennale. Artists kill to come here. So do semi-blind soldiers with mega connections in the US Army."

"Not funny," she says.

I picture her easel and paints set up at the far end of the small room directly in front of a French window, its shutters opened wide. There's a work-in-progress canvas set out on the easel and it's covered over with a paint-stained drop cloth.

The small college where she teaches in Albany keeps her pretty well tied down for most of the week, but when she doesn't have to teach art, she wants to be making it. It's one of the things I promised her when we first met five years ago. I would finally write something and she would make art and write beautiful poems and together we'd conquer the world.

That promise wasn't altogether different from the one I'd made Karen just before we married. I was going to leave the army for good. Become the man I always knew I could be. We'd travel, see the world. Live like Bohemians.

Then, on a hot summer afternoon in 2001, a police officer showed up at my front door.

I was devastated, because I never saw it coming.

Not long after that day, two airliners were purposely crashed into the World Trade Center. As the buildings fell one after the other, I wanted to run away. I wanted to run and I wanted to do battle, with myself and with the world. It was like a trigger had been pulled inside of me or a switch turned on inside my brain. The old soldier once again heard the piercing cry of Uncle Sam. But he also saw the pale body of his dead wife lying on a steel gurney in a basement hospital morgue, her long brown hair still soaked with river water. He saw a chance for escape and he took it.

"I can paint after dinner," Grace says, as she takes hold of my hand.

We're both still a little drunk, so I know full well what's about to happen.

She pulls me into her, like I used to do to her back when I could see her face and her green eyes veiled by her dark brown, almost black hair. But she's my guide now. We're standing together near the kitchenette, and as she leads me, hand in hand, toward the bed, I count the steps.

One through twelve.

She brings me to the bed, sits me down.

She takes both my hands in hers. Like the old-fashioned television tubes I recall from my childhood, it can take a few minutes for the light to fade away once the switch on my sight is turned off. All I see now is a blurry, dark silhouette of a woman surrounded by a glowing halo. She is not so much an apparition to me, but more like the last image I will see as I die, or perhaps the first thing I laid my eyes on when I was born.

Grace squeezes my hands.

I squeeze back.

It's then I realize I'm trembling. Me, the professional soldier. I'm trembling on the edge of the bed, my fiancée's hands gripped in mine.

"I want to try, Nick," she whispers, her sweet, quiet voice like a hallucination. Like something I'm imagining.

"I know," I say. "I . . . know."

My eyes wide open, I smell her rose-petal scent and feel her heart beating. Her touch is at once gentle, but explosive, as she runs her fingernails up the length of my forearm. It's like making love with a ghost or with a woman in my dreams.

She pulls on my hand, as if asking me to stand. I do. She moves my hands up toward her shirt, presses my fingertips against the topmost button. She doesn't have to speak a word for me to know what she desires.

I pop the button.

Then I undo the one under it.

And the one under that.

The light surrounding her begins to fade, her dark silhouette losing its human shape, like a droplet of blood introduced to a tiny puddle of water.

By the time my fingers reach the waist of her short wool skirt, I find that I can hardly breathe. I'm not seeing through my eyes, so I can only see within myself. The image of Grace's flat belly and the silver hoop piercing her naval fills my brain more vividly than if I were seeing it for real.

Gently running the edges of my fingertips against the smooth skin and up toward the space between her breasts, I bring both my hands around her back and unclasp her bra. I remove her shirt and the bra comes away with it. I kiss her breasts one at a time, her nipples erect against my lips and tongue. I see them in my mouth and grow rock hard. Once, I bite her slightly with my teeth, and she makes a sound that is both pain and ecstasy.

I open my eyes to make certain I am not dreaming . . . that I'm not about to awaken on my back on the gravel-covered ground of a battlefield, awaken anywhere else other than right here, right now. But for a second I do.

Click . . . *On my back . . . paralyzed . . . a woman's gloved hand caressing* . . .

I pull back, for a brief moment.

"You all right, Nick?" Grace whispers. "You okay? Do you want to stop?"

I breathe. "No, please let's not stop."

She moves in closer to me then, kisses me on the mouth. Our tongues dance and I gently bite her bottom lip. When we release, I place my hand on her bare breast, cup it, pinch it. I kiss her neck in the sweet-smelling place below her ear and hairline. She's breathing harder now, and I feel my heart pounding against hers.

Taking hold of my hands once more, she brings the tips of my fingers to her face. I touch her lips, her nose, her warm cheeks, her eyes. She runs my hands through her hair and she kisses my palms before pushing me onto the bed. I reach up under her skirt and slowly pull down her panties. She drops her skirt and then proceeds to undress me, one piece of clothing at a time. We crawl in under the covers and hold one another tightly. So tightly I can hardly swallow. I close my eyes, but somehow I am staring into her green eyes.

Outside the open window I can make out the sound of the water gently lapping against the stone walls. Positioning myself over her, I enter her and move in time with the motion of the never-still water, my face pressed to the nape of her neck, my teeth biting her skin and flesh.

The more I feel her, the more my vision turns to total darkness.

She moves with me, to the sound of the water lapping against the stone wall, and I feel myself coming to that place and we both breathe harder. She begins to cry out, her voice deep and loud in the studio apartment.

All vision fades.

"Please, Nick. Please, oh please, Nick. Please don't stop."

When I release, so does she and together we tremble for what seems forever, her whispered voice exhaling above the canals. I feel the sweat on my chest and forehead and the good tight pain in my arms. I kiss her mouth hard and settle my face against the warm skin of her throat and I listen to her heart beating.

"I love you," I breathe. "I . . . love . . . you."

25

Chapter 4

We lie on our backs with the covers off and listen to the water and the boats that paddle gently by. I soak up the sound of the gondoliers singing and in my head I see the wonder-filled smiles of the young couples. The sweat that coats my skin is quickly drying in the cool air and soon Grace's hand searches for mine. When she finds it, she squeezes it.

"Was it good for you, tiger?" she says, and together we start to laugh. Suddenly, I am no longer the tough guy I was playing at the outdoor caffè. No longer the man who imagines with perfect clarity what might have happened between Grace and her ex-husband on a single lonely night when I was away at the war. My dark mood has fled the scene, just like I left the concern over that overcoat-wearing, black-eyed stranger at our apartment doorstep.

Grace caresses my chest with her fingers, runs her fingertips over the jagged scar on my left shoulder.

"You never told me how you got this," she says.

"Honestly can't remember."

"Can't remember? A scar like that and you can't remember?"

I run my fingers over the scar. "Strange, isn't it?" I say. "You would think I'd recall precisely how I was cut, or even being sewed up later on. But . . ."

"But what, Nick?"

Once again, the dizziness sets in, as if it's triggered not by a memory that's fleeting, but one that isn't there at all.

"But," I go on, "I guess war is war. What I mean is, I've been in a thousand situations where it could have occurred. Hand-to-hand combat situations." I turn to her, as if I can see her. "War isn't always fought with guns and drones. Sometimes it goes down like it did two thousand years ago. Five thousand."

She nods, but I can tell she's not quite understanding me. But then, I'm not quite understanding me.

"Let's please talk about something else."

"Okay, Rambo," she says. Then, her hands back on my chest, "No dog tags. Isn't that a violation, Captain?"

"Sure," I say. "But then, so is going AWOL. And right now, I am AWOL. Technically speaking. Even if a friend or two in high places helped make this trip happen." I roll over and kiss Grace's mouth. "Listen, I'm sorry about this afternoon, babe. Sometimes I don't know myself."

"I'm still trying to get to know you too. Have been for quite a while now."

"Now . . . just now. I knew exactly who I was. Who I *am*. And why we're together and how I've got to put it all behind me, try to love you without all that shit in the way."

She circles her arms around my neck. "Put what behind you exactly?"

Click . . . *Karen and me in bed . . . Her head resting on my chest, her fingers rubbing my arm, my shoulder, the skin smooth, unblemished, uncut . . .*

My throat closes up. Dizziness returns. I want to answer her, but it's impossible. I don't like these visions, whatever they are. Something that comes free of charge with the hysterical blindness? I refuse to believe they're evidence that my brain isn't right. That I'm getting worse.

When the telephone rings, my heart seizes.

Apparently so does Grace's, because although I can't see her, I know she has shot up. "Who could be calling here, in this apartment?"

"I can't imagine. I don't even know the phone number to the joint. When my contact handed me the keys he didn't give me a phone number."

"We have mobile phones," she points out. "It must be for the owner of the apartment. But isn't that the US Army?"

"I think Uncle Sammy just rents it," I say. "Maybe we should let it go."

"But what if it's important? Like a family member in trouble?"

"Hope your Italian is sharper than it was at the caffè." I laugh.

The phone keeps ringing.

"That means I'm getting it?" she poses.

"I'm blind," I say, rolling over onto my side under the comfort of the covers. "Besides, I might stub a toe or something. It's a health risk."

"Oh, now I see what you're up to." She slides out of bed. "Poor, poor, pitiful me. Some G.I. Joe you turned out to be."

"Hoo Rah!" I bark.

She lifts the receiver. *"Pronto,"* she says. Then, after a silent beat, "Hello. Hello . . . No one there, Nick."

"Just hang up. Probably a wrong number."

She issues one more exaggerated "Hello!" and gives the nobody who's there a couple more seconds to answer. When it doesn't happen, she hangs up, and starts back toward our bed.

And then the phone rings again.

Chapter 5

Grace stops before she reaches the bed. I hear the sound of her bare feet stomping on the floor. In my brain, I see her rolling her eyes, shaking her head. She just wants to get back into bed and cuddle before we get up for good, pop the cork on a bottle, and make something fantastic in our kitchenette. Rather, before *she* makes something and I sit on the stool, drink wine, and listen.

"Whoever it is must be calling back," she says.

She lifts the receiver from the cradle once more.

"Pronto!" she barks. Grace isn't fooling around anymore. "Excuse me?" she adds. "I'm not understanding you."

I sit back up again. My pulse picks up. "Grace, do you want me to take it?"

In my head I see her waving her hand at me while she presses the phone hard against her ear.

"You see what?" she says. *"Non capisco.* I don't understand."

I'm sitting in bed trying to comprehend what's happening. Who is seeing who or what?

Silence fills the room for another beat. It's louder than the water splashing against the stone walls in the feeder canal outside the open window.

Grace hangs up the phone and shuffles back to the bed. I feel her climbing onto the mattress, curling up beside me. I feel her warmth, smell her sweet skin and hair.

"Strange," she says.

"Care to elaborate?"

"The man on the other end of the line. He kept repeating, 'I see. I see. I see.'" She snickers. "I had to ask him, 'What do you see?' But he just hung up."

I roll onto my side, facing her, as if I can see her. But then I *do* see her. I see her dark hair fluffed back, her green eyes open, staring into me, through me, onto some distant possibility.

"Did he sound Italian?"

"I'm not sure," she exhales. "The accent was different. I can't put my finger on it. But the sound was distorted. I don't think the call came from here. From Italy."

I turn onto my back, stare up at the ceiling. A big, black, blank nothing of a ceiling. "I'm guessing whoever owns this apartment made the call, thinking someone he knows is staying here. Must be they rent it to non–US Army people too."

"Sure," Grace says, after a beat. But I know what she's thinking. She's thinking she's weirded out, just like she was when the man in the overcoat stared at us this afternoon. Grace is in tune with her inner voice. Her mantra. Her karma. The man on the phone with the strange accent telling her "I see" falls into the realm of "be warned."

I pull the covers off.

"Vino rosso for the great artist?" I pronounce it *arteest*. "Or would she rather have beer?"

Grace slides off the bed, stands. "I'll get the wine."

"Grace," I say, "I'm perfectly capable of seeing in the dark, even if there exists the clear and present danger of stubbing my toe."

"On second thought," she says over the rustle of her slipping back into bed, "I think I'll lie here for another minute and drink up Venice."

"Splendid choice, Madame."

"I am your state of Grace," she says. "Never forget it."

Chapter 6

I'm dressed in a pair of jeans and a T-shirt, while Grace has tossed on one of my big green "Go Army" tees over a pair of silk black panties. Or so she informs me. But I run my fingertips gently across her bottom just to make sure, and the charge the touch produces in my body nearly causes me to take her back to bed. T-shirt and black panties is the standard Grace sexy post-romp uniform I remember so well, and that makes my heart skip a beat. The very outfit I would dream about while sleeping on the cold hard ground in Afghan country, night after lonely night.

I'm sitting on a wooden stool between Grace's easel and the kitchenette. To my right is the open window. To my left, a wood harvest table that's become a kind of catchall for our computers, spare eyeglasses, paper, smartphones, and Grace's shoulder bag, as much as it is a place to sit and eat together.

I hear the sounds of pots and pans banging, and already I'm smelling fresh garlic simmering in olive oil. I also hear Grace chopping up vegetables to make a salad.

An idea enters my brain. Without giving it further thought, I slide off the stool, position myself behind her, grab the French knife out of her hand. I feel for one of the vine tomatoes she bought this morning, slice and dice it as if I were a pro.

"Nick, what the hell," she barks.

"Couldn't resist," I say, flipping the knife so that the blade lands flat in my palm, the wood handle pointed toward her.

"Where'd you learn to use a knife like that?"

I sit myself back down. "Guess I learned it in basic."

Basic training comes to mind. Lots of target practice, self-defense techniques, and more roadwork than I could stomach. Though I honestly don't recall much fighting knife training, other than regulation maneuvers. Certainly I never trained with a blade while wearing a blindfold.

"Why do you think that man would say something like 'I see'?" Grace says after a long beat. Like I said, my fiancée is not the type to allow these, let's call them *life events*, to fade away easily. Always there must be a hidden meaning, even if there is none.

I sip my red wine, allow the liquid to rest in the back of my throat for a brief moment before swallowing.

"Maybe it's someone's idea of a sick joke," I say, following up with a nervous laugh.

The noise coming from the kitchenette stops.

"You did make a spectacle of yourself at the caffè this afternoon, Nick."

"Ouch."

"Okay, we both made spectacles of ourselves," she says, "and people couldn't help but stare."

"I get it," I say, sensing the conversation going south fast.

"You remember when we first decided to live together and I agreed to move upstate? If you call *living together* shacking up for a while after you got home from one of your deployments."

"That's still living together. My job is my job and it takes me away. And I've only had two deployments since we've been together. One in 2008. And this last one. A year."

"Your job is your life, Captain. Most people talk their day through when they get home from work." She picks up the wine bottle, sets it back down again. Hard. "You know, open a bottle of red, maybe sit out on the deck, talk about the day's highs and lows. But you're different. It's not that you *can't* talk about anything because it's classified. It's that you won't, because of whatever invisible barrier you've built around yourself."

In my mind I see Grace making quotation marks with her fingers when she says "classified," since I've witnessed her doing this on previous occasions.

I sip some wine. Wine always loosens my tongue. I have to be careful about that.

"Some shit is classified, Grace," I say. "Other things," I go on, shutting my eyes as a brief shot of dizziness sweeps in and out of my frontal lobe, "well, let's just say they do not bear repeating. Relaying war stories to the sig other is not my idea of a good time." I open my eyes. "Can we please, please, please talk about something else?"

"You still don't trust me."

"Can we talk about something else?"

"You still think I've been fucking Andrew for months."

I stand up, some of the wine spilling from my glass. "Grace, can we talk about something else, for Christ's sake? I trust you, okay? You were with him once and that's it. All's forgiven."

The place falls silent, only the food cooking on the stove filling the void.

"Maybe," I go on, breaking the quiet, "we can talk about how good it was when we first got together. How much we loved staying in bed all afternoon, watching Netflix, making love. How much we loved visiting museums, going to movies, going for jogs in the park.

How much we loved simply being together, trusting one another, not questioning silences or secrets or when I was going back to war or who might be sleeping with someone else."

I sit back down, drink down the wine. I would pour some more but I don't want to fumble around reaching for the bottle. Besides, I think my hands are trembling now.

"Tell me something, Nick," Grace says. "How unhappy was Karen when she died?"

My head spins. Pulse soars. The rage is coming on. As a soldier, you learn to recognize the signs. Why is she doing this to me? Pressing all my buttons?

Click . . . *Whatever was covering my eyes is gone, and I'm squinting painfully into bright light . . . "You need to breathe, Captain. You need to take a step back, recognize the situation for what it is. A discussion. Not a physical assault on your life, even if your first reaction is to come out swinging. Remember your training. The past doesn't exist for you anymore."*

"Can I have some more wine, please?" I say, a hoarse whisper.

She refreshes my glass.

"Let's not talk about Karen," I say.

"Here's an idea," she says. "Let's not fucking talk about anything at all."

She turns back to the stove, stirs the pot.

———

We finish the wine in relative silence and take our dinner to bed. We eat the pasta swimming in fresh tomato sauce and olive oil, and we open another bottle of red and drink that. When the food and the wine are gone we make love again. Maybe we make love to the evening breeze and to the sound of the boats on the canals and the gondoliers who make music with their voices, but it is a sexual act filled with both passion *and* more than its fair share of anger. We don't make love so much as we devour one another like angry lions. Exhausted, we lie on our backs on our separate sides of the bed, and fall asleep.

I'm climbing the hill that leads to the Taliban village. But when I reach the top, there's no village. I am instead back in my townhouse apartment in Troy. I'm dressed in full combat gear, helmet strapped to my head, M4 carbine gripped in gloved hands. I'm standing in the living room while Grace is sitting before her easel, which is positioned by the tall double-hung window. I can't see what she's painting since the back of the canvas is facing me, but I feel this overpowering need to see it. Like the fate of me and my men rests on what my love is painting.

"Grace!" I shout. "Get up!"

Her face is partially blocked by the canvas. But I make out her smile clearly enough.

"Darling," she says, "you're home. What a wonderful surprise." Then, as she stands, "Come, look what I've painted for you."

M4 aimed directly at her, I swallow something cold and hard, and I feel my heart beating in my throat while I slowly take it one step at a time.

"See, darling," she says, making room for me, "I can see inside your head."

I eye the canvas and see the face of my wife.

Karen.

She's sitting inside her car, the river water drowning her, her brown hair floating like the tentacles on a jellyfish. And something else too. Painted above her is a dark human figure strapped to a chair. A man being held against his will inside a dark basement. Above the seated figure is the face of the boy I killed. The face not really a face at all anymore.

"Do you like it, darling?" Grace says. "I think it's a masterpiece."

The rage boils inside of me. Shouldering the M4 I depress the trigger and blow the painting away. Then, with tears filling my eyes, I turn the weapon on Grace . . .

Chapter 7

I wake with a start. I'm no longer in bed. Instead, I find myself perched four stories above the feeder canal. The roof beneath me is shingled with clay tiles, some of which have been crushed under my weight.

The good news is that my sight has returned, however briefly.

Now the bad news: I'm sitting up on a severely angled roof, dressed in nothing but a pair of green US Army-issue boxer shorts, barely a few inches from dropping some sixty or seventy feet into a canal. That is, if I don't hit the narrow stone pavement that runs along its opposite side.

The obvious question is screaming inside my head.

How the hell did I get up here?

The answer is that I must be sleepwalking.

I've never been known to sleepwalk. I can't ever remember waking up somewhere other than where I laid my head prior to falling asleep. Be it the solid ground of an Afghan hillside or my queen-sized mattress back in Troy. So why should it start now at forty-six years old? The reason behind it must be the cause behind the blindness.

The dreaded PTS fucking D.

But I'm supposed to be improving. Forgetting the war. Forgetting that little boy. Forgetting about Karen. I'm supposed to be opening up and healing. Instead I'm up on a roof and I have no idea how to get down.

"Oh dear God!"

Grace.

"Oh Christ. Oh God. Don't move, Nick. Please don't move. Don't. Move."

"Good idea," I say.

She's looking up at me from the small stone terrace perched against the side of this old building, directly outside the open French doors.

"How in the world—?" she asks.

"I've been asking myself the same thing, babe."

Off in the distance, the view is spectacular. I see the Grand Canal, the early morning delivery barges coming and going from the different docking points all along the main water artery. Beyond that, and beyond the tile roofs of the buildings, I see the wide-open basin and the sea and the outlying islands and a rare off-season sun rising brilliant orange and warm. I see the birds. I see the sun. And it feels wonderful.

"Nick, do your eyes work?"

"Fleetingly, my dear."

"Great. Keep joking. You're about to end up in the bottom of that canal. I just might be widowed before my wedding."

I shift myself, just slightly. The tiles crumble beneath me. I begin to slide.

Grace screams.

"It's okay!" I holler. "I've stopped sliding. For now." Then, feeling gravity pushing against my back, "Grace, I need your help. I'm going to try and shift onto my stomach so I'm perpendicular with the edge of the roof. After that I'm going to lower my left arm and my left leg. If I can place my left foot onto the terrace railing, I can give you my left hand to hold tight. Make sense?"

"Yes, love," she says, her voice trembling.

Gently, slowly, I extend my right arm out and lower myself onto my belly. Then I extend my right leg out rigidly so it doesn't rest on the clay tiles so much as it holds me in place. Tiles break underneath my body, sending shards of sharp clay up into my skin. It stings like dozens of needle shots. But I'm trained to ignore the pain.

Now that I'm lying prone on the edge of the roof, I attempt to lower my left leg. I start by sliding it off the edge and then gently down toward the terrace's stone railing.

"How'm I doing, Gracie?"

"Almost there, love." Her voice is high-pitched, full of stress. My every movement bears its weight on her beating heart.

I feel it. The solid firmness of the banister.

"Okay, now for my arm," I say. "When you can reach it, take hold of my hand."

"Yes, love. I'm here. I'm here."

This time, in order for me to extend my hand down over the roof's edge, I have to stretch. I must bring my body so close to the steep edge that I find myself on the brink of dropping. It's as if I'm floating in midair. Makes me wonder how I managed to climb up here in the first place. But take it from a combat vet: The climb is always the easy part. It's getting back down that's treacherous.

"Can you reach it, Grace?"

"I'm trying!"

In my head, I see her struggling to make herself taller so she can reach my fingers and then my hand. I stretch until I feel our fingertips touching, and then our hands, and a second later, her tight grip.

"Gotcha!"

"Don't let go," I insist.

I pray I don't suddenly drop and pull her over with me. How will the headline look? Blind soldier and artist fiancée fall to their tragic death in romantic Venice. The news will be an international sensation. *Death in Venice . . . Tragedy in the Midst of Rekindled Love . . . Fiancé Falls for Fiancée . . .*

I press my weight onto my left foot.

"Grace," I say. "When I tell you, I want you to pull me in toward the door. You got that?"

She's already tugging on me. "Got it!"

"On three."

"I'm ready."

"One. Two. Three—"

She pulls me in toward the apartment and I slide off the roof, drop onto the banister and onto the slate-covered terrace floor, my hand still gripped in hers.

A wave of pain shoots up and down my spine and my butt cheeks since they cushioned the fall. But at least I didn't plummet to my death onto the stone cobbles or into a filthy, shallow canal.

Grace drops to her knees and hugs me. "You stupid jerk. What prompted you to do something so stupid? So selfish?"

Painfully, I peer into Grace's tear-filled eyes. I want to see them before I lose my sight again.

"I was sleepwalking," I explain. But the truth sounds ridiculous.

"We'll learn to lock the doors. I'll hold you all night long."

I draw her to me and, as I do, the light of the sun begins to fill the studio. I see the back of Grace's canvas. I see the couch and the harvest table and I see our bed, the blanket and sheets tossed about. As I soak in the vision, I sense the darkness coming on. It's like a total eclipse of the sun, only not as achingly slow.

We enter the apartment, hand in hand.

"When I was sleepwalking," I say, "I was asleep. But I could see."

"How can that be? What difference does sleeping make?"

We approach the bed and I sit myself on the edge, then lie back, feeling the small cuts and scrapes from the shards of broken rooftop tiles.

"Because there's nothing wrong with me," I say, my chest filling with a strange sense of optimism. "It's more like my brain is trying to reboot or something. But it keeps getting stuck every time it tries."

"How can there be nothing wrong? Lately you spend most of your life in the dark." She sighs. "Maybe the army did something to you, and you just don't know it."

I laugh. "There's nothing physically wrong. There's only my memory. Or a version of my memory anyway. I fell asleep last night to some bad remembrances. Had some bad dreams."

She lies beside me, curls into me.

"What remembrances, Nick? Open up to me."

I see a dead little boy. See Karen's drowned head. See a man strapped to a chair in a dark windowless room.

"Never mind," I say, closing my eyes. "I just . . . can't."

Grace doesn't respond, as if making another sound will somehow send me back up onto that roof. With the sun almost fully risen and bathing our studio in radiant warmth, I once more feel exhaustion invade the blood swimming through my veins, and I surrender to a deep sleep.

Chapter 8

When I wake up again, I smell coffee. I reach out for Grace, but she's not there.

As I crawl out of bed, I feel exhausted, but still energized, optimistic. The sight has left my eyes again, but it hasn't been replaced with complete blackness this time—as if a war is being waged inside my brain between the power of the light and the power of darkness.

Six steps to the center of the studio, and the blended smell of oil paint, turpentine, and freshly brewed espresso fills the air. The smells tell me Grace is painting. If I look in the direction of the open French doors, I can make out her silhouette sitting at her easel. She is surrounded by light. I can almost feel the fire burning off of her.

"Good morning, sleepyhead," she says, her voice free from the stress and panic that filled it just a little while ago.

"How long have I been asleep?"

"It's eight thirty, soldier. You slept for another two hours after I saved your life." She laughs.

"You saved my life?"

"That's my story."

I hear her get up from her stool.

"Coffee?" she says.

"Keep painting, Gracie. I can manage—"

"To burn up the building. That's a gas stove, my lovely husband-to-be. And must I remind you that at present we live above a book-shop? Real paper books."

"That place downstairs has been practically emptied out, last I looked. People read e-books on their smartphones now. On their Kindles."

"Last time you looked?"

"Very funny. If I'd lost a leg in the war would you call me Peg?"

"You've got to look on the bright side, babe." She giggles. "Oops, there I go again."

She makes the coffee for me, and I take it out onto the terrace. If I stare directly into the sun, my head fills with a light so profound it warms my entire body. Heaven must be like this. Light and warmth and happiness. I sometimes like to think the men killed under my command over the past two decades are staring back at me, cold beers in their hands, smiles on their faces, content voices telling me everything's okay now. That death isn't so bad. It's the dying part that's hard.

I drink my coffee with milk and soon I feel a hand on my shoulder.

"Come," Grace says. "I want to show you something."

Taking me by the hand, she leads me the three or four steps back inside the apartment through the French doors, past her easel.

"I think I'm done," she says, as she releases my hand. "I worked like a fiend while you slept."

"You're kidding, right? I'm blinder than Stevie Wonder right now."

It's true there have been times when I've been able to see with near 20/20 vision over the course of the past week. But during those times, Grace had always made sure to cover her work in progress with the drop cloth. She wouldn't take a chance on my seeing an unfinished piece. Now she wants me to see when I am blind.

"Here, Nick," she says, once more taking hold of my hands. "What do you see?"

Gently she lifts my hands and brings them so close to the painting it's as if I can feel the heat radiating off the canvas. She proceeds to move my hands in the exact shape of the object she has spent the past week, on and off, sketching and painting.

"Take your time," she says. "Try to see it."

I feel my hands making a kind of circular motion. Then she drops them just a bit, and my hands make a more oval motion. Next she moves my hands to the right, then to the left. She lowers them another few inches and moves them up and down, not once, but twice, as if to translate two parallel sticks or piers or even legs. I'm still confused. But, at the same time, something strange happens inside me. I feel like laughing, but I also feel like crying. Grace's hands wrap around my own. Her feathery hair brushes up against my face and I smell its rose-petal scent.

Somehow, I know that what she is painting has everything to do with us. But at the same time, she's being a tease, trying to make me wager a guess on something impossible to visualize. Is the painting a portrait of me? Is it a portrait of herself? Is it us standing together on the Ponte di Rialto in beautiful Venice? Is it a portrait of a total stranger?

"You're making me feel, really, really blind right now," I say.

"Stop relying on your eyes and rely more on your other senses." She kisses both my hands. "Now, Captain, what is it you see?"

"Use the force, Luke," I say. But at the same time, I feel as if a spirit or ghost has just passed through my worn body.

"I know this is crazy," I whisper. "But I see you and I see me. We're standing together, naked in an open field, facing the sun.

We've just made love and somehow, everything is different now." I face her. "So, Gracie, how close am I?"

Grace lets go of my hands and she holds me so tightly I feel our hearts beating against one another. The salt in her tears stings the tiny cuts and scrapes on my face. They remind me of how much I cannot live without her.

"You're seeing with your heart," she says. "For the first time in years."

"But how close was I to seeing what you painted?"

"Doesn't matter," she says. "What you saw was our future, and that's what counts."

My future wife. My life. My heart. My state of Grace.

———

We decide to get dressed and take the boat taxi to Piazza San Marco, where we can blow a day's pay on lunch and a bottle of Valpolicella at the outdoor caffè across from the cathedral.

Grace is happy with the idea.

Giddy happy.

I don't have to see her to feel her happiness. Her infectious delight. It's a hell of a lot better than the absolute panic she experienced when I nearly fell to my death. Better than the anxiety-ridden woman of yesterday afternoon when I gave her a hard time and the stranger kept us solidly in his crosshairs.

We grab our coats and Grace opens the door. It's like we can't escape the apartment fast enough. We step outside.

Then the phone rings.

Chapter 9

I came to Venice to regain my eyesight.

I came to live again and to heal. To make new memories. To forget some old ones. But you can never forget something entirely. No matter how bad. I recall the moment when Grace and I first met in 2007. Between Army Reserve deployments, I finally had time to work on building a writing career, something I'd made several false starts at prior to Karen's suicide. Which is how I came to attend a writers conference in New York City and a workshop dedicated to writing that first book-length work of fiction.

The large room was filled mostly with recent graduates buried in jobs they couldn't stand, student loans they were never going to pay off, and a quickly developing conviction that the nine-to-five life of sleep/video games/bed was the sure path to suicide. They were also convinced that the unfinished opus they had going on their laptop was the next great American novel.

A couple of seats over from mine sat a young, hopeful writer. A woman. Long hair that draped her shoulders, vibrant green eyes, and heart-shaped lips that made her dimpled cheeks glow like electric bulbs when she smiled. I found myself focusing in on her as if I'd traveled by train the one hundred forty miles from Albany to Manhattan to be with her and her alone. And maybe, in some kind of cosmic way, I had.

When the lecture was over and people began to disperse, I found myself searching for her almost frantically. I must admit, even then she reminded me of Karen. They shared the same long, dark hair, same womanly build. Not too thin. Not overly voluptuous. But just perfect. Even from two seats over I had been able to capture her scent. Rose petals. Had Karen smelled of roses, too?

But it was her eyes, entirely her own, that mesmerized me. They did something to me, those eyes. Did something to my head, I suppose. Opened a door in my brain to a place that I never knew existed until that very moment in time.

When I found her by the open doors, her leather bag hanging off her shoulder, standing behind the small line of attendees who were seeking out further advice from the speaker, I rushed over to her with all the urgency of a man who'd finally found what had been missing in his life.

I tapped her on the shoulder. She turned quickly, offered me a startled smile that made my heart beat and heat up and swell all at the same time. Her pale complexion flushed, as if something was happening inside her, too. I'd never met this woman before, but I felt like I'd known her my whole life.

"I'm sorry," I said. "I thought you were somebody else." But then, knowing how silly that sounded . . . "Correction," I went on. "You remind me of someone I knew a long time ago."

"I've never gotten that before," she said. "But this is a writers conference. Lotsa creative lines floating around this place."

Together we laughed. She was witty, and I liked that. The next panel was about to start, but I took a shot and asked her if she'd like to grab a coffee at one of the shops situated outside the tuna can of a chain hotel. She nodded thoughtfully, her face filling with more blood. As she pushed her bag strap up onto her shoulder, I caught a glimpse of her black lace bra through her low-cut shirt. Lowering my gaze, I watched her nervously cross one booted foot over the other. When I raised my head back up, her eyes were locked on mine. She was smiling.

I swear I wanted to ask her to marry me then and there. But I figured I'd probably better wait a while on that. Together, we escaped the conference, like our lives depended on it.

Her name was Grace.

And here was Grace's life according to her own invention: She was not only a poet and a would-be writer, but a painter who taught classes at the City College way uptown. She didn't drink coffee but loved tea, and other than red wine, wasn't much for the hard stuff. But she did like to smoke pot on occasion. I, however, confessed that pot made me so paranoid I would have to insist she stop looking at me, especially with those giant green eyes.

She wore a plain ring on her left hand.

"Married," I said, pointing at her finger as it tapped the tabletop outside the coffee shop. "All the good ones are."

Eyes wide, she shook her head like she didn't quite understand.

"I'm sorry," I said, staring down into my cappuccino, searching the white froth. "I shouldn't have said that."

She opened her bag then, pulled out a pad of pink Post-it Notes and a pen. "Married," she whispered, while jotting down the words. "All the good ones are."

"Hey, that's my line," I said, laughing.

"It just might end up in one of my poems," she said, with a wink. A sexy wink. Then, returning the notes and pen back to her bag, "*Was* married, as in past tense. Well, currently going through a divorce."

A spark of hope shot through my veins.

"You're *not* married?" she added, that red flush returning to her cheeks. "No kids?"

"My wife died," I said, holding up my lonely ring finger. What I didn't tell her was that when Karen had taken her own life, she'd taken the life of our unborn child with her.

She nursed her tea and I sipped my cappuccino and eventually she got around to asking if I wouldn't mind taking a look at some pages she'd written for what she hoped would be her first novel. She had them in her bag. In return perhaps she could read something of mine.

"I'd love to read your stuff," I said, finishing my coffee. "Maybe we can find some quiet space in my hotel. And something a little harder to drink. Like red wine, for instance."

New York City was congested with cars speeding past, hordes of suited workers and poorly dressed tourists crowding the sidewalks, and the din of thousands of conversations going on all at once.

But somehow the whole world stood still.

Grace got up, looked one way and then the other. With her eyes peering not at me, but up past the glass-and-steel towers at the blue heavens, she said, "Okay. Yes. Why the hell not?"

———

We weren't three feet inside the hotel room before our mouths were locked and I was undressing her and she was undressing me. Our trail of jeans, underwear, coats, and sweaters led to the queen-sized bed. It was awkward and first-timey until at one point, we both started laughing and I was able to feel more at one with her as I entered her, our hips pressed together, her wet heat surrounding my hardness, drawing me further and further in.

Afterward, she lay with her head on my chest and I ran my fingers through her hair. I asked her to tell me about her ex-husband.

She looked at me with frightened eyes. "Well, aren't you the master of apropos pillow talk?"

I laughed.

"What's his name?" I said.

"Andrew," she whispered after a weighted pause. "And I loved him once upon a time. Loved him very much."

He was a professor, she told me, and a musician. For a long time he was one of the most loving and open men she'd ever known.

"We were together sixteen years before we separated," she exhaled. "For the last couple of years, we had sex *maybe* four or five times at most. Currently, I'm thirty-three years young."

"Almost half of your life," I said after a while, my fingers still dancing in her thick hair. "That's an awfully long time to be with any one person."

"I never looked at it that way. But yes, half my life."

"You're beautiful, smart, talented," I said. "Even your brains are sexy."

She made a fist, lightly punched my arm. A love tap.

"For as much as Andrew claimed to love me, he just couldn't keep himself from offering extra office hours to a series of blonde, blue-eyed coeds."

"At least he kept his preferences specific. I guess I'd say I'm sorry if it wasn't such a cliché. But the professor's loss is my . . ."

"Oh no. Don't be sorry. He's the one who's sorry now that I walked out on him."

Afterward we got out of bed to take a shower together. I slipped on the porcelain and she reached out and caught me before I fell, but not before I tore the plastic curtain off the rings. We laughed so hard I found it impossible to comprehend that we'd only just met and that she'd loved a less-than-loyal professor named Andrew for half her living years.

We got out and as we dried off, the atmosphere began to take on a more serious tone. Without saying so, both of us were realizing that what we'd just shared, as beautiful as it was, was rapidly and cruelly fleeting.

Now fully dressed, she looked at her watch. "I have to get to work."

When she was gone, I felt the dreadful emptiness settle in. It'd been a long time since I'd been with a woman and an even longer time since I'd allowed myself to fall in love so easily. I thought about Karen. Her brown eyes, her dark hair, her never-ceasing optimism. The type of woman who wouldn't stress if we were broke, but instead would plant a beaming smile on her face and sing, "But we have each other, my dear." How she was able to hide her depression was and is beyond me. The courage and resolve it took for her to drive the car into the river on a hot summer afternoon surely paled in comparison to the strength it must have taken her to live each day, day in and day out, while planting that smile on her face.

Or maybe her depression had something to do with me and the things I couldn't talk about. The things I'd seen in the Persian Gulf War, things I carried with me as a professional soldier.

Then came her suicide and not long after that, the 9/11 attack on the World Trade Center. I was called back to fight, but I would have volunteered anyway. War was nothing if not the ultimate distraction. But that's putting it lightly. I felt a craving for going to war like a child craves candy.

During the hot summer of 2007 I was still a reservist, but instead of war and destruction, I was looking to do something creative with my days and nights. It was fate or providence or good luck that another woman had suddenly entered my life, not to take Karen's place, but to fill a long-empty void.

I stood in the hotel room smelling Grace's sweet, flowery scent and realized she hadn't even left me her phone number. At the thought that I might never see her again, that the lightness I'd felt, however briefly, would be gone forever, my stomach sank. Opening the door, I stepped into the hall and searched for her.

But she was already gone.

Turning, I saw that a pink Post-it Note had been stuck to the plastic Do Not Disturb hangtag. I peeled the note off and read it.

No longer married.
All the good ones are.

It wasn't a note at all, but a poem that made me laugh and tear up at the same time. Below the poem was her cell phone number and below that, an *XOX*, just like two young kids exchanging love letters.

Chapter 10

We've barely slipped on our coats, barely stepped out onto the landing when the phone rings. The clanging bell isn't just the sound an old phone makes. It's an alarm. An alarm that tells me there's been a breach. That someone or something has cut through our invisible barrier and is about to unleash something very unpleasant on us.

"Let me get it this time," I say, the excitement of heading out to lunch together now suddenly replaced with a dread. Like the floor is about to open up right out from under my feet.

I step back inside the apartment, shuffle the couple of steps to my right, to the wall-mounted phone beside the door. I feel for the cordless receiver, pick it up.

"Pronto."

My ear fills with white noise. Not loud white noise. More like the static that comes from a bad connection, or a cell phone with bad reception. I listen for a voice, but hear nothing other than static.

"Who is it?" Grace asks from the landing, her words echoing in the open stairwell.

I find myself turning in order to glance at her. But of course, this is just instinct kicking in. The sound of her booted feet shuffling against the stone tells me she's taking a step closer. "It's him again, isn't it?"

I hold up my hand.

Grace gets the message and goes silent. I think she's holding her breath.

"Who's there?" I say into the phone. Tone even-keeled, not at all threatening.

There is only the white noise. Until it's broken by a faint voice.

"I . . . see," says the voice. It sounds like a man. Perhaps an old man who is talking to me over the phone from a great distance away. But this is the age of satellites. He could be located on the other side of the world and sound like he's standing downstairs in the empty bookshop.

"What do you see?" I say, pulse now throbbing in my temples.

More white noise.

"I see," he repeats.

"Who is this? What is your name? Tell me your name, damn it." I'm lobbing the queries but they don't seem to be registering in the least. Not because the man on the other end doesn't hear me. But because he doesn't want to answer me.

Once more the receiver fills with white noise, and once more come the words, softly spoken: "I see."

Then the line goes dead.

"Hello," I bark into the phone. "Hello. Hello. Hello . . ."

But it's no use. The man on the phone is gone. Disconnected.

Grace steps inside the apartment. "May I?"

It startles me when she pulls the phone from my hand and punches in a couple of numbers. Instinct kicks in. I raise up my right hand, make a fist. But what the hell am I doing? It's Grace, not the enemy. In my throbbing head I picture her taut cheeks, her lips pressed together, her eyes bright and wide. It's the face she wears when she's angry or upset. I take a breath and try to calm myself down.

"What's happening?" I say. A breeze slips through the apartment's open door.

"Star sixty-nine."

"You sure that works in Europe? In Italy?"

"We'll soon find out."

I wait along with Grace, who holds out the phone so I'm able to discern the faint, tinny sound of the computer-generated operator speaking in rapid-fire Italian. I can't understand a word she's saying, but I sense Grace is trying her best to make sense of it all.

"Well?"

"Greek to me," she jokes. But I know it's not funny. Then she adds, "Something about the number I just dialed is not correct or can't be connected."

"The man is calling from a cell phone, maybe, his number blocked."

Graces reaches beyond me with the phone, her arm brushing up against my shoulder, hangs it up in its cradle.

The room fills with a hard silence.

"Does anyone know we're here, Nick?"

I shake my head. "Far as I know, almost no one. Just a couple of guys who helped me out."

"Do they often rent this apartment out to other wounded soldiers?"

Wounded soldier. I've never thought of myself as a wounded soldier or wounded warrior . . . a casualty of war. But I guess that's precisely what I am. A casualty.

"I doubt it. They reserve it for healthy officers. We're only here as a favor." I dig in my pocket for my cell. "I can make a call or two to DC—"

Grace grabs hold of my arm.

"Let's just go," she insists. "I'm sure there's a logical explanation for whoever's called to let us know he can *see* something . . . whatever that's supposed to mean."

"Maybe it's like I said. Some asshole's idea of a bad joke."

"Or bad timing." She heads for the door. "You coming?"

"Yes," I say, trying to imagine someone standing somewhere in the world speaking the words "I see" into a cell phone. I envision a bald, craggy-faced old man. Perhaps the man who used to own the rare bookshop.

"Close the door behind you," Grace says as she begins descending the steps to the first floor.

My hand on the brass knob, I feel the blood coursing rapidly through my veins. This isn't raw nerves so much as my gut speaking to me, telling me to be vigilant, to keep my guard up.

I close the door. Hard. And the building begins to spin.

Click . . . *My shoulder slams against the concrete floor . . . a steel door slams closed behind me . . .*

Panicked, I reach out for the railing, hold on to it with both hands.

"Nick, what's wrong?" Gracie calls up to me from down below.

Jesus, get it together, Captain. Shut off your goddamned brain.

I peel my left hand away from the rail, begin feeling my way down the stairs, like I'm the blind man descending into hell. But what I'm beginning to realize is this: the hell is in my mind.

"Be careful," Grace reminds me.

"Grace, cut it out!" I bark, my voice echoing in the stairwell.

I stop my descent.

Silence ensues. Weighted and dreadful.

"I'm sorry," I say. "Those phone calls . . . They're getting to me."

"Just . . . take your time," she says.

"I will," I say, now once again feeling my way down each step, my hand securely on the rail.

Chapter 11

The waiter is formally attired in a white shirt, black trousers, and matching jacket, a clean white towel draped over his forearm. Or so Grace tells me. He escorts us to a table that overlooks the San Marco Basin and the small islands set in the near distance. Torcello and Murano among them.

Torcello.

Where Papa Hemingway fell in love with a beautiful Italian countess by the name of Adriana. He was not much older than I am now, and still licking his wounds from World War II, where he reported from the front lines in the dreadful, deadly Hürtgen Forest. She was nineteen and ravishing, and her family fortune was dwindling. Hemingway fell head over heels for her and even asked her to marry him, though he was already married at the time. She said no, of course. He worshipped her anyway and spent many lonely days and nights in Venice writing a novel in which their love became more real than if it had truly happened, but for which he was badly maligned by the New York critics who suggested he'd become a poor parody of himself. Plagued by severe memory loss resulting from a series of electroconvulsive shock therapy sessions, he would eventually shoot himself in the head with his prized Italian side-by-side twelve-gauge shotgun. The Italian countess would later hang herself from the rafters in her apartment overlooking the Grand Canal.

The wind picks up off the basin.

It seems to seep right through my leather coat into flesh, skin, and bone. I try to hold my face up to the sun while the waiter takes our orders. Grace orders a single glass of vino rosso along with a pancetta and cheese panino. I forgo the Valpolicella and order a Moretti beer and a simple spaghetti pomodoro.

We sit in the calm of the early afternoon, the sounds of the boat and vaporetto traffic coming and going filling my ears. People surround us on all sides. Tourists who have come to San Marco for the first time and who've become mesmerized. The stone square, the cathedral, the bell tower, the many shops and high-end eateries that occupy the wide, square-shaped perimeter. The pigeons. The people. Always throngs of people coming and going amidst a chorus of bells, bellowing voices, live music emerging from trumpets, violins, and guitars, and an energetic buzz that seems to radiate up from underneath all that stone and sea-soaked soil.

It's late November.

Here's what I know about Venice: in just a week or two, the rains will fall even harder and more frequently and this square will be underwater. The ever-sinking Venice floods easily now. The only way to traverse the square will be over hastily constructed plank walkways. Many of the tourists will stay away and the live music will be silenced. But somehow, that's when Venice will come alive more than ever. When the stone is bathed in water.

The waiter brings our drinks and food.

With the aroma of the hot spaghetti filling my senses, I dig in and spoon up a mouthful. I wash the hot, tangy, sauce-covered pasta down with a swallow of beer.

"Whoa, slow down, Captain." Grace giggles. "Eating, smiling, making love to me. What's next? Writing something? Maybe even opening up about the past?"

"Don't press your luck, Gracie. Just don't start asking me to identify engagement rings."

She laughs genuinely and I listen to the sounds of her taking a bite out of her sandwich. But then she falls quiet again. Too quiet, as if she's stopped breathing altogether.

"There's someone staring at us again," she says under her breath.

The tickle on the back of my neck . . . The *click* in my brain that signals and awakens my senses . . . My right hand reaching for a sidearm that isn't there . . .

"Man or woman?" I say, trying to position my gaze directly across the table at her, but making out nothing more than her silhouette framed against the brightness of the sun. Later on, when the sun goes down, the image of her will be entirely black. Like the blackness of the Afghan Tajik country when the fires are put out, the lights extinguished, and you lie unmoving on your back and you feel the beating of your heart and you pray for morning.

"Man," she whispers.

"What's he look like?"

"Jesus, it's him again. The man in the overcoat who was staring at us yesterday."

I put my fork down on my plate. "You sure?"

"He's wearing sunglasses this time. But it's him."

"What's he look like?"

"I'm afraid, Nick."

"Slow down, take a breath, tell me what he looks like. I just want to be sure it's him. The same man."

I hear her inhale, exhale. "He's thin. A little taller than you. He's got a dark complexion."

"Black?"

"No. More like Asian or Middle Eastern. It's the same man, Nick. He's wearing sunglasses and that same dark, brownish overcoat and a scarf. His hair is black and cut close to his scalp. His beard is trimmed." I hear her take a quick, nervous sip of her wine. "He keeps staring at us. At me. Just like yesterday, Nick."

"How do you know he's staring at you? It could be something behind you. We're in Venice. Lots going on behind you. Lots to see."

She's stirring in her chair. Agitated.

"Because I can feel him. His eyes . . . I feel his eyes."

Just like I felt them yesterday and feel them again right now . . .

I wipe my mouth clean with the cloth napkin, and then I do something entirely silly. I turn around in my chair to get a look at the man. When will I ever stop doing that?

"What are you doing?" Grace asks, the anxiety in her voice growing more intense with each passing second.

"Trying to get a look at him."

"You're joking, Nick."

I turn back, try to focus on her without the use of my eyes. "You think?"

We sit silent.

Once more I am helpless and impotent.

"Sorry," she says after a time. "But this man is at the same caffè we're at two days in a row? This is really starting to creep me out, babe. Really scaring me now."

My pulse begins to race. Two steady drumbeats against my temples. I find myself wanting to swallow, but my mouth has gone dry. What I wouldn't give for a little vision right now. I take a sip of beer, thinking it will help calm distressed nerves.

"He's coming toward us, Nick. I don't like it."

A second distinct *click* in my head. Heart pounds against my sternum. Blood speeds through the veins. Battleground conditions.

"Are you sure?" I'm trying not to raise my voice, but it's next to impossible.

"He's looking right at me. His hands are stuffed in the pockets of his overcoat. And he's coming."

I feel and hear her pushing away from the table. That's when the smell sweeps over me. A rich, organic, incense-like smell.

Then comes the sound of Grace standing. Abruptly standing. I hear her metal chair push out. Hear the sound of her boot heels on the cobbles. Hear the chair legs scraping against the stone. Hear the clink of her wineglass wobbling, tipping.

"Grace, for God's sake, be careful," I say. But my entire being is filled with confusion and fear.

She doesn't respond. I hear no sound at all other than the boats on the basin and the constant murmur of the thousands of tourists that fill this ancient square.

"Grace," I say. "Grace. Stop it. This isn't funny. Grace."

The smell of incense is gone.

I make out gulls flying over the tables, birds shooting in from the basin to pick up scraps of food and then, like thieves in the night, shooting back out over the water. I hear and feel the sound-wave-driven music reverberating against the stone cathedral.

"Grace," I repeat, louder now. "Grace. Grace . . . Grace!"

Nothing.

It's like she's gone. Vanished. But how can she be gone? She was just sitting here with me. She was sitting directly across from me, eating a sandwich and drinking wine. She was talking with me.

The waiter approaches. "The signora is not liking her food?"

I reach out across the table. To the place where she was sitting. She is definitely not there.

"Is there a toilet close by?" I ask. "Did you see my fiancée leave the table and go to the toilet?"

The waiter pauses for a moment. "I am sorry. But I did not. I was inside the caffè."

"Then maybe somebody else saw her. Maybe you can ask them."

"Signor, there are many tables in this caffè and they are filled with people. And there are many people who walk among the tables. No one seems to be concerned about anything. Sometimes there are so many people here, it is easy to get lost. Perhaps she did go to the toilet, and she got lost among the people. I will come back in a moment and make sure all is well."

The waiter leaves, his footsteps fading against the slate.

I sit and stare at nothing. My heart is pounding so fast I think it will cease at any moment. What I have in place of vision is a blank wall of blurry adrenaline-fueled illumination no longer filled with the silhouette of Grace.

I push out my chair. Stand. My legs knock into the table and my glass of beer spills. I cup my hands around my mouth.

"Grace!" I shout. "Grace! Grace!"

The people surrounding me slip into quiet alarm as I scream over them.

The waiter comes running back over.

"Please, please," he says, taking me by the arm. "Please come with me."

He leads me through the throng of tables and people. He is my sight now that Grace has disappeared.

"She's gone, isn't she? Did you check the toilets?" I beg.

"We checked the toilets. They are empty. I am sorry. I am sure there is a reason . . . a, how you say . . . explanation."

"A man took her away," I shout. "How could no one have seen it?"

"You're frightening the patrons, signor. Please just come with me and we will try to find her."

I reach out for the people sitting at a table beside me. I know they must be looking at me, gawking. Maybe they're as frightened as I am.

I reach out, grab at nothing. But when I reach out again, I feel an arm. A man's arm.

"Did you see my fiancée leave?" I plead.

The man yanks his arm away. He speaks something in a language I do not recognize. It is most definitely not Italian.

"Anyone," I say. "Did anyone see the woman who was sitting across from me leave the table? Did she leave with a man who wears an overcoat and sunglasses? Somebody speak to me. In English. Somebody."

But all I get are confused, murmured voices, as if the people who were sitting so close to Grace never noticed her vanishing into thin air.

The waiter puts his hand on my shoulder.

"Please, signor," he repeats, "the patrons seem to know nothing. It will be better if we discuss this somewhere else."

I slap his hand away from my shoulder.

"Grace is gone," I say. "Don't you fucking understand me? My Grace is gone."

Chapter 12

By the sounds and feel of it, I'm led through a dining room into a small room located in the very back of the caffè. The wooden door is closed behind me, and I am offered a chair. After I give him permission to look through the many photos I have of Grace stored on my mobile phone, the waiter pours me a snifter of brandy, tells me to drink it.

"It will make you feel, how you say, all the better," he insists in somewhat broken but surprisingly good English.

I do it.

In the meantime, with the waiter's help, I speed-dial Grace's cell phone. While he checks for her in the area surrounding the exterior portion of the caffè, I press the phone to my ear. I get only the voice mail. After leaving five messages begging her to call me, I'm connected with an automated recording telling me her mailbox is full. I imagine that the man who took her away from me has tossed her phone into the Grand Canal.

When the waiter returns, I know what he's about to tell me before he says it. I don't need eyesight to see his ashen face. I hear the sad sluggishness of his gait and the defeated shuffling of the soles on his leather shoes on the wooden floorboards.

"Perhaps the time is here to call the police," he whispers.

My heart plummets.

Chapter 13

He introduces himself as Detective Paulo Carbone and he's a somewhat burly, well-dressed Venetian police official of middle age. Or so I picture him, judging by his excellent English and the smooth, low tone of his voice. Like a pack-a-day smoker now trying to quit and succeeding. When I hear him lighting up with a good old-fashioned Zippo-style flip-top lighter, I'm confident the picture I've painted in my head is not entirely inaccurate.

I'm seated in a wooden chair before his desk inside the Venice Polizia, or the Polizia di Stato, headquarters. I was transported here by a uniformed policeman who, despite grilling several of the caffè patrons, insisted that a crime-scene investigation was not yet in order since it is possible my fiancée simply disappeared of her own accord. A notion that not only fills me with dread, but that makes my already-ailing heart nearly quit on me altogether.

After the detective orders hard-copy prints of several photographs of Grace from the batch on my phone, he makes note of her vitals: name, age, weight, height, eye, hair, and skin color. He then begins probing into what he defines as "the situation."

"We were having lunch at the caffè outside the cathedral in Piazza San Marco. Grace spotted a man staring at us. A middle-aged man with a dark complexion who wore sunglasses. He was thin, a little taller than me. In good physical shape anyway. He had a trim beard and he had on a long brown or brownish overcoat. It's possible he's been following us."

"Why do you say that?"

"Because we spotted him staring at us at a different caffè not far from here. If only you could have seen his eyes."

"You say he wore sunglasses. How could you see his eyes?"

"I saw his eyes yesterday afternoon, goddammit." My voice rises. "They're dark eyes. Like the whites are missing. Or burned away from constant exposure to the sun."

"You've spotted the man before."

"I just told you that, Detective." Then, "Listen, instead of sitting here doing nothing, don't you think it would be a good idea to check my apartment? Maybe Grace went back there after she disappeared?"

"My men have already checked your apartment above the bookshop. She's not there. No suspicious activity reported around the place." He smokes a little. "But let's get back to his eyes. What color eyes did you say he had?" I feel like I'm back on the line. Like I've just spent two weeks in hostile territory and some West Point hotshot who can't tell the difference between the caliber on his sidearm and the diameter of his asshole is grilling me over why I didn't bring him enough scalps to make him look good to command.

"Black. Or dark brown. Shall I tell you what color they are a third time?"

He laughs. "Maybe. It's just that I'm confused. The man you saw today was wearing sunglasses?"

"That's correct. But it was raining yesterday."

"Yes," he says, writing something down. "It was raining. And you think the man you saw yesterday and today is the same man and that it is possible this man might have taken your fiancée? Kidnapped her right before your eyes? The eyes of one thousand other people who occupied that area of the caffè and the square?"

"If you haven't already noticed, I'm blind."

"That contradicts what you stated in the written police report."

"Correction," I say. "I am undergoing a temporary blindness due to—"

"Due to what, Mr. Angel? Or do you prefer Captain Angel?"

"Due to the war. In Afghanistan. I'm a soldier, like it says in the report. Or was a soldier. I'm a writer, too. Or would like to be a writer."

I feel him nodding, writing something else down.

"I, too, was a soldier, Captain Angel. I served in the Persian Gulf with the First Draghi and later with NATO."

"I've been serving on and off, Detective, but I'm not here to trade war stories. I'm here to find my fiancée."

He goes silent for a moment while he smokes. "You should know that thus far, no one has reported seeing your fiancée being abducted from the caffè. This would have been a couple of hours ago in the plain light of midday, you understand."

"I understand. I was there."

"But you could not see anything."

I exhale. "Yes, I couldn't see."

"Do you ever experience the eyesight anymore?"

For a split second I consider revealing my recent sleepwalking incident, but just as quickly think better of it. I don't want to give him the impression I'm nuts or emotionally disturbed.

"On occasion. When I least expect it, my vision returns to me."

"I've heard of this kind of thing before. Not an uncommon malady for soldiers suffering from post-traumatic stress disorder or perhaps traumatic brain injury. But I must assume you already know that."

"I'm aware of the complications prolonged combat presents."

"Tell me, Captain, have you ever felt like killing yourself? Killing someone else?"

At this point, I want to reach across the desk, grab him by the necktie, and scream at him to leave this place and go find Grace. But I know I would get nowhere, other than a jail cell or, worse, a hospital bed in the Venice nuthouse.

"No," I answer. "No on both counts."

The sound of a door opening interrupts us. I listen to the sound of footsteps. Boot heels on the stone floor, followed by the scent of woman. A pleasing fragrance. She says something to the detective in Italian and immediately leaves the room, closing the door behind her.

I hear the detective quickly shuffle through the paperwork she's apparently dropped onto his desk. When he's finished reading, he stamps out his cigarette and exhales the last of the smoke. The noise of the squeaky springs on his swivel chair fills the room when he leans back. Maybe he's resting the back of his head in his hands.

"Your story checks out, Captain Angel. You are a soldier and a writer. Are you published in Italy?"

"I'm not published anywhere yet," I tell him. "The war sort of stalled my career."

"War tends to kill more than just people."

Click . . . *Climbing the hill to the village, my troops behind me, the motor-oil-like smell of detonated explosive fills my senses along with black smoke from the fires . . . I hear the moans and groans of the wounded . . . I smell the dead . . . As I pass by a dead cow with green-bellied flies buzzing around its open wounds, a little boy emerges from*

around the corner of a stone building that is still standing. There's some-
thing in his hands . . .

I take a moment to breathe, to stop the room from spinning. Then, "What about Grace? It's possible so many people were gathered in the square no one actually noticed her being taken away. But does that mean you won't search for her? Can't we at least check out some CCTV video somewhere? There's got to be dozens of security cameras in the square."

"Yes, we will search for her, Captain. We will check out the CCTV. We will scour the entire city with a fine-toothed comb before we are done. But first, allow me to ask you a few more questions."

I nod, exhale.

"How well did you and your fiancée, Grace Blunt, get along?"

"Very well."

"Very well," he repeats. He's questioning my answer.

"Okay, the past year since Grace and I announced our engagement has been difficult. There were the normal stresses and strains of being apart, being out of communication sometimes days at a time, and even then, communicating mostly by e-mail and texts." But what I'm not telling him is how Grace and her ex-husband, Andrew, rekindled their friendship while I was away. How the friendship turned into something else one night. How Grace called me the day after, left a message for me in a fit of tears and remorse. How for weeks after that, I wouldn't talk with her. Wouldn't talk on the sat-phone. Wouldn't Skype. Wouldn't text or e-mail. About how I thought very often of leaving her and never returning to the US after the war.

"And now you are suffering from a . . . malady."

"Yes, a *malady*, as you call it. But it's going to go away one day soon. And I will be good as new and Grace and I will be married."

"I understand," he says. "But first she must come back to you and you must make the decision not to go to any more wars. That is, the decision is yours to make."

My insides drop. I want to call the detective a son of a bitch and walk out the door. But I am at his mercy and he knows it.

"Yes," I say, holding back my rage . . . my fury. "Grace must come back or be found by you good people."

He picks up a piece of paper. Probably the paper the female officer brought in for him.

"We have witnesses who say they saw you both in a caffè yesterday not far from here. And that you were arguing."

I recall the engagement ring dropping to the cobbles. I recall spilling my drink. I recall our heated words and picturing Grace and Andrew together in bed and all the people who were staring at us. People who watched us argue, but who then went blind to Grace's being kidnapped from our table this afternoon.

"Yes, we argued," I say. "I assume you argue on occasion with your wife?"

The detective issues a subtle laugh. Like he's grinning about something humorous that happened years ago.

"Yes, we did argue quite often. She was an American from Los Angeles. Which is why we divorced. Happily."

"So that explains your excellent English," I say. "I've been married before, too."

"Your first wife," he says to the sound of more paper rustling. "Her name was Karen?" Pausing to, I imagine, glance down at the notes set on the desktop. "She committed suicide in July of 2001?"

Me, feeling the not-so-strange tightness in my chest at the mention of Karen. At the mention of her death and how she died.

"Tell me," he says. "Soldiers . . . combat soldiers . . . are under a great deal of stress and strain both on and off the battlefield. Did you and Karen argue a lot, just like you and Grace?"

He's testing me now, pushing my buttons. He's testing my stability. Trying to gauge my sense of guilt and remorse. Reading my face and my reactions.

"Stress," I say. "You should know all about that, Detective, shouldn't you?"

"I am the one asking the questions. I am not the one looking for my wife. In fact, I am still running away from her."

"Sure, Karen and I argued like all married couples. But I had nothing to do with her death, if that's what you're getting at. That's why in the end, it was determined a suicide."

"In the end," he says, like my choice of words means something more than it does. "Did you know that oftentimes, when a person disappears, her significant other is responsible for making it happen? Soldiers, especially those suffering from acute psychological repression from the prolonged effects of combat, can be especially volatile."

I lower my head, peer down into my lap. I don't want him to see the expression on my face, my need to jump out of this chair, wrestle him to the floor, dig my thumbnails into his eyeballs.

"You are some years older than Grace," he observes. "Eight years, if my math is correct. She could be attracted to someone younger. Someone not affected by the war or wars. Someone more stable. Someone she was married to before, perhaps?"

"Yes." I swallow. "Grace was married once before. What's your point, Detective?"

"My point, Captain Angel, is that Grace may very well have simply walked away from something she no longer wanted in her life. Something she was afraid of. It's possible she is frightened of committing herself to only one man for the rest of her life. This is an entirely human response to the prospect of marriage."

He must by now recognize the expression of stone-cold anger radiating from me. It must be painted on my face.

"Walked off," I say. "Walked off without a change of clothes. Without luggage? With the clothes on her back and no warning? What about the stranger?"

"With all due respect, Captain, do you have any idea how many men walk away from their wives while vacationing in Venice? How many wives walk away from their husbands, never to return? Honeymooners, Captain Angel. Couples who are supposed to be in love."

He's right, of course. I'm not oblivious to spoiled love or love gone suddenly wrong. I'm not completely out of touch with a man or a woman experiencing a one-hundred-eighty-degree change of emotion. Sometimes walking away from something just seems easier than attempting to climb an impossibly steep and slippery slope. Sometimes driving your car into the river is easier than living. Sometimes you shoot and ask questions later. Maybe dealing with my blindness this past week has been too much for her. Maybe she's still hopelessly in love with Andrew. Or maybe the man in the overcoat has taken her and is hurting her right now.

"Detective Carbone, I know what you are trying to tell me, and despite some arguments, I assure you, Grace and I are very much in love and very solid. So maybe it's time we stopped talking and you go out and find her. For God's sake."

"Very much in love and very solid," he says, lighting another cigarette. "Well then, you are sure about the strange man you saw yesterday and today?"

"Sure I am."

"Have you seen him at any other time while in Venice?"

I pretend to think for a moment. But there's nothing to think about.

"I can't recall. But we definitely spotted him yesterday and today."

"But you yourself did not actually see him with your own eyes."

"Grace got a very good look at him. I managed to catch a glimpse of him when my eyesight returned for a brief time. He wasn't hiding from us."

"No other strangers have come your way, then?"

"No," I repeat. But then I catch myself. "Wait. Phone calls. We've received some phone calls at the apartment we're renting. When we answered the phone, the person on the other end simply said, 'I see.' In English. To be honest, I thought it was some kind of prank or joke because of my condition. My . . . malady."

He's writing something down. I hear the scribbling again.

"How often has this man called?"

"A couple times. Maybe three."

He writes that down. "What is your number?"

"I don't know. We don't use that phone. I use my mobile. But we can find the number easily enough and trace the calls."

"Yes, landlines are becoming extinct. Like the old paperback books and vinyl records."

"You think there could be a connection between the phone calls and Grace's disappearance?"

"Perhaps. But we will have to trace the calls first and find their origin. We can do that now when we escort you back to your apartment."

Finally, some progress. Some action. Not a full-frontal assault. But at least it isn't a retreat.

"One more thing, Captain. Does Grace have any family? Sisters, brothers, parents?"

"An older sister and a younger brother. Parents are dead. She doesn't communicate with her siblings as far as I know. Or maybe they do know something. How the hell should I know at this point?"

"Hold off on notifying them for now, assuming you were thinking of it. We wouldn't want to alarm them unnecessarily. The same goes for Grace's ex-husband, again, assuming you are thinking of it."

The detective stands.

I stand.

He comes around and takes my arm. As he leads me toward the door of his office, he asks what the prognosis is for the permanent return of my eyesight.

"Fifty-fifty."

He issues another one of those light laughs like something's real funny.

"If I were a betting man, Captain Angel," he says, "I would enjoy those odds. I would be optimistic."

As he opens the office door, I consider asking him what the odds are of finding Grace. Instead I yank my arm from his hand and keep my mouth shut. Chances are, I'm not going to like the answer.

Chapter 14

I'm escorted back to my apartment above the bookshop in a wooden police boat that might pass for a sleek Gar Wood motorboat back in upstate New York's lake country. Or so my memory tells me. They are permanent floating fixtures on the ripples of the Grand Canal.

The two uniformed cops doing the escorting don't speak a word to me other than what's necessary. Things like "Watch your step," and "Watch your head." But I sense their suspicions, their distaste for me . . . the unstable soldier. The wounded vet with no visible wounds. A bad captain is fully capable of losing his squad either through bad decisions or bad orders he can't possibly carry out. But only a sad son of a bitch is capable of losing his fiancée in broad daylight. A blind, sad son of bitch anyway.

They walk me up the flights of stairs to the studio. I open the door for them and they enter. Since I don't require the overhead lamp at present, I don't bother turning it on. But one of the cops hits the wall-mounted switch. I sense the light as soon as it's triggered. But not much else.

"Where is the phone, Captain Angel?" one of them asks.

"Help yourself," I say, pointing to the wall beside the apartment door.

The handset is plucked off the wall, some numbers punched in. That's followed by a pause until the cop starts barking something in rapid-fire Italian. My guess is he's speaking with the operator. The phone is hung up with a heavy plastic slap. The cop approaches me.

"We have a trace being conducted on the last number to have called this line," he informs me. "The detective will contact you with the information when he receives it. In the meantime, is there anything we can get for you? Food? Water? Wine?"

"A dog for the eyes?" barks the second cop in his heavy accent. "A stick for the walking?"

The two officers laugh like this is one hell of a party.

"Please, do me a favor. When you look around the apartment, does anything look disturbed?"

They take a minute to glance around.

"Nothing seems out of place," says the first cop, whose English is better than the second cop's. "But then, this isn't our place to begin with."

"Beside the bed you'll find our luggage. Does it look like it's been opened?"

"There is one suitcase and one backpack. They both seem to be undisturbed."

If Grace came back here on her own to retrieve something . . . anything, she wouldn't have bothered to close the suitcase on the way out . . . But what about her painting? Would she have taken her painting?

"Behind me," I say. "Do you see a painting set up on an easel?"

"Yes," says the first cop.

"Can you do me a favor and look at it?"

"Look at it?"

77

"Please," I say. "What's painted on it?"

The second cop stifles a laugh. But I hear shoes shuffling until they're standing in front of the oil painting.

"It is a woman with long dark hair, and green eyes. Her belly is pregnant."

The wallop to my chest feels like taking a bullet.

You see our future, Grace said. Did she want me to feel her painting because that's the future she wants for us? Or am I entirely wrong? Is she pregnant with Andrew's child, and this was her way of telling me?

Grace, have you left me to run back to Andrew's arms? Have you been lying to me all along?

"Now," says the first cop, "if there is nothing else you would like from us, Captain, we will be leaving you."

"My fiancée," I say. "You can find her and bring her back."

"We will find her," he says, no longer laughing. "If she *wants* to be found."

With that, the two officers leave, closing the door behind them.

I make my way to the bed, drop down to my knees, feel for Grace's suitcase. The cops were right. The simple carry-on bag is zipped closed. I pick it up, set it on the bed, unzip it. I feel my way through the contents, but what good is the act when I can't see a damn thing? Closing the bag, I set it back on the floor.

Returning to the living area, I run my hands over the harvest table, feeling for anything that might belong to Grace. All I feel are our computers. Turning, I go to her easel, but I'm so panicked I've forgotten to count my steps. I collide with the edge of the canvas and it tumbles to the floor.

"Christ!" I shout, kicking the table that holds her paints, just the way she left them earlier.

Weaving unsteadily to the couch, I sit down. The heavy silence weighs on my shoulders. I feel numb and suddenly beyond exhausted. Pulling my phone from my coat pocket, I feel along the screen, attempt to press "Redial." But I can't see what I'm doing and I press the wrong buttons. I should have had the cops try Grace from my phone while I had the chance. But then, shouldn't Grace be calling me if she's lost?

Not if she's being held against her will or worse, already dead.

I shove the phone back into my coat pocket, feeling the weight of her absence like a hole in my heart.

I lie down on my side, close my eyes.

Darkness prevails.

Chapter 15

My men break down doors, gather the people hiding inside the stone buildings who haven't been hit by the bombing run or are not engulfed by fire. The soldiers drag them out, make them assemble near the well in the center of the village. Some of the troops search the untouched buildings for contraband. Weapons, explosive devices, and unspent rounds hidden inside the walls and under the floorboards. When they find them, they will toss in a live grenade and blow the structure sky-high.

Suddenly, a small boy emerges from around the corner of a surviving building. It looks like he's carrying something. But after a second or two, I can see that he's not carrying anything so much as something is strapped to his chest.

The fine hairs on the back of my neck stand straight up.

Without hesitation, I shoulder my M4, take aim with both eyes open . . .

Chapter 16

When I wake I find myself not on the couch, but standing on the opposite end of the apartment at the kitchenette, in the process of stacking dishes on the counter. I can see. I have no idea why I am doing this or if it means anything at all. Just like this morning when I woke on the roof.

I repeat, I can see, over. . .

I turn away from the stacks of boxes, cans, dishes, cups, wineglasses, drinking glasses, knives, and forks, and peer outside the open French doors. Beyond the painting situated on the easel is the dark night of Venice. I glance at the back of the canvas, and listen to the pleasant sounds of the ever-active city of water until the realization hits me like a cement block.

Grace is gone.

I have my eyesight. I need to call her again while I have my eyesight.

Digging into the pocket of my leather coat, I retrieve my phone.

I stare down at the screen. I've received no phone calls in the time since I've returned to the studio. Nothing.

I try speed-dialing her.

But I get the same automated "mailbox full" message I got before. I set the phone down on the harvest table, beside a stack of white bowls and a tower of cereal boxes.

Taking a step back, I survey the room.

In the light of the naked overhead bulb, I see piles of white plates on the small kitchenette counter. In between the pillars of plates are carefully positioned boxes of pasta and rice set beside towers made from canned goods. The boxes, cans, and plates don't seem to be randomly placed there. It's like I was arranging them in that position on purpose.

It's the same story for the harvest table.

I've made myself a model city of boxes, bowls, plates, with knives and forks placed end on end to mimic roads or maybe a river . . . canals. The dream I was having while I was sleepwalking must have really been something. Now I'm designing cities. Or making a map anyway. A 3-D map.

I start to return the boxes and plates to the shelves and cupboards, but as soon as I lift the first stack, I decide to leave them be. My gut tells me that something is happening inside my head besides the effects of PTSD. I'm working out the problem of Grace's disappearance in a somnambulant state. A sleepwalking state.

I look at the 3-D map on the floor.

I have no recollection of building it. I only know that I must have built it.

But why?

I know damn well what I'm searching for . . . what the police should be searching for. But why do I have this stone feeling inside my stomach that tells me I am hiding something from myself?

When the phone on the wall explodes in a cacophony of ringing bells, my heart nearly pops out of my chest. I make my way to the phone, yank it off the cradle.

"Yes!" I bark. "Grace!"

The receiver fills again with static or bad reception. Maybe both.

"I see," says a voice. A man's voice. "I see."

My heart pounds.

"Is Grace with you?" I say, trying with all my strength to keep calm. Not piss him off.

"I see."

"Do you have Grace?"

"I see," he repeats.

"Listen to me, please. Do you have my fiancée?"

I'm trying to hold back from screaming into the phone. If he does have Grace, I don't want to take a chance on him causing her pain. I don't want to give him an excuse to break off contact.

"Please, please," I beg. "Who are you? Have you taken my Grace? Please."

"I see," he says yet again.

"Please!" I scream, but the phone goes dead.

I pull the phone slowly away from my ear, and my eyesight begins to bug out. Everything around me becomes clouded. Like I'm trapped in a fog.

Chapter 17

I pull Detective Carbone's card from my pants pocket, stare down at it.

You're a dumb son of a bitch, Captain Angel...

Of course I can't read the card. My eyes won't make out the numbers. Not even when I hold it just a few inches away from my face.

I never thought to add his number into my mobile. But then, he never offered to do it for me. Maybe they think I'm faking it. My blindness. Maybe they think I'm making it all up. I guess I don't look like a blind guy. If they don't believe me, I suppose it's possible they think I had something to do with Grace's disappearance. Or maybe I'm just being paranoid.

My mobile rings.

I nearly drop the phone trying to answer it. Instead of issuing a "Hello" or the customary *"Pronto,"* I shout out, "Grace!"

It's not Grace. But by the grace of God, it's the detective.

"I'm sorry to bother you, Captain Angel. I have some information I would like to share with you."

"I was just about to call you."

"You just received a phone call. Is that correct?"

"Yes, that's correct."

"We traced the number."

I breathe into the phone.

"It's a cell phone and a local number," he goes on. "But the owner of this phone . . . one Francesco Cipriani . . . might not fit the description of the man which you provided us with earlier."

"I don't understand. What are you trying to tell me?"

"We have made contact with Mr. Cipriani. He is relieved we have found his cell phone. He and his wife spent their ten-year wedding anniversary in Venice just a couple of weeks ago. The phone was pickpocketed from out of his coat, perhaps by your overcoat man. Thousands of visitors pour into and out of Venice on a daily basis. So you can imagine the endless opportunities if you are a thief."

My throat constricts, chest grows tight. "Where does this leave us, Detective? What does it all mean?"

"It means I have no reason to disbelieve Mr. Cipriani's story. As you say in America, he checks out. I contacted the hotel where he stayed and they confirm his reservation. Mr. Cipriani is an accountant working in a private practice in Milan. He hardly fits the description of a man who would kidnap your wife, Captain."

"Does he have any connection to this building? Would the number have been stored in his phone?"

"How did you find the apartment in the first place?"

"The US Army found it for me."

"How very interesting. Perhaps that is the answer. Perhaps the caller is connected to the US military. Perhaps he's even been inside the apartment in the past. In any case, it is something to ponder." He pauses, the sound of him lighting a cigarette oozing over the receiver. "Tell me, have you received any text messages or calls from your fiancée since we last parted?"

I tap my fingers against the phone. "I think I would have told you that already."

"Indeed, you are still sharp, Captain," he exhales, "despite your blindness. We have our police keeping an eye out for her throughout Venice. But until she is missing for forty-eight hours, we do not consider her an official missing person."

"Well, I consider her missing. Very fucking missing. Invisible missing. Gone-baby-gone fucking missing. I consider it official that she is not sitting here safe and sound with me right this very minute."

"I'm sure you do. However, as difficult as it is to believe, I'm afraid it is still quite possible she has simply left you. And if that is the case, we have little right to interfere."

"Unbelievable." Making a fist, I punch my thigh. I'd toss the phone against the wall if I didn't know how stupid a move that would be. Like tossing my M4 into a river just because I missed my target.

"But do not worry, Captain," the detective goes on. "In consideration of your condition, and your being a member of a NATO military force, we have issued an early alert to every airport, train station, taxi operation, and bus depot in the country. Even bicycle and motorbike rentals will be notified. If your fiancée's passport shows up at any of these places, she will be questioned and, if need be, detained."

"Her passport," I repeat. "Jesus, her passport."

"She did take her passport with her when you went to have lunch at the caffè in Piazza San Marco?"

I try to think. It's been our habit since arriving in Venice to carry our passports wherever we go. It's the safe thing to do should the studio get robbed while we're gone. But I had no vision when we left the room earlier this afternoon and we were in a rush.

"I can't be sure," I say. "I can try to check."

"Please do so. In the meantime, Captain, get some rest. I know this is difficult to believe, but nine times out of ten, the person who goes missing returns within twenty-four hours. It's no different from a child running away from home."

"A child," I repeat, my blood boiling. "This is my fiancée we're talking about here. Not a spoiled kid. She was abducted, Detective. Abducted by a creep in a long overcoat. Go find her!"

"Keep your mobile phone charged. I will be in touch if we discover anything else."

He hangs up without a good-bye.

Chapter 18

I walk the six steps to the bed, grab hold of Grace's suitcase, flip it
back up onto the bed.

For the second time, I open it and once more start rummaging
through the neatly folded clothing. I recognize a pair of jeans and
a skirt. Some T-shirts, socks, and underwear. Unlike the last time,
I run my fingers along the fabric-lined interior walls and along the
bottom.

No passport.

There's also no sign of the emergency cash and credit card that
Grace stored inside the case, which means she took that with her
as well. A droplet of cold sweat slides down the length of my spine.

I sit on the edge of the bed.

Maybe the real question I need to ask myself is this: Did Grace
leave the apartment with her passport, emergency credit card, and
extra cash because it was the safe and prudent thing to do? Or did
she do it because she had every intention of leaving me?

—————

My feet are pressed against the floorboards, but I don't seem to feel them. My head is a buzzing beehive of adrenaline. I don't know what feels worse, the possibility that Grace was kidnapped right before my blind eyes, or that she simply left on her own, abandoning anything she could replace.

I think about the police. Detective Carbone believes it's entirely possible Grace took off on her own. He's seen it happen dozens of times, he said. Lots of lovers leave one another in Venice. Breakups happen even in the most romantic of places. Maybe it's me who's being blind to the possibility of Grace going because she *wanted* to go. Maybe it's me who is refusing to believe the truth about Andrew.

Maybe it's not over between them.

But then, if it isn't over, wouldn't Grace have been very unhappy with me? Wouldn't she have wanted to run away from me instead of accompanying me to Italy? Maybe she came with me only out of loyalty. Or worse, guilt. Maybe I missed the signs with her the same way I did with Karen. I'd always assumed she was happy just because I was happy. By the time the cops fished her out of the Hudson, it was too late.

But Detective Carbone doesn't know Grace like I do. He doesn't understand how in love we are. How much we need one another. Yes, the past year has been wrought with the difficulty and heart-break caused by my being absent—and having needs go unfulfilled. From my being at war. From Grace fighting a war of loneliness.

But I'm not at war anymore.

Correction. That's not exactly right.

I'm not at war in Afghanistan, I should say. But that doesn't mean I'm not still at war with myself. The blindness proves it. A bullet has never so much as grazed me. The shrapnel from exploded ordnance never came close. Other than a knife wound, I am a casualty of my own frayed nerves and memories that are not always complete. Not always reliable.

I recall a time not so long ago, but that now seems like another lifetime: a warm, pitch-dark summer morning. I was packing for the embarkation to Frankfurt. I would be gone for at least six months. Grace lay on the bed, dressed in her T-shirt and panties, her face buried in the pillow.

"Why do you have to go?" she begged, in between sobs. "Why must you keep running away from me? I fucking moved up here for you. Gave up a good life in the city. My life. Why do you have to go, Nick?"

How do you answer a question like that when you're going off to war?

I remained silent while I packed. My leaving had nothing to do with what was in my heart or whether I was being selfish or not. In my head, I felt a physical need to leave. To lock and load. To defend against the enemy.

While Grace wept I packed until my backpack could hold no more. When I was done and dressed in my travel camos and combat boots, I came around to her side of the bed and sat down beside her. For a time I held her, pressing my face into the soft space between her shoulder and her neck.

"Listen," I said. "I know you miss New York. I know you miss your friends. Your art shows and poetry readings." In my head, picturing her ex-husband, his long hair, his natty attire, his brains. "But I promise, I will make it up to you when I get back. We'll go to Paris. Or maybe we'll rent an apartment in the city for a while."

"Do you know what my horoscope said today?"

"No, what did your horoscope say?"

"It said to beware of giving myself over entirely to a lover. That the joy would soon be replaced with heartbreak. You must give to yourself first, it said, before you can give to someone else."

"What's that supposed to mean?"

But she wouldn't answer.

"I love you," I said, raising my head just a touch, whispering into her ear, feeling the wetness of her tears on my freshly shaved cheek. When she didn't respond, I said it again. "I love you."

But she wouldn't say it back.

The horn blared outside the bedroom window, announcing the arrival of my ride, and I had no choice but to go. But then, I wanted to go. It wasn't that I had been trained for combat. It was more a case of my having been born for it.

I got up from the bed and left Grace alone in the cold dark silence of the morning.

Now, I stand up from the bed, stumble the twelve steps toward the kitchenette. My right arm swipes a stack of plates on the harvest table. They come crashing down, the noise combining with a deafening *click*—

—*They've stolen my clothing again. I'm inside a square room. Not exposed concrete and steel, but padded walls and floor. Bright overhead lights flash. Piped-in battlefield noises blare. So loud, my eardrums bleed. "Stop it! You're killing me!" But only the camera hears my screams . . .*

I make it the last few steps to the counter. My head is pounding, like I've just slammed my forehead against the wall. I fumble blindly for the whiskey bottle, knocking over boxes and some coffee cups, one of which shatters.

But I find the bottle.

Unscrewing the cap, I drink deep, set the bottle back down. The whiskey burns as it goes down, but it has an immediate calming effect on my heart.

I slam my fist against the counter.

My eyes well up with tears. Anger, fear, sadness, confusion, fury . . . *fury* . . . I am a cesspool of battered emotions. I am helpless. Grace is out there somewhere. For all I know, she's gagged and bound, being held captive in some rancid basement. Maybe she's hurt. Maybe she's been raped. Maybe she's dead already.

Dead already . . .

The two horrid words resonate inside my brain.

I'm up here in this apartment by myself. I'm doing nothing while Grace is out there alone. I'm a useless sack of rags and bones. Doing nothing. It goes against everything I know . . . everything that I am . . . everything they conditioned me for.

I slam the counter again.

Grabbing my keys, cell phone, and coat, I leave the apartment, blind to the possibilities of what can happen.

Chapter 19

I step out into the cold damp darkness of Venice. The cobbles bump beneath my booted soles; the moist air coats my face. The only thing I can remotely make out are small, indiscernible blobs of light when I peer directly at a lamp or one of the moving lights mounted to one of the motorboats slowly cruising the nearby feeder canal. I hear the footsteps of tourists passing by in both directions. I feel their presence the same way a psychic feels a world full of ghosts and spirits surrounding her. They make my pulse soar and steal my oxygen.

Taking a deep breath, I take a step forward. Then another. Until I run directly into a brick wall of a human being who is passing by. The collision nearly sends me to the ground.

"Watch where you're walking, mate!"

It's a man. An Australian, judging by the accent. I've fought beside hundreds of Australians over the years. They are born voyagers. Also born fighters. I regain my balance, try desperately for a point of focus. But without hearing his voice, I can only make it appear like I know where he's standing.

"I'm sorry," I say, trying to pretend I'm looking into his eyes. But I could be aiming my gaze in any direction. "Clumsy of me."

"You okay, mate? You don't look so great, you don't mind my saying. Your eyes are rolling around in their sockets."

I tell him I'm fine. But I don't dare take another step, or else risk knocking into someone else. I can feel the Australian standing before me. I smell the liquor on his breath. I feel stupid and exposed.

"You sure you're going to be all right? Because you don't look all right. Maybe a little too much to drink."

I recall the whiskey I drank. Not enough to make me drunk. But he can smell it on my breath. I know the man isn't going to leave until I walk away first. So I take a step, and then another, until I feel two hands clutching at the collar on my coat, and I'm down on my back.

"Jesus, mate, you were about to walk right into the canal. You're blind to the world."

Footsteps. A crowd is gathering. Voices. Some of them in languages I cannot understand. Others in English. This was a big mistake. Venturing out. What the hell was I thinking? I'm a soldier. I'm used to taking action, not sitting around on my ass, useless.

"Call a cop!" somebody barks. An American.

"Please," I beg. But it's no use.

"You must be bloody soused." The Australian laughs. "Blind and drunk. Just stay down, before you fall down again."

From out of the distance, sirens. Didn't take the cops long to respond to my desperation. My stupidity. They are coming by boat. Coming for me, the blind man. The man who took aim at a little boy. The man who lost his fiancée. The man who lost his wife and unborn child. The man whose world has become a dark private hell.

Chapter 20

When the boat arrives, I hear an English-speaking, Italian-accented, bullhorn-amplified voice insisting everyone clear the area. Then I hear the pounding of jackboots on the cobbles.

"Mamma mia!" comes a voice I vaguely recognize. One of the uniformed police who escorted me to my apartment a few hours earlier. The first cop. The one with the better English. "Call the detective," he adds. "Tell him he is about to have company."

A short boat ride later I am once more sitting in front of Carbone as he lights another cigarette.

"Tell me, Captain Angel," he says, exhaling a stream of what I imagine to be blue smoke. "What exactly were you trying to prove by going out on your own without the use of your eyes?"

"My fiancée is missing. Unlike you, I was trying to find her."

"All you would have accomplished is drowning yourself. I don't need another one of those."

"I would have been doing something."

He smokes for a minute. Then I hear him stand up.

"Captain Angel, how long have you been a soldier? Please remind me, if you would."

"I don't understand the relevance. Grace is gone. We need to find her."

"Entertain me, please."

I swallow a breath. "Twenty-plus years. Off and on. I'm a reservist now. After the Persian Gulf, I went stateside and was assigned to the Tenth Mountain Division at Fort Drum in upstate New York."

"What did you do there? If you don't mind my asking."

I do my best to peer into his eyes, without being able to see his eyes. "I do mind. But if you must know, I beat the shit out of new recruits."

He laughs. "You were, how do you call it, a hard-ass?"

"I also pushed a lot of paper."

"Maybe you were waiting for a good war to come along to free you from the boredom."

"What I can tell you is I left the army in early 2000 and became a reservist. I met the woman who was to become my wife by chance at a bar in upstate New York. We got married after only a few months. But a year later, she drowned. September 11th, 2001, arrived shortly thereafter and . . . well, you know."

"Your plans were somewhat shattered with the death of your wife?"

"Plans and outcome don't always share the same intent."

"And why was your wife's death ruled a suicide?"

The pressure in my head goes from dull ache to sharp pain. "What the fuck, Detective? I thought we already covered this."

"I'm just trying to get a clearer picture of the past."

"Because after all, it has everything to do with my missing fiancée. Why aren't we talking about that?" My temperature rises. My pulse soars. He's antagonizing me while an ugly black spider spins silken possibilities inside his head. "Has there been any word out on the street about Grace? Has anyone spotted her?"

"I'm afraid not. But our eyes are wide open." He smokes a little more. "Were you ever wounded physically in combat?"

I pat my left shoulder. "Knife wound. Aside from that, not a scratch."

"How did you get that? Which campaign?"

When I attempt to recall where, I see only a gray-black blur. Like a television that has lost its picture, the image is there all right. It's just irretrievable. For now.

"Again, I don't see the damn relevance in your questions."

"You don't see anything. Which is why you are sitting here."

"That supposed to be funny?"

"No, it is not. My apologies to you if you thought it was. But truth is, we have not spotted anyone who fits the precise description of your fiancée, nor a man with a long brown overcoat and a closely cropped black beard or the black eyes."

"What about the phone calls? They must mean something, especially calls to an apartment used often by military personnel. What if the asshole we're looking for thought he was harassing someone who'd stayed here before us? Maybe even as early as last week? Maybe another soldier?"

"I've already told you, we traced the phone call that came to your apartment landline. The call was placed from a cell phone that was pickpocketed. There's nothing more we can do with that."

"You can search the location of the phone with GPS."

He laughs. "Yes, we can do that if we are in Hollywood. Which we most definitely are not. Although the famous Woody Allen owns a penthouse apartment on the Grand Canal not far from here. His movies are very funny."

I let that comment sit for minute. Then, "Why are you asking me if I've been injured in combat?"

"Because we have a man who knows the phone number to the landline at your apartment. I have made inquiries to the US Army.

97

The military people who have stayed at the apartment over the course of the past few years check out. They do not fit the description of our kidnapper, should a kidnapper exist at all." He plants himself behind his desk, stamps out his cigarette. "Also, I spoke with your company psychologist and while he couldn't comment specifically on your condition, he did tell me that you show signs of having undergone significant trauma. Such as a serious battlefield injury or even a car wreck. He indicated that the severity of your PTSD is often found in prisoners of war."

"Oh for God's sake, Detective Carbone, for the last time, I was never injured in combat and I wasn't a POW." I start to stand and there comes the *click* or snap inside my brain and—

—*Bare chested. Camo pants stuffed into combat boots. A sun-baked dirt yard. A razor-wire fence surrounds me. Surrounds him. A man, a little taller than me. Darker complexion—from exposure to the sun or . . . ? The knife in his hand lashes out and I spin—*

"Captain Angel," he says. "You still with us?"

When have I ever been inside a prison yard? Engaged in a knife fight? These memories don't belong to me. It's like the sleepwalking dreams have wormed into my waking state. Like my subconscious is now FUBAR. You know, fucked up beyond all recognition.

"Yes," I answer, my head beginning to pound.

"There is one thing I am having a great deal of difficulty with."

"And that is?"

"If your fiancée was abducted in broad daylight, directly in front of you and literally hundreds of people, why didn't anyone see it? How is it that not one single soul took even the slightest notice of something that seems so obvious?"

My already-pounding head fills with blood, panic, and fire. As if it's about to explode. "He must have been quick about it. Maybe he's a professional. A professional kidnapper or killer or soldier trained in close-quarters combat or all of the above who's been following us. Waiting for the right time to make his move!"

I'm shouting now. The door opens.

"*Come stai*, Detective?"

"*Molto bene,*" he responds. "*Bene.*"

"Listen," I say, lowering my voice, "is it possible to get some aspirin? And a glass of water?"

"But of course." Carbone gives the order to his aide. The aide comes back with the aspirin and water. I devour both immediately.

"Please refrain from shouting, Captain. It upsets my support staff."

I offer no apologies.

"It's not that I don't believe you," he goes on. "It's just that I have a hard time believing there would not have been a struggle . . . a physical resistance. Or, at the very least, a scream."

"Doesn't matter that you don't believe it. That doesn't mean it didn't happen."

"Like you say, it would take a kidnapper in possession of the skills required of a great assassin or political enemy. Your Grace doesn't fit the description of an enemy of state. Did she have any enemies?"

"Of course not," I insist. But naturally, I have no idea if Grace had any enemies or not. Certainly no one who would go to the lengths necessary to kidnap her.

"Then I must tell you, Captain Angel, as much as it hurts to hear it, I believe it is more likely than not that your fiancée left of her own accord. It might be the most reasonable conclusion."

I shoot to my feet. "I've already told you that's impossible. Grace would never leave me for anyone. We're in love."

I'm leaning over his desk when the door swings open again.

"It is the only explanation!" Carbone barks.

I hear footsteps and suddenly my arms are snatched up in the grasp of not one but two men.

"Get off of me!"

But they tighten their grip.

"I want to speak to someone from my embassy. The American Embassy."

"Why? They can do nothing for you."

"My fiancée is missing. They damn well will do something. It's their job to protect Americans in danger in a foreign country."

"Captain Angel, please calm down. You are not in danger. I told you before, if Grace left of her own accord, no one, not even your embassy, can do anything about it."

I struggle against the arms that hold me. "Call them. Do it. Do it now."

I hear the detective pick up the phone, while exhaling a frustrated breath.

"The American Embassy, *per favore*," he speaks. Then, "Let him go, Fredo. Set him down."

The men shove me back into the chair. "Now please behave, Captain. Or you will be speaking to your embassy official from a jail cell in Venice." He laughs. "Of course, that would be quite the story to tell your grandchildren one day."

Chapter 21

But I am not tossed into a jail cell. Rather I am escorted to a small waiting area upstairs where I am afforded a view of the Grand Canal that would easily cost five hundred euros per night if this were a hotel. Or so a young woman tells me as she escorts me up the stairs. It's a damned shame I can't see it. Staring out onto the canal with the never-ending boat traffic moving up and down its narrow man-made banks would help the time pass faster, maybe take my mind off Grace's disappearance even for a moment or two. Instead I sit on the leather couch situated up against the far wall, and close my eyes.

Despite the aspirin, my head still aches. Pulse remains elevated. Grace is gone and along with her, my sanity. I try to remember her lying right beside me in the studio apartment over the bookshop, as if the overcoat man never invaded our life in the first place. As if we were still alone in Venice to heal.

For a brief but wonderful moment, I create a fantasy of what I want for Grace and myself. I can see it perfectly. From where my head is propped on a stack of down pillows, I survey the entire studio. The kitchenette that makes up the far wall. The leather couch and the long harvest table. Grace's easel to the right by the always-open French doors. Grace lies beside me on her right side. She's fast asleep, her naked body curled into a question mark of loveliness. She has become so much a part of me now that I ache at the thought of ever being separated from her again. I only want what she wants. I want to promise her that I will never go back to the wars again.

For a while, I daydream with my eyes closed, until sleep overtakes me.

I am no longer lying beside Grace inside our studio. I am no longer at peace. I am sitting at a table at an outdoor caffè in Piazza San Marco. It is noon with a warm sun shining on my face on an otherwise cold day. To my left is the wide-open basin, and the supply barges and boats that bob in its never-ending chaotic wake. To my right are the hordes of tourists who compete with the thousands of pigeons fighting over their tiny slice of real estate outside the stone steps leading up to the cathedral.

Across from me, I see Grace as plainly as I see the black-suited waiter approaching our table. He's carrying something on a tray. Something we've ordered for lunch. He sets the tray down onto one of those aluminum foldout tray stands. On the tray is a severed head. Grace's head, her long black hair waterlogged and draping her face like a veil, a pool of blood collecting on the place below her cleanly sliced neck.

I shift my eyes to where she is seated across from me. Her headless torso occupies the chair. But she is not dead. She raises her hands, calmly crossing her arms, like she is simply soaking up the view. When I shift my gaze back to her head, her eyes open and she shoots me a smile.

"I see," she whispers.

Chapter 22

Startled awake.

I open my eyes. What had been nothing but a gray-brown blur interrupted only by the rays of the sun and, later on, the manufactured light radiating from your average longer-lasting lightbulb, is now gradually replaced with vision.

Real vision.

There's a connection here. Sleep and sight. Sight and sleep. And dreaming, too. I'm not ignorant to the medical possibilities, the physiological reasoning. The more I rest, the more I heal. But I can't exactly rest while Grace is out there somewhere.

Christ almighty, maybe I should have stayed in America like the army wanted. If I'd stayed put, Grace would not be missing in action and none of this nightmare would be happening.

I look up to see a man standing in the center of the small room.

"I'm sorry to disturb you, Captain Angel," he says. "You seemed to be caught up in a dream."

My thoughts shift to Grace's severed head. *It was only a dream,* I try to convince myself. But it's like pretending the knife I'm plunging through my chest into my heart isn't real either.

I sit up straight, face the man.

He's younger than me. Taller, thinner. Dressed in a finely tailored navy-blue suit, white shirt, and gray silk tie. His gray hair is slicked back with something that Grace would refer to as "product," and he is clean shaven, as though immune to five o'clock shadow, even when it's more than three hours past that time. A diplomat to the core, blessed with an assignment any federal government worker with warm blood in his veins would die for.

He drags over a chair, holds out his hand.

"Dave Graham. US Embassy. How can I be of service?"

I take the hand in mine, amazed I can actually see it and feel it. I grip it tightly. Like a soldier should.

Releasing my hand, I stare down at my palm. He's no longer holding my hand, but I still feel his grip. When Graham grows a big smile, I get that feeling like I've been here before. A déjà vu.

"We've met before?" I say.

"But that would be impossible," he says, his face beaming. "However, guess how many Dave Grahams there are in the Manhattan directory alone?"

I can see that he is an expert at smiling, no matter his mood.

"So how do you like Venice so far, Captain?"

Is he fucking kidding me?

"It would be a hell of a lot better if my fiancée hadn't disappeared this afternoon."

His smile dissolves. It's another good trick he's acquired: the ability to shift his moods in a half second.

"I understand there was some trouble at the caffè near the cathedral in San Marco earlier today."

I lean forward, to add emphasis to what I'm about to tell him.

"Look, Mr. Graham," I say. "My fiancée was abducted by a man wearing a long brown overcoat. He has short black hair and a black beard. He was wearing sunglasses and staring us down. He knows the phone number to our apartment, so I'm thinking, maybe he's a soldier. A US soldier."

"Or perhaps someone who very much dislikes US soldiers."

"Maybe. But whatever he is, he approached our table and then, just like that, Grace was gone, which tells me he bears the skills of a highly trained combat soldier. Someone familiar with the art of extraction."

"The art of extraction," he repeats. "How interesting."

"I have reason to believe this same man has been following us for some time and placing calls to my apartment. He whispers 'I see' into the phone before he hangs up."

Graham bites down on his bottom lip, nods.

"I've been briefed by Detective Carbone, so I am fully aware of what he says to you on the phone." He pauses. "I understand you are just back from the Afghan war. You've also done numerous tours in Iraq. Must have been hard out there in the field, engaged in combat again and again. Most difficult."

"Yeah, it was hard. But I had a job to do and I did it. No questions asked. I'm a good soldier. I'm a patriot. My country called me again and again and I heeded the call again and again. Now my fiancée is gone."

Clasping his hands together, Graham nods once more, and peers down at the tops of his polished leather lace-ups.

"I further understand, Captain Angel, that you've had your share of trouble with PTSD and you are here in Venice to recuperate."

"The brass would rather I recuperate in the States. But let's just say, I'm not the Federal Veterans Administration Hospital type. Essentially I defied an order, which I now regret."

"So you came to Venice of your own accord." A question.

"I pulled some strings, called in a few favors. Like I said, I was ordered to the States, but some orders you can blow off."

His brow scrunches. "I should think a move like that might irritate the higher-ups, Captain. Maybe even get your rank busted."

"Are you a military man, Mr. Graham?"

"Never mind," he says.

"Truth is," I go on, "I think the army is more afraid I'll turn my back on the red, white, and blue. And to be honest, I don't give a rat's ass about rank, since I may never go back to the army again. Right now . . . right this very minute . . . I want my fiancée returned, understand?"

There's that big public relations smile again. Graham is like a lamp you can turn on and off.

He says, "How are those eyes of yours? You've been suffering from temporary bouts of blindness, I'm told. How have you been dealing with that?"

I'm staring at him standing inside the room. A few feet behind him is the picture window with that amazing view of the Grand Canal I was informed about earlier. I could also stand up and get a look at it, but I'd rather focus on him while I have the chance.

"Grace has been my eyes while I've been here. She helps me. She guides me. Christ, man, we've had our problems, but the woman loves me and I love her, and I'm going to get her back with or without you, with or without the Venice cops, with or without my eyes."

"Must be especially tough on you now that she's gone." Pursing his lips. "Of course, you can always head immediately back to your base hospital in Germany. We would take care of working out your safe transport." He looks away. "It would be the prudent thing to do, don't you agree?"

Just the sound of him stating the reality of it all in quite that manner and tone is enough to send my insides on a nosedive south.

. . . The concrete room. Seated in a chair. Rubbing my wrists as though . . . as though I'd been strapped in. A man seated before me. Impossible to make out his face. "Tell me what you remember about . . . the torture," he says.

I shudder. Fuck. Torture. I've never been captured. Never been a POW. What damned torture?

"Are you all right, Captain?" Graham says.

I nod, rub my forehead with my thumb and index finger.

"I'm okay," I say, a wave of nausea passing through me. "I've been getting headaches."

"Must be the stress. You really should go back to Frankfurt. I can arrange it for you."

"I'm not leaving!" I bark. "Not until I find Grace. Don't you get it?"

He bites down on his lip, issues me a slow nod. He gets it, all right, but he doesn't like it either.

"Can you help me find her, Mr. Graham? And can you promise me you won't talk to the army about what's happening? Carbone has already spilled enough about the situation. He fill you in on that too?"

Another nod. More biting down on the lip.

He turns to peer out the window onto the canal. "I understand your frustration in the matter, Captain. But it's really a police issue now. Even if you had come to me first I would have sent you here. Should your fiancée become detained by the police for any reason, or should she be officially reported missing, then the embassy will do everything in its power to cooperate with local authorities and Interpol. But until that time, her *disappearance* is still a local police matter." He turns to me.

"I'm not leaving," I say.

"Perhaps it's best you go back to your studio, get some rest. There's nothing more that can be done here."

I stand. "The detective believes she ran off on her own. Some people witnessed us arguing in a caffè yesterday afternoon, and that's what he bases his assumption on. But I don't believe Grace has left me. She would never do that."

But then, I never imagined she'd fuck Andrew, either.

"Yes, that would be a difficult pill to swallow. Especially in your condition." The smile once more paints his face. "It's been a long day, Captain. Is there anything I can do for you while you wait and see what transpires over the course of the next forty-eight hours? Can we give you a lift back to your place?"

I slide my hands down the length of my face, breathe in. "No thank you. I have my eyesight back for now. I'll see myself home."

Graham nods, goes for the stairs. But before descending them, he turns to me once more. "Captain," he says, his brow scrunched with concern. "Please don't do anything foolish. The police will do everything in their power to see that Grace is located. The best thing for you is to go home and get some rest. Should Grace go officially missing, you'll need all the rest you can get."

"I will," I tell him. But it's a lie and he knows it.

Chapter 23

By the time I make my way back downstairs into the main reception area, the precinct has been reduced to a nighttime skeleton crew. Venice has never been known as a beehive for major crimes like kidnapping, rape, and murder. In the detective's office situated at the end of the open square room, two men are standing, talking. I see parts of their torsos through the opaque glass panel embedded into the wooden door.

Detective Carbone and Dave Graham from the US Embassy.

Talking isn't the right word. They seem to be arguing, the detective waving his hands up and down, as if to stress his point. I can only wonder if they're arguing about me. About Grace. Maybe they're arguing over where to go for a drink and dinner. Maybe they're not even arguing.

I know the detective expects me to return to his office so he can once more assume the responsibility of escorting a part-time blind man back to his hotel. But I'm not blind right now. I can see. Seeing means I'm not helpless. It means I can do something. I can attack the problem. I can try to find Grace.

The front doors to the precinct are directly before me.

I turn away from the detective's office, descend the small flight of stairs, and head out into the night.

Chapter 24

Out on the cobbled walk, I spot the Route 1 Vaporetto as it's about to depart the bobbing dockside stop. I pay my seven euros at the window and hop on just as it's pulling away, squeezing in amongst annoyed tourists and evening commuters. I do my best to balance myself in the never-ending chop of the Grand Canal while the boat heads deeper into the old city.

At the stop for Piazza San Marco I get off, crossing over the short but precarious steel-plated gangplank along with half the boat's passengers. I follow the crowd through several passages and over two or three narrow pedestrian bridges that span thin feeder canals until I come to a large building set on a foundation of arches and pillars.

I make my way through the open arch and enter into the piazza.

This is the first time since the late 1980s that I have actually focused functioning eyes on the ancient cathedral, its lamp-lit Asian-inspired stone exterior, tall arches, and minarets. In the time since I arrived in Venice with Grace, I've walked on the hard cobblestones of Piazza San Marco, but never actually seen them. I've felt and rubbed up against the hordes of tourists, but I've never set functioning eyes upon them.

I don't waste any time. I have no idea how long the seeing is going to last. If I lose my sight here, I will have no way of getting home in the dark through the maze of alleys and walkways.

I head directly for the cathedral and the caffè located to its right alongside the basin. As always, the place is full. Every single one of the two dozen or so tables is occupied with patrons eating and drinking under the electric lights and the heat from the tall, gas-powered braziers set in between the tables.

I have no idea what I'm looking for.

The truth is that I'm living a fantasy. I half expect Grace to still be seated at the table we occupied this afternoon. I expect to see her face ignite with a relieved smile when she sees me. For her to stand up, hold out her open arms to me.

"Where have you been, baby?" she'll say, as if I were the one who went missing. "I was worried sick."

But she's not sitting at that table.

Another couple is sitting there instead. A young, well-dressed couple. Americans. They sound like they're from New York City. Probably enjoying their honeymoon.

I move on past the tables, scanning the cobbles as if Grace might have left something behind for me to find later on. Something that would tell me I'm not crazy in thinking she was abducted by a man in a long brown overcoat. I scan the ground, but I see nothing. Only cigarette butts, paper wrappers, bits of food that have fallen from the tables, and the pigeons who brave the stomping feet of caffè patrons in order to snatch them up.

When I raise my head, he's standing at the far end of the outdoor caffè.

He's positioned himself under a black wrought-iron lamp, bathed in an inverted arc of white lamplight. He's not wearing his sunglasses, so he stares at me with eyes that are glossy black, even from a distance of thirty feet. My breathing goes shallow and my temples begin to pound. I move toward him. But the moment I start walking, he takes a step back and disappears into the darkness, like he was never there in the first place.

I run.

Run in the direction of the lamp. When an oblivious caffè patron pushes out his chair, I crash into it, sending him and me onto the pavement.

The man lies quietly on the ground while I roll onto my knees, peering in the direction of the lamp. The overcoat man is nowhere to be found now. The scattering of people who were sharing the table with the man I ran into are trying to help him back up onto his feet. They are speaking German or Swiss; I can't really tell. They shoot me angry looks.

My eyes are beginning to lose their focus.

Sight fades in and out like it's controlled not by my brain but by a pair of batteries rapidly losing their juice. I've caught the attention of the entire caffè now. Or so it seems. It's late and they're drunk. Some of the patrons have gotten up from their tables and are approaching me. Someone takes a picture of me, the flash blinding me further.

My vision is entirely black when I feel a pair of strong arms attempt to lift me up off the cobbles and drag me away.

Chapter 25

"Please," he says, "just try to walk without running into something or scaring someone else away."

I know the voice.

It's the waiter who helped me earlier this afternoon. Once more he's leading me through what I assume is the dining room of the quiet caffè to the back, where the office is. He sets me down in a chair and gets me a drink of sherry, which he puts in front of me, placing my right hand around the stem. As if I need him to do this for me.

"Drink," he insists. "It will calm you."

I give the alcohol time to settle in before saying anything.

"What's your name?" I ask.

"Giovanni," he answers. "Why did you come back here?"

"I saw him, Giovanni. I saw the man who took my fiancée."

"What did he look like?"

"He's a tall man in that same long brown overcoat. This afternoon he was wearing sunglasses. But tonight he was without them.

He has black eyes. Striking black eyes, as if there are no irises. No whites. Do you know the man?"

"I see lots of men come and go through this caffè every day. Inside and outside. He could be anyone."

"You would know him if you saw him. He looks like a dead man who is alive for only one purpose. To steal Grace."

He pours me another sherry, tells me to drink. "And what is your name?"

I tell him.

"Nick," he says. "It's possible I know this man. I recall a man standing around the caffè this morning, this afternoon, and tonight. Never does he sit down to eat or drink. But always just standing. Like he is expecting someone."

"Like me for instance, Giovanni."

"Yes, like you, Nick."

I drink the sherry, set down the empty glass. Looking up into the light, I discover my blindness is no longer absolute. I'm not enveloped in darkness like I am during the blind periods. Instead, I am seeing shapes and the blurry movement of those shapes. It's as if every time I experience a bout of full eyesight, a little of the temporary blindness disappears.

"I take it you have been talking with the police," Giovanni goes on. "They have been here off and on all afternoon. And someone from the US Embassy. A well-dressed American who was accompanied by the detective."

I recall Dave Graham. He never mentioned visiting this caffè. Why would the distinguished diplomat keep that kind of information from me? And why would he come here at all if he was so convinced that Grace's disappearance was simply a police matter?

The calming effects of the sherry are kicking in enough to slow my beating heart to almost normal levels. Something dawns on me.

"Giovanni," I say. "Why are you helping me like this? Why not just call the police and be done with me?"

Through a hazy blur I see him fill the sherry glass once more. Only, instead of handing it to me, he drinks it down. Setting the empty glass onto the desk, he exhales.

"Because I found something," he says. "Something that must be very important to you. But before I show it to you, I suggest another sherry."

Chapter 26

First I drink another glass of sherry. Then, after setting the empty glass back down onto the desk, Giovanni asks me to hold out my hand. Palm up.

He puts something into my hand.

It's small and hard. A metal band topped with a stone. An engagement ring. Grace's engagement band.

My heart skips a beat. "Where did you find it?"

"In between two cobbles near the table where you were having your lunch. But the question, Captain, is *why* did I find it?"

I grip the ring in my fisted hand. It's all that I have left of Grace.

"What are you suggesting?"

"If your wife—"

"Fiancée."

"*Si*, if your fiancée was taken from you by this man we have both seen, perhaps it is possible she slipped off her ring and . . ."

He hesitates.

"And what?" I say.

"How do you say, release the ring? Or allow the ring to fall?"

"She *dropped* the ring, you mean."

"Yes, that's it. She *dropped* it, hoping someone would find it and report it missing. It would perhaps be her way of screaming for help. Like she was leaving you a marker. Like someone who is lost in the forest might leave behind a handkerchief or a piece of clothing. Something that tells you she's become lost and wants to be found."

I squeeze the ring harder, if that's possible. In my mind, I see Grace being dragged away while she struggles to free the ring from her finger. I try to ignore any thoughts that suggest she knew she was going to die, and that's why she left the ring behind. For me to have something to remember her by.

"Of course, there is another possibility," Giovanni says.

"What is it?"

"If your fiancée was not abducted . . . if she was merely leaving you . . . then perhaps she removed the ring from her finger and dropped it onto the cobblestones before walking away for good. A final, physical act that would represent the end."

I loosen my grip on the ring while my heart once more nosedives south. But I must admit, as painful as it is to hear what he's suggesting, he still makes perfect sense. I recall just yesterday afternoon when the ring fell to the cobbles beside our table in a different, quieter piazza not far from the Grand Canal. I recognized the sound of the metal smacking against the stone. That wasn't the case in San Marco, which is always crowded, always loud, always confusing and distracting. Especially for a blind man.

"I refuse to believe she dropped the relationship *and* the ring, Giovanni," I say after a time. "If she dropped it, she did it because she wants to be found. Rescued."

"But no one saw her being taken. You must accept that as a possibility."

"I understand it as a possibility. But I don't believe it as a reality."

We sit in silence for another few seconds, until Giovanni asks me if he can escort me home. "But first," he adds, "should we not alert the detective to our discovery of the ring?"

He's right. We should alert the detective. But then, if the worst has happened and Grace has been abducted, the ring will be confiscated as evidence. I squeeze the ring harder, as if it's possible to embed it into my skin and flesh. It is all I have left of my love.

Standing, I shove it deep down into my pants pocket. "For now I'll keep the ring. Until we get to the bottom of what happened to my Grace."

Giovanni lays his hand on my shoulder and squeezes, and for the second time tonight, I experience a flash of déjà vu.

"You and I, Captain," he says. "We are more alike than you know."

"How's that?"

"I do not always trust the police either."

Chapter 27

After I explain where I'm staying, Giovanni escorts me home. Not over the water but through the series of back alleys and narrow stone walkways too impossibly connected to describe. He holds my hand the entire way, like I'm a lost child in a hedge maze. Or maybe I'm just a blind mouse. For a man who works as a waiter, his hand is remarkably cold, and hard.

When we come to my building, I fumble for my keys and manage to unlock the building's front door on my own. Giovanni leaves me, but not without handing me a card with his cell number written on it.

"If you need me," he stresses, "please call me. I am not far away, as you can see."

As I can see . . .

"Wait," I say, recalling my mistake in not getting Detective Carbone's number earlier. "Do me a favor and pop your number in my phone." Pulling out my cell, I hand it to him. "You don't need a code to access the dialer. I turned it off a while ago, as soon as I started experiencing the blindness."

"No problem," he says. When he's done, he hands me the phone, then bids me farewell and walks off.

I carefully climb the stairs to the empty apartment over the bookshop, let myself in, find my way to the couch, and collapse onto it. A lonely soldier losing the battle to desperation and grief.

Chapter 28

I'm not sure exactly what time I fall asleep. But when I wake up, the sun is emerging as a red-orange haze over the distant basin. Not only can I see the sun, but I feel the warmth of its rays shining on my face through the open French doors. I've slept all night, but not lying down. Fact is, I'm no longer lying on the couch. Instead I'm standing on the terrace that overlooks the feeder canal and the narrow alley that runs perpendicular to it, all the way to the Grand Canal.

I've been sleepwalking again.

Sleepwalking and dreaming.

Staring at the sun, I try to dredge up the dream, piece it together as if it were a mirror that's shattered into a hundred pieces.

I'm sitting in a brightly lit room. It's a classroom of some kind. Two other men occupy the room with me. There's a fourth man standing at the head of the room, in front of a screen. Slides being projected on the screen. Images of World War II showing the execution of Jews by Nazi Gestapo, the barrels of their Lugers pressed against the backs of the prisoners' heads

*as they kneel before an open mass grave. Images from Vietnam. US Army
soldiers lighting a village on fire, children screaming all around them,
their skin charred and burned from napalm. Images of Saddam Hus-
sein's army gassing the Kurdish children, their chubby, white, doll-like,
open-eyed faces covered in dust and insects. Images of the two passenger
jets crashing into the World Trade Center, the buildings burning from
the top down, young men and women standing on window ledges, making the sign of the cross before leaping to their deaths . . . The man at the
front of the room is bathed in these images, so that it's difficult to make
out his face. "How do you feel when you view these images, gentlemen?"
I'm sitting in between the two men. As if on cue, we glance at one another
over our shoulders, then face the front of the room once more. "I don't feel
a thing," I volunteer. "Not a goddamned thing . . ."*

But is it really a dream?

Feels more like a memory. A distant, but still-vivid memory that
has returned to me. But how can something return to me if I never
experienced it in the first place?

I'm not naked, but I've undressed during the night. I'm wearing only my pants and nothing else. The air is cool on my skin, but
the sun warms it enough that I am not the least bit uncomfortable.

I stand facing the sun, until I sense something behind me.

Turning, I peer into the apartment. Something has happened
while I've been asleep. The couch has been moved, along with Grace's
painting. Stepping inside, I can see that I've rearranged the living
room so that the harvest table is now pressed up against the end of
the couch to create one long continuous object. I've laid out the
plates and bowls on the floor opposite the couch and table so that,
at first glance, it gives the appearance of an S-shaped path.

Like a child who's occupied himself on a rainy day by using
everyday household objects to create a small city on his bedroom
floor, I find myself walking this little S-shaped path until I come to

its end. On the floor, centered directly in between the plates to my right and the farthest edge of the couch to my left, is a card. A card containing a painting of a woman.

Bending at the knees, I pick the card up. It's a mass card that must have come from one of Venice's many churches. The image is of a young woman dressed in a Renaissance-era gown. Her hair is pulled back into a kind of bun, and she's staring up at the heavens, rays of light beaming into her eyes, which are no longer there. Rather, her eyes have been set on a round silver platter, which she holds in her left hand.

I shiver, recalling an earlier dream: Grace's severed head set on the waiter's tray.

Below the image are the words *Santa Lucia*.

"Saint Lucy," I whisper.

I try to recall if Grace and I visited a church dedicated to Saint Lucy during this past week. For certain I know that we haven't. We haven't visited any churches or museums. So where did this card come from and why is it on the floor in the middle of a path I've created in my sleep out of couches, tables, silverware, and plates?

I stare down at the card, turn it over.

A short bio of Saint Lucy is printed on the back. Having sworn her devotion to God, Lucy refused to give up her virginity to her pagan husband. In turn, the evil bastard gouged her eyes out with a silver spoon. The Italian translation for Lucia means "light." Lucy became patron saint to all those who could no longer see the light because of their blindness. I guess in a small way that makes her my patron saint, even if I've never heard of her until now. I wonder if I have to believe in God to believe in Saint Lucy.

I slide the card into my pocket, and once more stare out the open doors into the light of the sun.

"Dear Saint Lucy," I pray aloud, "help me find my Grace today."

My words sound empty inside an infinite and expanding universe. But I am not entirely without faith. I find my clothes and dress while I wait for an answer. A sign. A voice, a warm breeze, a tickling sensation inside my empty gut. Anything. But nothing happens.

I wonder if the little boy I killed in the Tajik village sees God. I wonder if Karen and our unborn child see him. If the men who died while following me into battle see him. If the enemy sees him.

Chapter 29

I check my e-mail and my texts. Nothing. I call Grace's phone and get the same prerecorded message telling me her mailbox is full.

Slipping the phone back into my pocket, I think about my next move.

I decide to start from the beginning. When we first arrived in Venice, my come-and-go blindness seemed irreparable, and it was placing a more than considerable strain on a relationship already tested by time, separation, distance, faded dreams, war, and, yes, infidelity. Depression had sunk deep into my bones. That's not all. I felt I deserved to be blinded. I deserved to have my sight robbed from me for what I did to that boy. If that small child had to lose his face, then it was only right I lose my eyes. Maybe it's even right that I lose my fiancée. Lose her back to her ex-husband. I've already lost my first wife. Maybe it's my fate to be forever on the losing end of the stick . . . my penitence for heeding the call of the gun.

Grace didn't see it that way.

I was only doing what I was told and trained to do. Obeying orders. We're at war. My calling in an airstrike on that village might have saved the lives of dozens or even hundreds of other soldiers and innocents alike. I'd bombed other villages and towns just like it over the years, so why should this one be any different? I'd killed countless times and never once questioned my actions, because after all, we're at war. Sure, the death of a little kid was tragic, but I wasn't the one who turned him into a living bomb. Grace insisted I had to believe that or else I would never recover my eyesight. But as we walked the alleyways and passages of Venice during those first few quiet days, her arm wrapped around my own, I sensed what she was really saying was this: you have to believe in your innocence or you will lose me.

We didn't talk much those first couple of days.

Grace tried to paint and she tried to transcribe the scattering of pink Post-it Notes shoved in the pockets of her leather coat into some poems. But, in her words, "Nothing will come." She encouraged me to try and write, but I told her I couldn't see the words. I didn't want to write if I couldn't see the words themselves, and I didn't want to write if that little boy didn't have a life.

"That little boy and what happened to him is not your fault," she said. "You did the right thing."

I did the right thing, but what was it about this boy that his death affected me so much?

In my head, I saw him coming toward me. Coming toward my men, that bomb strapped to his chest. I saw myself acting on instinct. I wasn't seeing a little boy at that point. I was seeing imminent destruction. My training dictated that I show no sentimentality toward the enemy. No hesitation or prejudice when it came to pulling the trigger on a danger so volatile it not only threatened to eliminate my life, but the lives of my men. All of them.

I thought about Grace's words.

Not your fault.

For all our troubles, Grace believed in me. And maybe she was right. Maybe she understood what was happening more than I did. The malady. The malfunction. The short circuit that was not only causing me temporary blindness, but also a kind of confusion.

A pressure was building up inside my brain that was inexplicable and at worst it felt like hell. At best it made me want to sleep. As if I were suffering from the results of a concussion.

Question is, what's memory and what's dream? What's imagined and what's real? My brain feels like a computer that's been invaded with a virus and now it produces nothing fluid, nothing logical, no single series of threads that I can piece together. Just snippets of events, emotions, fleeting visions. Like shadows that catch your attention during the deep night and send a cold shiver up and down your spine. The shadows are you. But they don't feel like you. They feel like strangers. Strangers out to get you.

I never know when the shadows are going to arrive.

But one thing is certain: the moments the shadows come are the moments I'm beginning to fear the most.

⌣

Grace and I were trying to strike a balance between the darkness and the light. Until the day before yesterday when, finally, we had it out at that caffè. If I was going to be blind, then Grace was going to try and work with the darkness. She tried to make me see things with my hands, my ears, my five senses. While a stranger stared at us from a distance, she placed the ring into the palm of my hand and she asked me to tell her what I felt. I told her it made me angry that she assumed I was blind to something so plainly obvious as an engagement band. But the ring, I now realize, had nothing to do with what she was asking me.

She was asking me if I felt her love.

Reaching into my pocket, I pull the ring out, stare down at it, feel the short hairs rise up on the back of my neck.

"You left this behind for me to find, didn't you, Grace? Because if you no longer loved me . . . if you wanted to leave me, you would have done something else. You would have tossed it into the drink, and disappeared forever."

Squeezing the ring, as if Grace were the one pressing it against my skin, I return it to my pocket.

A buzzer goes off, and I nearly jump out of my skin.

I go to the door, depress the intercom mounted to the plaster wall beside it. *"Pronto."*

"*Scusi*, Captain Angel. It is the police. May we come up?"

It's Detective Carbone. My stomach muscles constrict. If he has news of Grace, why couldn't he just call me about it? Why make the trip over here?

"Come up," I say into the intercom while pushing the door release.

It dawns on me now, I can see. But my gut is telling me not to let the detective know. I'm not sure why. Maybe it has something to do with my waiter friend, Giovanni. Like him, I'm not so sure I trust the police.

Chapter 30

A knock on the door.

"Captain Angel," barks the detective.

"Coming," I say.

I open the door. I've slid on my sunglasses, but even with the tinted lenses hiding my eyes, I try not to connect directly with the stout, bearded man's gaze, nor that of the uniformed cop who accompanies him. The cop with the better English, I think.

I tell them both to come in, while I step aside. The door shuts behind them and the uniformed cop whispers something into the detective's ear.

"You have been doing some redecorating, I'm told," Carbone comments.

My stomach tightens for the second time in as many minutes.

"Tell me, Captain Angel," he says. "How do you manage such maneuvers in the dark?"

"I'm sorry," I say, as if I don't understand his question.

"Isn't it a dangerous proposition to be moving heavy furniture when you are blind?"

I laugh. But nothing's funny.

"Now I understand, Detective," I say, pushing the sunglasses farther up on the crown of my nose. "I've been trying to work with my blindness. Testing my skills without the use of my eyes. It's a way for me to train myself for a life of no sight, should it come to that."

I'm not looking directly at him. But out of the corner of my eye, the detective nods, and shoots a glare at the uniformed cop. The cop returns the glare. The puckered-ass expressions on both their faces scream of suspicion.

"Do you mind if we sit down?"

"Of course," I say. "I'm sorry I don't have any coffee brewing. I can try and make some."

"No, *grazie*. We've already had ours."

I move slowly, guiding myself with the fingers on my right hand, until I pretend to locate the couch's armrest, where I perch instead of sitting beside the detective. Behind me, the uniformed cop remains standing at the apartment door, as though guarding it.

"Who is the painter?" the detective asks.

"Grace is the painter," I answer. "And a poet. You should know that by now."

"A self-portrait," he says. "Then she is pregnant, Captain?"

"It's possible," I say. Grace, tracing the image on her canvas with my hands, knowing what she was trying to reveal to me was far more precious than a work of art. What I find impossible to believe is that she would so willingly abandon our future.

"Whatever the case," he says, "she wears many hats, including that of your wife-to-be."

"Yes, she does. It's all a part of what makes her beautiful."

"Endearing, Captain. How interesting she should fall in love with a soldier."

"I don't see your point."

"I'm having trouble picturing an artist as accomplished as Grace falling in love with a military man. Usually artists seem to attract artists. They tend to shun the military type."

He smiles, but I pretend I can't see him smiling. I know he's trying to bait me. But I'm not sure why he's doing it.

"You might recall I'm a writer," I say. "Or, hoping to be a writer one day. I might not be a visual artist. But there's definitely an art to what I aspire to."

"A blind writer," he says, as if it's a punch line. "You'll have to excuse me, Captain. I forgot about your book-writing aspirations. Of course you are an artist. Now it all makes sense."

Sliding off the armrest, I face the detective without actually looking into his eyes. "Please tell me. Do you have news?"

"Yes," he says, half under his breath. "I'm afraid I do."

My limbs tremble. I try not to look directly at him when he reaches into his pocket, pulls out a passport.

"Hold out your hand," he says.

I hold out my hand, palm up. He sets the passport into it. I feel the familiar, flexible plastic-coated cover. It's wet. It's been dunked in water, or left out in the rain or both.

"Do you know what you are holding?"

"A passport." I swallow.

"That's correct. Your fiancée's passport."

"Where . . . where did you find it?"

He stands. "It was fished out of the Grand Canal by tourists during their gondola ride."

"What does this mean?"

"It means we know for certain now Grace is not leaving the country. We also know it's possible harm has indeed come to her."

I try to avoid looking directly at Grace's picture when I open it, and pretend to scan the pages with my fingers.

"I'll need that back, of course," Carbone adds.

Before handing it back to him, I thumb to the first page and run my fingers over Grace's face. My eyes fill, and I find it hard to swallow. With an unsteady hand, I return the passport to him.

He pockets it and stands in silence for a moment. The silence makes me feel uncomfortable. Exposed. Like I'm standing inside a fishbowl.

"What are you doing to find Grace?" I say.

He reaches into his pocket for his cigarettes. Holds them up to me, as though asking me if he has permission to light up.

"It's okay," I assure him. "You can smoke."

He lights up with his flip-top Zippo, returns the lighter to his jacket pocket. I tell him there's an ashtray on the counter of the kitchenette. Slipping past me, he locates the ashtray and hovers over it while he smokes.

He says, "With your permission, I'd like to list Grace as officially missing before the required forty-eight hours have passed. Now that we have evidence, however circumstantial, of foul play."

A part of me wants to scream, "It's about time!" But another part of me wants to show him that it's time we started working together to find Grace.

"Please," I beg. "What can I do to help?"

I see him glance at the uniformed cop, then to me, and back to the cop.

"I'd like you to come in for more questioning. Say later today. If that's okay with you." Smoking, laughing wryly. "I can't imagine in your condition, you have much in the way of plans, Captain Angel."

He once more glances at the cop standing by the door, who is also smiling wryly.

"No," I say. "I don't have much in the way of plans."

He stamps out the cigarette.

"I'll have someone pick you up. Say about fifteen hundred?"

"Three o'clock. That's fine."

He begins making his way toward the door. "Oh, and one more thing, Captain. You have not received any more strange phone calls over the landline? Anything my people and their tracing might have missed?"

I tell him I haven't.

He nods, and I pretend not to see it.

The uniformed cop opens the door, steps out. The detective follows. Until he stops and turns once more.

"Captain," he says, "I never actually asked you if I could smoke."

The comment nearly robs me of my breath.

"I'm sorry," I say. "I'm not sure I understand."

"I merely pulled out the pack of cigarettes and gestured to you like I *wanted* to smoke. I never actually asked."

"Since I've lost my eyesight," I say, "I've learned to recognize the sounds of things. I know you are a smoker, and I heard you go into your pockets for your pack of cigarettes. I heard you take out your lighter."

He nods, once more shoots a glance at his colleague.

"Of course," he sighs. "How silly of me."

He steps out and politely shuts the door behind him.

Chapter 31

Stealing a moment to collect myself, I walk to the French doors and stand out on the terrace. Below, people are crossing the pedestrian bridge that spans the feeder canal.

I wonder how long my vision will last. If the blindness is finally disappearing for good. The detective almost certainly saw through my act and, if that's the case, it's possible he believes I have been faking my blindness all along, regardless of what the US Army states about me in their reports. If he believes I am faking my condition, he will consider me a suspect in Grace's disappearance. No two ways about it.

I find the card bearing the image of Santa Lucia. I also take out the card with Giovanni's cell number and recall that he added his number to my speed dial. The police will be here to collect me at three o'clock. That gives me seven hours to try to find out what might have happened to my fiancée before I drown in this shit storm and something horrible happens to Grace. That is, if something horrible hasn't happened already.

———— ————

Giovanni isn't expected at work until the evening. In the half hour it takes him to get here, I shower and change my clothes. For now, it is far safer to go out in the world with someone who can look after me when and if the lights go out. I meet him down in the street and together we share a coffee at a cramped bar before heading toward the Ponte di Rialto, where we'll cross over onto the opposite side of the Grand Canal into what used to be the Jewish ghetto.

"Let me get this straight," the tall, black-haired Giovanni says as he sips his caffè macchiato. "The police have located Grace's passport, and now they believe she was indeed kidnapped. But they still have no witnesses to the event."

"Other than me," I confirm, taking a careful sip of my caffè Americano.

"But you were blind at the time. So you are, how you say in English . . . an unreliable witness?"

I nod. "That about sums it up."

"And now you see again."

"But I don't know for how long."

"And why do we want to visit the church where the blind Santa Lucia rests in her peace?"

"Because that's what I told myself to do in my sleep."

He nearly chokes on his coffee.

"*Scusi?*" he says, wiping coffee from his lips with the back of his hand.

I drink some more coffee, explain to him in as few words as possible about my three separate bouts of sleepwalking during the past three nights. During the first night, I climbed onto the roof. On the second night, when Grace was gone, I began to build a city inside the apartment. A 3-D map out of boxes, spoons, knives, forks, and dishes. I didn't know what city I was building until I completed it and it most definitely became a model of Venice, complete with the Grand Canal in its center. And at the very head of the canal was placed a mass card depicting the eyeless face of Santa Lucia. It's as if my subconscious has been trying to give me directions.

"Are you suggesting," he says as he finishes off his coffee in one swift pull, "that you can see things in your head before they happen?"

I shake my head.

"Not exactly," I explain. "But what if it's possible that Grace is trying to communicate with me? Like two people who are so connected they anticipate one another's phone calls before they happen. They call one another at the exact same time. So exact that the phone doesn't even ring. Suddenly that person is there, on the line."

"You and Grace are that close."

I down the rest of my coffee.

"Not as close as we're trying to be," I say. "I suppose I can't read her mind exactly. But I believe it's possible to somehow feel her trying to communicate with me. It's a matter of believing she wants to come back."

"But you might be all wrong in your beliefs. It's also possible that Grace doesn't want to communicate with you."

He's right, of course, and it's a possibility I must accept. My sleepwalking could be just that, sleepwalking and nothing more. The city I've built out of those boxes and plates could simply be the work of an anxiety-ridden soldier trying to cope with the horrible effects of PTSD. End of story. Maybe I placed the mass card of Santa Lucia on the floor or maybe there's some other explanation of how it got there. The apartment is rented to lots of military men and women. So I'm told. Many of them must visit the church where Santa Lucia lies inside her glass coffin. It is a Venetian landmark. Maybe the occupant of the studio prior to Grace and me paid a visit to the blind saint and carried the mass card home with him.

"I understand what you're trying to tell me. It's possible my logic is broken, but then even a broken clock can be relied on to tell the right time twice a day."

Giovanni nods, then places a couple of euros on the counter.

"Your blindness," he says, laying a hand on my arm. "It might make you more in tune with her thoughts. You try harder to feel what she feels. To see what she sees."

"My blindness can provide me with a special tool," I agree. "But I need my eyesight in order to find her."

"You need both. You need the dark and the light."

As we exit the coffee bar, I find myself praying for the onset of blindness. But not yet.

Chapter 32

We walk along the cobblestones that line the flat banks of the Grand Canal, until we come to the Ponte di Rialto, the white-marbled bridge of stairs spanning the canal's head. Descending the steps on the opposite side of the bridge, I spot the train station to my left and the pedestrian street that leads deep into the old Jewish district, now filled with artists, shops, student housing, and restaurants. Tourists cram into the cobbled passageways along with gelato and fruit venders. As we pass a small piazza, a group of clowns are performing magic tricks with metal hoops, rope, and long walking sticks. Not much farther up the way from them a violinist plays a sad harmony. He's an old man dressed in wool jacket and matching trousers. On his head, he wears a black wool skullcap. For shoes, old leather cordovans that now are riddled with holes and held precariously together with strips of filthy gray duct tape. Laid out on the cobbles is his open violin case. Fumbling inside my pocket, I find a ten-euro note and drop it into the case. He nods, smiles.

We move on in the direction of San Geremia, where Santa Lucia lies in state, the blind seeking out the blind.

We find the church nestled at the far end of a square that's book-ended by feeder canals. Some children are playing in the square, kicking a soccer ball back and forth. It's going on nine in the morning and the sun has risen, warm and bright. Raising my face, I feel it seep in through the thin skin that covers my eyes, and into my eyeballs. I've been able to see now without interruption for more than three hours.

I follow Giovanni to the wood doors of the stone-faced, Gothic church. He pulls the door open and we are greeted by a barred ticket window. I dig out another ten-euro note and pay for the both of us. We're handed two entry tickets attached to the same card containing the image of Santa Lucia holding her extracted eyes that I found on my apartment floor. When I hand my ticket to the ticket taker, he tears the card, or stub, off at the perforated seam and hands it back to me. I stuff the card into my pants pocket along with the one I found this morning. Giovanni hands over his ticket, gets the card back in return.

Then we enter the church.

The old church smells of burning incense and, aside from Giovanni and myself, there are no other visitors to be found at this hour of the morning. The pews are empty, as are the small chapels that flank the main altar. Placed in the center of the altar is a glass coffin that contains a red-robed body laid out on a bed of silver. It immediately grabs my attention the same way a hot fire can suddenly rob you of your breath.

"What do you wish me to do?" Giovanni whispers, his voice taking on a slight echo despite its soft tone.

"Just stay close to me. Keep your eyes open for Grace."

"But the church, she is empty."

"Not everything is as it appears, my friend."

The church comes alive with the sound of our leather soles slapping the hard marble floor. It makes me feel like I'm about to wake the dead.

As a born and bred Roman Catholic who long ago abandoned his church and its rules, I'm not a praying man by any means. I've seen too much death and devastation, and I've witnessed too many men and women willingly blow themselves up in the name of a God who promises them paradise and dozens of vestal virgins as a reward. But when we come to the altar, I intuitively drop to one knee and make the sign of the cross. It takes me by surprise when Giovanni does the same thing. Standing, we approach the glass tomb.

Santa Lucia was a small woman. Smaller than small by today's standards. She can't occupy more than four and a half feet inside the glass coffin in which she is laid out, her more than five-hundred-year-old body somehow nearly perfectly preserved, as if touched by God the moment her heart stopped beating. In the place of her gouged-out eyes are a pair of fake, glass eyes. They are strikingly green, just like Grace's. Peering at them through the glass coffin, I find myself growing dizzy and out of balance.

Is this why I was drawn to this place in my sleep? To witness this old saint's fake eyes? Eyes that look back at me from the dead? Eyes that look like Grace's?

For a brief moment, I feel like I might lose consciousness. Sensing my fall, Giovanni grabs hold of me.

"Are you all right, Captain?"

I nod. At the same time, I feel my vision begin to fade in and out of focus. I know I will soon lose my ability to see altogether. But not yet. I must make a sweep of the entire church before that happens. It's exactly how I explain it to Giovanni.

We search the church and find no sign of Grace.

In the end, I feel thoroughly exhausted and consumed with grief, as if I came to this place only to realize that Grace is already dead. I sit inside the final row of pews, close my eyes, and feel the onset of dread. When I open my eyes again, a single wet tear falls down my cheek and I see something through the haze of rapidly diminishing eyesight.

I see a man wearing a long brown overcoat.

Chapter 33

He's standing at the altar, facing the rows of pews, his back to the glass coffin.

The man who took my Grace.

He's staring directly at me, those black eyes reflecting the firelight from the candles. At first I think I might be seeing things. Maybe I fell asleep and now I'm conjuring up his image in a dream. A vivid dream. But I know this is not a dream when Giovanni gently elbows me.

"There is the bastardo," he says loudly.

Standing, he jumps over the pew, and takes off after the overcoat man.

Chapter 34

I follow on Giovanni's heels, both of us sprinting the length of the aisle toward the altar.

"Stop!" I shout, the demand sounding entirely inadequate despite an amplifying echo.

It takes only about a second and a half for us to reach the altar. But when we get there, the overcoat man has vanished.

Giovanni turns to me.

"Other side of the coffin!" I bark.

Coming from behind me, the shouts of the church guards. They are yelling at us to stay where we are. They're running toward us, blaring voices and stomping boots reverberating against the stone walls. Giovanni disappears behind the glass coffin. I follow.

We eye one another. *Where the hell did he go?*

Until I see the sacristy door only a couple feet away from Giovanni.

"There!" I say, lunging for the solid wood-paneled door.

I open the door and Giovanni and I both slip inside. Closing it, I grab hold of a chair leaning up against the wall and shove the chair back under the handle. Just in time. The guards converge on the door. They attempt to plow through it by shoving their shoulders into the panel. But the door and the chair are holding.

The sacristy is like a pantry for dozens of robes and cassocks. The shelves store gold chalices, incense burners, crucifix staffs, and wine bottles. The room transports me back to the days when I was an altar boy. It's long and narrow and leads to an exterior door.

The door is open.

Without having to utter another word, Giovanni and I sprint for the open door and head back out into the salty Venetian air.

Chapter 35

We stand on the narrow walkway. Directly before us is a feeder canal, its water calm and undisturbed. To our right and left, nothing but empty, cobblestone-covered walkway.

"Do you believe we really saw the man in the brown overcoat, Captain?" Giovanni whispers after a time.

"We saw him," I answer, my heart just beginning to dislodge itself from my throat. "We saw him and he got away."

"How did he know to find us here?"

"I'm not looking for him. But he's most definitely got his eye on me. Maybe even had his eye on me *and* Grace since we arrived." I pause. "There's something else that bothers me."

"What is it?"

"The card with Santa Lucia that I found on the floor of my apartment this morning. Maybe I found it because the overcoat man put it there."

"*Mamma mia*, Captain, he was in your home? Last night? I thought you put it there in your sleep."

I look into his eyes.

"He was here waiting for us, Giovanni. How could that be unless he led us here?"

But Giovanni doesn't have time to answer. Making their way toward us on foot, in the direction of the church entrance, are three uniformed police officers being led by Detective Carbone.

"Stay where you are!" the detective shouts. "You are under arrest!"

Chapter 36

"What makes you think you would find your fiancée inside that church?"

I remove two identical cards from out of my pocket and hand him the older one I found on my floor. "This morning I found a card on the floor of my apartment. It has the face of Santa Lucia painted on it, and it comes from that church where you unjustly arrested my friend and me."

The detective glances down at it, sets it aside on his desk. "I will hang on to this for now. Perhaps have it tested for prints."

"Knock yourself out," I say.

"Your friend has been released pending further questioning. He's been escorted back to his caffè in San Marco."

"Kind of you, Detective. Why haven't I been afforded the same courtesy? I am a guest in your country."

"Indeed you are, Captain Angel, which makes what I'm about to tell you all the more sensitive."

"I hope you are about to tell me you have developed a solid lead on the whereabouts of my fiancée."

Carbone stands, comes around his desk, pulls out his cigarettes, and lights one with his silver lighter. Staring out the window onto the Grand Canal, he smokes. Contemplatively.

"This morning, Captain," he says, while staring into his reflection, "you could see me. Yet you chose to fake your blindness."

My eyes leave his backside and refocus on his desktop. Grace's waterlogged passport sits on top of it. A voice inside me screams, *Grab the passport and make a run for it.* But I know that would be like committing suicide.

I shift my eyes back to him.

"I'm not sure why I did it," I confess. "It's the truth. I panicked. I was afraid you might think I've been faking it all along."

"Your strategy has had the opposite effect. Indeed, it makes me believe perhaps you have been faking it. Taken together with the argument you had with Grace the afternoon before she disappeared, plus your severe post-traumatic stress disorder, we have reason to believe the proper course of action is to detain you under police custody for the time being."

I shoot up from my chair. "A man in an overcoat took Grace. He's been calling my apartment. He's been tracking us. It's quite possible he left a card with the image of Santa Lucia on it on my floor while I was asleep. I saw him inside the church this morning. So did the damn waiter. He's following me, Detective. Baiting me. Playing with me."

I'm shouting, without trying to shout.

Carbone turns, stares me down.

"Allow me to better explain, Captain," he says, coming back to his desk, sitting down on the edge of it, one foot planted firmly on the floor, and the other hanging off the edge. "You are not being

149

arrested . . . yet. But you are under suspicion in the disappearance of your fiancée."

"You have no right."

"Please sit, Captain, and calm down. It's not as bad as it may seem."

"How much worse could it get?"

"When I say you are under suspicion, it simply means you have not been eliminated as a suspect. You have no alibi and you've already been caught fabricating your blindness. Taken together with the argument you had with Grace only hours prior to her disappearance, we find we simply cannot rule you out as a suspect."

"My blindness is real, and it's temporary. My US military record reflects the truth."

"Indeed it does. But that does not take away from the charade you carried on this morning."

"I'm trying to protect Grace from any further harm."

"You are only managing to cause her further harm by interrupting my investigation into her disappearance." He holds out his hand. "Now if you don't mind, your passport, please."

"I want to speak with Mr. Graham at the embassy."

"He's been alerted and he's aware of our decision. He can't help you, Captain, but you're free to contact him at your convenience." He gestures over his shoulder toward his desktop. "By all means, use my phone."

But I decide not to give him the satisfaction. Reaching into the interior pocket of my coat, I retrieve my passport, hand it over to him. What the hell choice do I have?

"As usual, Captain, I am happy to provide you with a lift back to your apartment."

I stand. "No *grazie*, Detective. I'd rather walk. For now, I can see." I turn for the door.

"But what if you should go blind in the meantime?" he asks, some sarcasm sprinkled in his tone. "I would feel terrible unleashing you into Venice without the benefit of your eyes. As you are already sorely aware, this city can be a confusing place even with perfect vision."

In my mind, I'm picturing the overcoat man leaving a picture of Santa Lucia on my apartment floor while I'm asleep on the couch. Maybe he was the one who arranged the plates, bowls, knives, forks, and boxes to resemble the water city of Venice. Maybe he somehow baited me up onto the roof of my building in the early morning before he was to kidnap Grace. Maybes. Possibilities. Or perhaps, just wild assumptions on my part.

"Nor is it without its dangers," I say.

"Never a truer word has been spoken, Captain. We'll be in touch."

"Find Grace, Detective Carbone. Do your job."

"It will be our distinct pleasure. Believe me."

Chapter 37

Turns out I barely make it home before the lights start going out in my brain. I'm seeing through a foggy blur of distorted shapes by the time I reach the stairs up to the apartment. Unlocking the door, I step inside, feel my way to the repositioned harvest table, then feel my way to the couch and sit down.

I barely feel the blow to the back of my head before I'm face down on the floor.

Unconscious.

Chapter 38

The three of us are led outside to a yard surrounded by a concrete and razor-wire fence. From where I'm standing, it looks like a yard belonging to a maximum-security prison. Suddenly, two uniformed soldiers come out of nowhere, tackle the two men beside me, and force them down onto their knees while their wrists are bound behind their backs with plastic ties. I'm ordered to stand behind both men by the taller soldier. He pulls his sidearm, forces it into my hand.

"Do it," he barks. "Do them both."

I look at him, dumbfounded.

"They're my friends," I say. "We fought together in the Persian Gulf. We were just kids, really."

"They're the enemy," he barks. "And now they're dead."

Heart pumping in my throat, tears blurring my vision, I slowly raise the pistol to the skull of the first man. I thumb back the hammer, release a breath, squeeze the trigger.

The hammer comes down.

I scream.
But there are no rounds in the chamber.

Chapter 39

When I come to, I'm lying on the bed, face up.

It's dark out, the time on my watch barely five o'clock in the morning. An hour before the dawn. I've been asleep for more than ten hours. As usual, when I wake up these days, I can see. Perfectly. Clearly.

I reach around to the back of my head and feel for a lump, or an abrasion, or a cut. Something to confirm that I was hit over the head when I came back home by someone who'd been waiting for me. The overcoat man maybe. No, scratch that. For certain, the overcoat man.

There's a lump rising from the back of my lower head above the spine. It's a bruise and tender to the touch. I pull back my fingers and examine them for blood. There's no blood, but someone definitely hit me with something.

My head throbs. Head aches.

Concussion? Maybe. Not my first.

Whoever hit me was waiting inside my apartment.

Whoever hit me has a key to the place.

Whoever hit me doesn't want me dead. He wants to antagonize me. Torture me. Prove to me he's more powerful than I am.

Why?

I have no idea, other than he is not satisfied with simply abducting Grace. He wants something more. But what exactly does he want?

Without a note or a phone call or an e-mail detailing a list of demands, I haven't the slightest clue. But there's one thing I do know. Best that I take advantage of the sight I've got for now.

I start by habit, speed-dialing Grace's number, and get the usual song and dance. Setting the phone back onto the table, I slip out of bed, turn on the bedside lamp, and in the dull glow of the lamplight, view something extraordinary. The furniture has all been put back in its rightful place. The couch and the harvest table take up the center of the room, the length of the table pressed up against the back of the couch. The plates, cups, bowls, spoons, knives, and forks have been returned to the cupboards, the boxes and jars of food replaced on the shelves. Grace's unfinished painting remains undisturbed and ready for more brushwork, should she ever return to it.

I stare out the open French doors and feel the cool, fish-tainted air seeping in. In the distance I can make out the occasional electric light, but no voices or purring motors or footsteps. No Grace.

Stepping around the table and couch, I slide past the easel and close the doors. Then I decide to take some aspirin and make some coffee. When the coffee's done, I take it to the couch and try to figure out exactly what happened when I arrived home yesterday afternoon. Did the overcoat man hit me over the head, then leave? Or did he clean up the place and, if so, why the hell bother? Why didn't I wake up on the floor or on the couch? How did I get to my bed? Or maybe I woke up on the floor and then, in a sleepwalking state, cleaned up the studio and got in bed, fully clothed, and fell into a deep, dreaming sleep.

I'm reminded of the Santa Lucia card I found on the floor yesterday morning.

If it wasn't placed there by the overcoat man, then how did it get there?

Maybe it was inside the apartment all along, courtesy of the previous tenant. Maybe when I discovered it, I immediately interpreted it as a clue. Maybe the overcoat man simply followed me to the church instead of the other way around: me following him.

My mind is spinning with questions for which I have no answers. Why am I not calling the police right now? Because they'll think I'm lying. At the very least, they'll use the attack to detain me inside a cell. For my own protection, they'll insist. Grace is still out there somewhere, at the mercy of the overcoat man. I can't allow myself to be locked away. I can't risk it.

I sip my coffee. It's hot, but the unanswerable questions that buzz around my brain like flies around the dead fill me with an ice-cold dread.

The coffee cup nearly slips from my fingers when the phone rings. I set the cup down, sprint to the wall phone, pick it up. I don't utter a word. I just listen. The earpiece provides a near silent static. Like air blowing through the line. Then I hear the voice.

"I see."

"What the fuck do you see?" I respond, as if at this point, I'm going to get an answer. "Tell me what you see, you son of a bitch."

"I see."

His refusal to say anything but those two words is my cue to begin rattling off the obvious questions. Questions that have no chance in hell of being answered.

"Do you have Grace? Do you wear a brown overcoat? Did you follow me to San Geremia church? Have you been up in my apartment? How'd you get a key to the place? How'd you get this number? Did you hit me over the head? For Christ's sake, answer me."

"I see" is all he says. And then the line goes dead.

Goes . . . dead.

Chapter 40

I slam the phone into its cradle, wondering if the police have traced the call and if there is anything they can do about it at this point. I run my hand behind my head. Just touching the tender skin and flesh unleashes shock waves of pain. The smart thing to do is get myself to a hospital. But that would only waste precious time . . . prevent me from finding Grace.

Outside the French doors, past Grace's painting, I make out the first rays of the sun exploding over the horizon. Soon it will be first light, and another day of Grace gone missing. My eyes drift to the bed and the baggage stacked beside it. I see my computer bag. It's gone untouched since I unpacked my laptop after I first arrived in Venice.

I listen to my gut. It tells me that maybe it's time to go online and do some detecting of my own.

Dozens of times while in Iraq and, to an extent, Afghanistan, we used the power of the press to our advantage, sending out false leads and stories on enemy combatants we wanted flushed out in the open. It didn't always work, but the general rule is that people love fame, no matter how humble, no matter how fleeting. Maybe the asshole who took Grace is no different. So then, why don't I put the story out there? I'll put it up on all the social media sites. I'll alert the news. Christ, I'll even start a blog.

If the overcoat man is following me, he'll take notice of it.

I set the laptop on the harvest table, boot it up, wait for an Internet connection. When it arrives, I bring up CNN world news. I scour the site for the latest headlines. I search through the global headlines and the world news. Another suicide bomber in Kabul. The military withdrawal from Iraq. A passenger jet crashes in Nigeria. Then I take a chance and type in, "US woman goes missing in Italy."

At first I don't believe Grace's disappearance will make the news that fast. But then, unlike my memories and dreams, the words don't deceive. The small sidebar story consists of just a few paragraphs. It's not even accompanied by a photo.

The piece, written by a journalist named Anna Laiti, simply states that a US citizen by the name of Grace Blunt, an artist living in Troy, New York, was reported missing yesterday by authorities in Venice, Italy.

Having traveled to Italy with her fiancé, Captain Nick Angel of the US Army Reserves, Blunt is said to have disappeared from a popular tourist caffè in Piazza San Marco. It's still too early to tell if her disappearance was the result of her own decision to leave what witnesses describe as a "troubled relationship," or the result of foul play. The detective in charge of the matter, Detective Paulo Carbone, has reported that Blunt's passport was located floating in the Grand Canal. While the US Embassy states no US officials have yet committed to the search for the American, they do not rule out the possibility.

That's it.

No mention of my temporary blindness. No mention of the overcoat man. No mention of the strange phone calls. No mention of the overcoat man having followed me to the resting place of Santa Lucia. Nothing.

My heart races and my brain buzzes with adrenaline. Why didn't the reporter contact me for my side of the story? And who fed her the not-entirely-accurate information about Grace and me having a troubled relationship?

I click on Anna Laiti's byline.

The link offers up her bio. No contact info. Not even an e-mail address.

Maybe it would interest her to know I have an opinion on the matter of my missing fiancée. But then, how can I possibly contact her? I see a place where I am invited to comment on the above article.

It's not the same as knocking on Anna Laiti's front door, but it will have to do.

Chapter 41

Here's what I write: *My name is Nick Angel. The woman you are writing about, Grace Blunt, is my fiancée. She was taken from me while we were having lunch at a caffè across from the cathedral in San Marco. I have been suffering a recurring, temporary blindness since my participation in the war in Afghanistan and had no way of seeing her being taken, nor the individual who did the taking. But only moments prior to her disappearance, Grace had been complaining of a man in a long brown overcoat who was staring at her. He was a man with a cropped beard, black hair, and very dark eyes hidden behind sunglasses. He's been following us. He approached our table, which upset Grace. Within seconds, she was gone. Please contact me here as soon as you see this. I am desperate.*

I click "Send" and wait for a reply.

The e-mail comes almost two hours later, when the light of day is splashing down on the terrace.

Dear Mr. Angel, please contact me with your phone number at this e-mail address as soon as possible.

I reply with my cell phone number.

Moments later, when the phone rings with a number I do not recognize, I sense that it must be her. Holding Grace's engagement ring in one hand, I answer the cell phone with the other. For the first time in two days, my heart begins to fill with hope.

"Hello," I say.

"Is this Captain Angel?" the voice asks. British-accented, soft and low toned.

"It is. Thank you for calling."

She's not alone. Nor is she in a quiet place like her home or an office. Coming from over the phone, the sounds of a busy, congested place. People shouting in the distance. Laughing. Voices coming from over speakers, announcing arrivals and departures. An airport, more than likely.

"I'm at De Gaulle in Paris," she explains. "I'm about to board a plane for Venice now, where I'm following up on this story and another, separate story. I cover Italy almost exclusively for CNN online."

I glance at the article on the computer. It came out only last night. How could she write about Grace if she's in Paris? It's precisely what I pose to her.

"Welcome to the Internet age, Captain. I can write about anything from anywhere so long as I've access to the proper information. Surely you must realize that as a military officer."

"You're absolutely right. But what I mean is, in this case, you don't have all the information, Ms. Laiti. You never bothered to contact *me* about the situation."

"I didn't have any way of contacting you, and police refused to give out your number. Can you meet me this afternoon?"

"I can try. If my eyes hold up."

"Where are you located in Venice?"

I tell her.

"I'll come to you," she says. "Three o'clock."

"That will work," I tell her. But she hangs up before I get to the word "work."

⎯⎯⎯ ⎯⎯⎯

I sit in silence for the better part of an hour, stealing occasional sips of whiskey to calm my nerves. But the alcohol doesn't prevent my heart from skipping a beat when my cell phone rings again. I fumble for the phone on the harvest table, answer it.

"Hello!"

"Nick," the voice says. "Nick, is this you?"

A wave of confusion sweeps over my body. A man's voice. I've heard the voice before, that much is for sure. But I can't recall where or when. Until it comes to me like a slap across the face. It's Grace's ex, Andrew, calling from New York. It's four o'clock in the afternoon in New York.

"Andrew," I say, "how the hell did you get this number?"

"Grace goes missing and you don't call me?"

I don't have his number. Nor would I have called him anyway. I'm guessing Grace gave him my number. In case of emergency.

Emergency.

I swallow something cold and bitter, then clear my throat.

"Funny you should ask," I say. "I thought professorial types like yourself were all-knowing."

"Don't start, pal. I'm not calling for a fight."

"Then why are you calling, Professor?"

An exhale. "You really have to ask?"

I take a second to gather myself together. What's the point of arguing with the guy? "The police asked me not to call anyone just yet. They didn't want me to alarm anyone unnecessarily. Even you."

"What a load of crap. I had to find out about it on CNN. The bloody Internet, for God's sake, Nick."

Andrew is panicked. Or still in love with Grace. Probably both. Flashing through my brain: the image of them lying in bed together. Naked. Pressed up against one another. I try to remove the image, but it's like yanking a bullet from out of my thigh with a pair of rusty pliers.

"Calm down, Professor. The cops tell me it's very likely she'll show up in a day or two. In the meantime, I'm having her face printed on some milk cartons while I staple some eight by tens to the telephone poles. Oh shit, no telephone poles in Venice. I'll just have to climb the bell tower in the piazza and shout out her name like Hansel and Gretel."

"You've got real issues, Nick, you know that? Too much violence. Too much time spent with those who wish to wage war rather than seek out peace. You're a goddamned killing machine. The United States Defense Department rings the dinner bell and you come running like Pavlov's dog, isn't that right?"

"You finally figured it out, Professor. I'm a slave to my work."

"So what happened, you two have a fight? You get all fired up on Jack Daniel's? You hit her? You try and drown her, maybe? It *is* Venice."

. . . *Water filling the car . . . Shouting, "Karen, get out!" But she's calm as the water rises above her head—like she wants to die . . .*

"Nick? You there?"

"None of your business," I snap, the image of Grace's and my argument at the caffè replacing the memory of Karen dying. "But let me tell you this: it's a very good thing you're thousands of miles away from me right now."

"That's a direct threat coming from a trained assassin, which I am jotting down for my records."

"That's what professors do. Jot things down at their desks."

"You know what I hope has happened, Nick? I hope that Gracie got smart and left you for good. Maybe she got sick of waiting around while you're off playing cowboys and Indians in some desolate country we've unjustly invaded."

"Hey, wait just a minute, Professor. Only I get to call her Gracie."

I could tell him about the overcoat man, about my fear that he's kidnapped my love . . . his ex-love. But then he'd be on the next flight over here and the detective would have no choice but to put me in jail after I beat the professor to a pulp with my bare hands. Instead, I say, "I'm a soldier. It's what I do. And maybe it's time you got used to the fact that I'm with Grace now. Not you, pal."

He's silent for a moment. Then he lets out a deep sigh. "Tell me the truth, Nick."

"You mean like, have Grace and I been fighting a little? Sure, we have our spats. It's not easy coming back from the war. My eyesight comes and goes these days. But then, that's what happens when you man up and defend freedom for asshole professors like yourself. Grace has been under a lot of pressure, too—she feels like hell about what happened with you while I was away. She knows how wrong it was. What a mistake it was."

I feel his exhale more than I hear it. "So you think she took off to be alone?"

Though it kills me to say it, as if I believe it . . . "It's entirely possible, if not probable."

"And what exactly are you doing about the situation?"

I picture him with the phone pressed against his ear, running fingers through his long hair, while the other hand fingers the keys on his laptop inside his university faculty office, perhaps some adoring female students waiting outside the door. Blonde, blue-eyed, female students.

"I'm working with the police and being patient. I'm told to be patient."

"Patient. Isn't that what you asked of my wife when you decided to go off and be John Wayne once again?"

"Hey, John Wayne was cool, pal."

An electric hum fills the connection before Andrew says, "Call me back when you know something."

"And when exactly is my assignment due, Professor?"

He hangs up.

Setting down the phone, I lie on the couch, my open eyes staring at a ceiling that looks much better when I'm blind.

"She's not your wife anymore," I say. But there's no one around to hear me.

Chapter 42

By three o'clock that afternoon, I have heard neither from Grace, which is expected, nor from the police. What is unexpected is that my eyesight has lasted all day without interruption. The buzzer goes off at exactly two minutes after three. I go to the intercom, depress the Speak button.

"Yes," I say into the unit.

"Good afternoon, Captain. It's Anna Laiti."

Unlocking the front door, I tell her to come up.

A minute later the journalist is standing inside my studio. She is an attractive thirty-something woman, with short red hair that's parted over her right eye, smooth pale skin, and deep brown eyes that afford her an air of inquisitiveness and seriousness. She's dressed in a short black skirt, black tights, and knee-high black leather boots, like lots of women in Italy wear this time of year. For a top, she sports a thin gray sweater under a brown leather jacket.

She's carrying her travel bag, which I assume contains her computer. It also tells me she came here straight from the airport. Reaching into her bag, she pulls out a notepad and a pen.

"You don't mind if I take a note or two," she says, more like she's telling, not asking.

I nod. Of course she can take notes. "Would you like a coffee?"

"Please."

Happy I have something to occupy myself with while she's asking me questions, I walk the few steps to the kitchenette and fill the pot with tap water.

"Now," she exhales. "I would like you to start from the beginning."

"From my time here in Venice?" I ask, spooning espresso-blend coffee into the top chamber of the pot. "Or prior to that? Grace and I have had many beginnings."

The studio goes silent while she thinks.

"Tell me about the war, Captain," she says. "And how it took away your eyesight."

"That beginning," I say. I set the pot onto the stove, switch on the gas burner, and turn to face her. "There was a village way up north," I tell her. "I called in the airstrike that destroyed it . . ."

I speak about my war in Afghanistan. But I do not tell her everything. I tell her about the village filled with Taliban who would raid our encampment night after night, causing multiple casualties. I tell that we were like fish in a barrel. That not even the Hesco defense barriers could stop all the bullets raining down on us some nights. Then I tell her about the airstrike. But I do not tell her about what happened to the little boy. What was strapped to his chest.

I fill her in on how the blindness began almost immediately after the incident in the village, and how I was medevacked to Kabul, and from there flown to Frankfurt, where the psychologists went to work on me once it was determined from numerous MRIs that nothing was physically wrong with my brain. Then I tell her about how Venice proved an opportunity for me to not only regain my eyesight, but also for Grace and me to get to know one another again.

By the time I'm done telling the writer my story, we've gone through two pots of espresso. Despite the caffeine, my eyes are getting tired and beginning to lose their focus. Maybe it's exhaustion that triggers the blindness. Maybe it's memories that trigger it. Memories, that for some reason or another, I'm not meant to recall. Not without doing some kind of damage to myself. Without inflicting some kind of pain in my head.

Anna stares down at her notes, bites the nonbusiness end of her pen with her teeth. She looks very young when she does this, like a college student trying to come up with the answers for a midterm exam.

"Please allow me to get my facts straight. The waiter at the caffè . . . this Giovanni . . . he believes you. Yet he did not see Grace being kidnapped." It's a question.

"But he has seen the overcoat man on two or three different occasions. A couple of times outside his caffè, and then yesterday inside the church of San Geremia. That's why I suspect he might have been following Grace and me not just for a couple of days, but all week."

"The police have Grace's passport." Another question.

"Yes. They found it floating in the canal. So they tell me. And I have this." Reaching into my pocket, slowly I withdraw Grace's diamond. "Giovanni located it stuck in the cobblestones under the chair she sat in before she was taken."

"May I?" She holds out her hand.

"Please."

She takes hold of the ring, examines it. I can almost hear the gears spinning in her brain.

"Captain, do you trust me?" she poses.

Her question takes me by surprise. Why shouldn't I trust her? She came here of her own accord directly from Paris. I can only assume she is interested in more than just filling in the missing pieces of yesterday's article. She sees something else going on with Grace's disappearance. Something larger. Deeper. Or perhaps this is just what I want to believe. A man who is desperate for help. Any kind of help.

"Sure," I say. "I suppose I can trust you. Why do you ask?"

She stands, returns her notebook to her bag.

"Because I'd like to take the ring with me and have it tested for prints."

My tired eyes go wide. "You mean at the police station? If they know I have the ring, it might make me look—"

She shakes her head. "I have friends on the inside, as they say, who can test the ring for prints tonight when things are not so busy. I can have it back to you in the morning with my findings."

"Seems to me you're not going to get a hell of a lot from a ring."

She holds up her hand. "You would not believe what crime labs can pick up nowadays with digital holography and new imaging workstation advances. Traces of prints on the tiniest of spaces. I wrote a series of articles on the subject not too long ago. Perhaps there are more prints on the band than yours and Grace's. Perhaps there is a set of prints matching those of a man who wears a brown overcoat."

"But Giovanni and I have handled the ring since. It's likely worn off any prints that the overcoat man could have left, if he touched it in the first place."

She tilts her head in acknowledgment. "It's a long shot, because the ring surface is small. But trust me, not that small. If it does turn out it's possible to uncover the print of a third party and then cross-reference it on the Interpol database, you might have a solid ID on the man who stole Grace. The investigation would be over before it begins and you would no longer be a suspect in the eyes of the police. You might even be able to locate Grace before any further harm comes to her." Another backhanded wave. "In any case, looking into the prints won't do any harm."

She's got one hell of a point.

"I will take good care of it, Captain," she assures me, storing the ring in a pocket on her jacket. She walks to the door. "I promise you, come morning, I will have some answers for you. One way or another."

"Thank you," I say, looking into her eyes.

"I understand your frustration over the Italian police," she offers. "How do I begin to fathom your fear?"

"You don't," I say, opening the door for her. "You just don't go there."

Chapter 43

The journalist isn't gone for more than thirty minutes when my blindness returns. I'm convinced if I can force myself to sleep, rather than wait for sleep to overtake me spontaneously, I will regain my eyesight far quicker than if I stay awake.

Inside my Dopp kit in the bathroom, I find the bottle of sleeping pills I use on long-haul transatlantic flights to knock myself out. I take a pill with a shot of whiskey. Then I shuffle the twelve steps across the studio floor to the bed and lie down on it. In no time at all, sleep takes over.

My eyes open. I can see. Focus on the ceiling above me.

I can see but I cannot move.

It's as if I am glued to the mattress, my limbs, head, and torso impossibly paralyzed. I can breathe, swallow, and I can feel my heart drumming against my ribs. But I can't lift a finger any more than I can speak or shout. My voice, my ability to make any kind of sound whatsoever, has vanished.

I'm not alone.

There's someone else in the room. I can't see, touch, or speak to him. I want to shout out. But I can't. Still, I know he's there, the same way a bird will sense the onset of an earthquake minutes before the ground opens up.

But wait, I've got this sight thing all wrong. It dawns on me that I'm not staring at the plaster ceiling. I'm staring at the inside of my eyelids.

The sound of breathing.

Then come the words "I see." He pronounces the word "see" like "seeeezzz."

The words come from the end of the bed. The smell coming from that direction is wormy and moldy, mixed with a hint of burning incense. His presence is overwhelming. Like meeting my maker. Or in this case, my destroyer. My and Grace's destroyer. I want to jump up, grab him, throw him down onto the floor. I want to slam his head on the floor-boards until he gives up Grace's location. Then I want to choke him with a full forearm hold until his heart and lungs stop.

I want to neutralize him.

But soon I feel myself drifting.

Falling and drifting.

Until I am once more unconscious.

Chapter 44

When I open my eyes again, my eyesight has returned. Daylight is pouring in through the French doors. I slide out of bed, look for any signs of an intruder. There are none. And something else. Judging by the position of the furniture, I didn't sleepwalk last night. At least, there doesn't seem to be any evidence that I did. I woke up in my own bed. Mine and Grace's. Everything seems to be in its proper place.

I check the door.

It's locked, the bolt engaged. I check the French doors. They too are closed and locked, just as I left them last night. Standing by the couch, I recall the presence of a man standing at my bed in the middle of the night. I recall the smell of a strange mix of sweat and incense. I recall the words he spoke. *"I see."*

I recall not being able to move a muscle. Not being able to utter a sound. I recall being entirely paralyzed, as if I'd been injected with a drug that rendered me immobile, but allowed my senses to thrive.

But then, why does the sensation of being paralyzed suddenly take on a greater significance? Have I been paralyzed before? Drugged? Made to endure something unspeakable?

The world is off-kilter, unbalanced. The pain shoots into my head. I feel sick. Running into the bathroom, I lean over the toilet, release a mixture of clear bile and stomach acid that burns the back of my throat, sends me into a fit of coughing.

When I've calmed down enough to straighten back up, I wipe the sweat from my brow, the snot from my nose, and the spittle from my lips. Turning, I catch my image in the mirror. The concave cheeks covered in stubble. The bloodshot eyes, the pale complexion. Who the hell is this man?

Then, in the mirror, a shadow. A shadow that appears and disappears as quickly as it registers. Ice water replaces the blood in my spine and I react to the threat, throw a swift punch at the mirror. The crack of fist against glass means I've hit my target.

Alert to a second attack, I turn on the balls of my feet, peer into the studio. "Who's there? Who the fuck is there!"

But the apartment is silent.

Turning back to the sink, I avoid my face like it belongs to the devil. I don't want to look into the cracked glass. But something makes me look. The fury boiling up from deep inside me. From a source that isn't entirely my own. As if it's a small separate part in my system. It's not something I can easily resist, but it's something I have done my damnedest to keep from Grace. In war, the fury keeps me alive. In peacetime, the fury makes me a dangerous man.

My head spins, and something snaps in the gray matter.

. . . I see not one, but dozens of mirrored reflections in the jagged, triangular slices of cracked glass. I don't see myself standing before the sink in the bathroom. I'm lying down in a brightly lit room. A man enters. A big, bulky African American. But I can't move. Can't talk,

175

can't open my eyes . . . When the man returns, I hear him set down two objects. One of them sounds like a metal bucket sloshing with water. The other, a wood board . . . "Refreshments are served, Captain," he says, in a happy voice. "Hope you're thirsty . . ."

"Stop!" I scream, pulling myself away from the mirror, sitting down on the toilet lid.

Breathing in and out.

My fingers are cut. Bleeding. I pull the towel from the rack, apply pressure. The cuts are not deep, but the pain in my head goes endlessly deep. Maybe this whole thing is an elaborate dream. A lucid nightmare. I've never been waterboarded, so why does my mind insist on recalling something so false?

I'm no stranger to vivid dreams. Soldiers who spend enough time in the field will eventually experience one or two of them. Dreams in which the line between reality and the subconscious becomes confused and undefined. Exhaustion and stress will do that to a man. You find yourself standing guard in the middle of the night, then suddenly you see eyes looking back at you in the darkness and the flash of a shadow or the movement of a figure. Maybe several figures. The figure is carrying a weapon and he's about to ambush you.

You don't think twice.

You empty an entire clip into the darkness. When the morning comes, you realize the eyes you swear you saw in the dark were nothing more than the white flowers on a bush reflecting the moonlight. The movement was the wind on the willows. The bittersweet smell of fear was entirely your own.

Or maybe you're behind enemy lines, crawling uphill on your stomach toward an enemy encampment. The fear is concentrated entirely in your heart, because it pounds like a bass drum in your head. But still you keep on moving until you come to the edge of the encampment where you spring yourself on an armed bandit, and slice his neck without the slightest hesitation or emotion, other than fear.

Fear cripples, but only if you allow it to.

Loneliness kills, but only if you let it take hold of heart and soul.

Sanity is fleeting when you've experienced enough battlefields. But then, I experienced more than just battlefields.

Dreams . . .

Dreams are the strange bedfellows I fear the most. Dreams you don't control so easy.

Dreams will tear you apart . . .

. . . even when you try to kill them.

⎯⎯⎯

After I clean the blood from my hand, the cuts require three Band-Aids. Thank God a good soldier is always prepared with a travel-sized first aid kit.

As usual, I check my cell phone.

Nothing.

I call Grace's number.

Now I don't even get a computer voice telling me her mailbox is full. I hear only a prerecorded announcement telling me the number I've reached is out of service or temporarily disconnected. So please check the number and try calling again, or check with an operator for assistance.

Screw you and the digital line you rode in on.

I decide to calm down, before I become so frustrated and pissed off I do something FUBAR, like toss my cell phone through the French doors and into the canal below. I wash my face, brush my teeth, make coffee. While the espresso is cooking on the stove, my eye catches my laptop. I go to it and refresh the page. It's still open to CNN and the short sidebar article about Grace's disappearance. I peer down at it, not sure what to expect. The article is still the same article. But something is different. I see my comment, and I see the comment that Anna Laiti made in response to it. But now there's a third comment also.

It says, "I was there at the caffè. I saw what happened."

It's signed simply "Geoff." And following that, his e-mail address.

My pulse picks up. I open my e-mail and write:

Dear Geoff,

I am Grace's fiancé. What did you see?

Please write or call or both. Please!

Nick Angel

I add my phone number, then click "Send" and wait. Realizing that an immediate answer is highly improbable, I drink my coffee and try to stay loose. But it's no use. I think about what day it is. It's Wednesday. I recall when I was a kid in grade school, how I would come home off the school bus and watch ancient reruns of *The Mickey Mouse Club*. Wednesday was "Anything Can Happen Day."

Soon, Anna will be here with the results of the print tests on Grace's diamond. That is, if the reporter is true to her word. Perhaps at the same time, I will hear from the man who saw Grace being taken away. Maybe I'll also hear the progress of the police investigation. My God, maybe it's possible I'll also hear from Grace.

Wednesday.

Today, anything can happen. Today my life will never be the same. But maybe, if I'm lucky, just a part of what I have lost will be returned to me.

Chapter 45

I'm not halfway finished with my coffee when my cell phone rings.

"Captain Angel?"

"Yes, it's me. You saw what happened?"

"I did. But I'm not comfortable talking about it over the phone."

"Why? What difference does it make? What . . . difference?"

"They're listening."

"Who? Who's listening?"

"Meet me at the Ponte di Rialto. Fifteen minutes. I can't stay long. The missus and I are leaving on the noon train. She won't know I'm meeting you."

"How will I know you?"

"Don't worry. I'll know you."

He hangs up.

Chapter 46

As always when I step out into the daylight of Venice alone, I never know when my blindness is going to return. But I'm taking no chances. I call Giovanni, ask him if he has some time to accompany me this morning to the Rialto. Ten minutes later he meets me outside the door of the bookshop, a smile beaming in his round face. I sense that this is an adventure for him.

He peers down at my hand.

"But you have injured yourself?"

Without asking he takes hold of my hand, the cuts on my fingers stinging for a quick instant. Instinct kicks in and I pull the hand back. Something washes over me then. There's the *click* in my head and a quick flash of a face. *A round, almost cherubic face, smiling . . .*

I shake the image off.

"I'm sorry," he says. "I did not mean to be so abrupt."

I make a fist with my injured hand. "I cut it by mistake, stumbling around in the studio."

The noise of the many outboard motors fills the wet Venetian landscape. I start walking.

"Finally, you have a witness," the leather-jacketed Giovanni says, but he's not following me. "I knew it. Only a matter of time, Captain." He pulls out a cigarette, lights it.

I don't share his optimism.

They are watching . . .

The man I communicated with over the phone sounded nervous and unsure. Like he was being watched or, worse, warned against talking with me. Or maybe my imagination is playing tricks on me again. When you spend more than half your time without the use of your eyes, you learn to see things in your head. You learn to dig up the memories buried there, no matter how painful. Dig them up with hammer and chisel if necessary. But the things you see are not entirely real. They are a collage of what you remember and what you believe to be true. More often they are a cob job of fact, fantasy, and paranoia. Things happen. Events pile up, one on top of another, like a cairn of rocks, differing shapes and sizes, weights, and colors.

There's just no pattern or predictability to anything. No logic. It's possible you built a replica of Venice out of boxes, spoons, and plates. It's possible you are somehow communicating with your missing fiancée.

Or maybe something else is going on.

Maybe you are being set up by the stranger who stole Grace in the first place. Maybe the overcoat man has a key to the apartment. Maybe he's the one who's trying to drive you insane. Terrorize you.

Or maybe you are just plain crazy and delusional. A casualty of war. A *malady*. Maybe you should have stayed put in upstate New York like the army insisted. Maybe Grace was beginning to see the madness in you, and she had no choice but to leave you for good.

But then, what choice do you have other than to keep on looking for her? Looking for the truth?

"We should go," I say, pointing in the direction of the Rialto, "while I still have my vision."

But the vision I have for now is not one-hundred-percent clarity. Not even close. My sight is okay for maybe ten or fifteen feet. Beyond that, all objects begin to lose their shape, all edges blur.

"It's your dime, Captain."

I start walking again, praying my eyes don't fail me as much as my mind seems to be.

Chapter 47

Just like the Bridge of Sighs and the Ponte degli Scalzi, the Rialto is said to be one of the most romantic bridges in Venice. A bridge for lovers and suicides. Therefore it is constantly occupied by tourists, their cameras, and video cams. Giovanni tells me he'll wait for me at the bottom of the bone-colored marble steps while "You do what you have to do." He won't be far should the darkness suddenly return to my eyes.

I climb the steps, my eyes scanning the men and women I pass, none of them paying me any particular attention. Until I spot a man standing at the top of the stairs. He's a short man. Pudgy. Stocky. His head is bald and his blue eyes lock onto mine the closer I come to the top.

I stop on the stair tread just below his, making us the same height.

"Captain Angel?" A question for which he already knows the answer. "My name is Geoff Miles, from Cleveland. My wife and I are here on vacation. A second honeymoon, really." Smiling. "You can call me Miles. All my friends do."

"What do you know about my fiancée?" I ask. "Who stole her away?"

The near panic in my voice increases with intensity with every word I speak. I want to grab hold of this little man, shake him, scream at him, demand he tell me what he knows. But that's the last thing I should do.

He steps up onto the landing of the pale stone-covered bridge, approaches the marble banister. I follow, and together we stand at the top of the Rialto looking out through the marble arches onto the Grand Canal and the near-chaotic boat traffic that approaches and disappears beneath our feet.

"I was having lunch with my wife," he begins. "We were seated a couple of tables away from yours. Forgive me for saying this, but I couldn't help staring at you. Truth be told, you were . . . *are* . . . a handsome couple. But it was the way you spoke to one another that captured my attention."

"My blindness."

He nods, and turns to me. He peers into my eyes as though distrusting them more than I do.

"You're not blind right now, are you?" he asks.

"It comes and goes. The condition is not physical. Only the result of the condition is physical."

He shakes his head. "I don't understand."

"I've been involved in quite a few military actions," I explain. "The most recent conflict, the war in Afghanistan. Things happened there. Bad things."

Now instead of shaking his head, he begins to nod.

"I'm sorry," he offers. "I was deployed with the Marines in Vietnam. I was at Tet in the summer of '68. Just in time for my eighteenth birthday. I saw some things, much like you, I imagine.

Things I'd rather forget. But I tend to forget my anniversary more than the human beings I killed. Their faces. Their eyes."

"It's not your fault. You didn't start the war. You did what you were told." Grace's mantra. "Now tell me, what did you see, Miles?"

He thinks about his answer for a moment while staring out at the busy canal and the bobbing of the boats on the endlessly upset water.

"Your fiancée seemed fixated on a man," he says after a beat.

"What did the man look like?"

"I was just about to tell you. He was a tall man, wearing a long brown coat. Dark complexion, dark hair. Sunglasses masked his eyes."

I gently take hold of his arm with my right hand. His eyes widen, but he is not so much alarmed as he is surprised.

"Did this man kidnap my fiancée?"

I remove my hand, as if it's impossible for him to answer otherwise.

"There were so many people in the piazza that day. So many people surrounding the tables."

The blood inside my brain begins to simmer.

"Did he take her or not? Please, Miles, please."

"To be perfectly frank, Captain, I'm not sure."

I stare into his round face, feel his eyes glued to mine.

"How can you not be sure when you were looking right at us? At her? At him?"

"The man approached the table. This seemed to cause some alarm in your fiancée. She spilled her drink and started to rise out of her chair as the man came within two feet from you. Behind you. So close he could have simply reached out and touched you on the back of your head."

"But you didn't see him taking her?"

"Yes, or, I mean . . . no."

I take hold of his arm again. Harder this time. "Which is it?"

He struggles to free himself. But he can't.

"A group of people stepped in front of my table right then. A Japanese tour group. There must have been twenty or thirty people suddenly streaming in between our tables. By the time they finished shuffling through and I was able to get another unobstructed view of your table, the man and your fiancée were gone."

My heart sinks to new depths.

"Did you see them walking? Could you see them in the crowd?"

"That's just it. They were gone. Vanished. I truly looked for her. For him, since it was clear they had abandoned you. But it was no use. They were gone. And when I looked back at your table, you were still talking, as if she were seated there across from you."

"Still talking," I say, releasing his arm again. "Until I realized she wasn't seated there any longer."

"I could tell when it dawned on you that she was gone. You stood up. When you shouted, the waiter came and took you away." Exhaling, staring down at his feet. "My wife started to cry. We finished our lunch and waited for the police to arrive, thinking they would come right away. But it took some time. Enough for us to finish our lunch, and then some. Not that we had much of an appetite by then."

"But you told the police your story."

"They wouldn't listen to us at first. In fact, they wouldn't talk with us at all. They weren't the least bit interested in what we saw that afternoon. And, far as I could tell, we were the only ones they spoke with at the restaurant."

"How can they not take your statement? It doesn't make sense."

"Exactly. It bothered me enough that, later in the day, I paid a visit to the Venice metropolitan police and asked to see a detective. A big, bearded, well-dressed man saw me immediately. A Detective Carbone."

"I know him," I interject.

"He escorted me into a small interview room and listened to what I had to say. I *thought* he was listening to me. I was convinced that man had kidnapped your wife somehow. But the detective told me that in all likelihood there was no abduction. No kidnapping. That it was more likely your fiancée left of her own accord."

"That's impossible," I insist. "We love one another. We were getting married soon . . . we *are* getting married soon."

He holds both his hands up, palms facing me, eyes closed, like he's surrendering. Surrendering to my emotions. Agreeing and commiserating with my sadness, frustration, and confusion.

"Detective Carbone wouldn't listen. He just smoked and stared out the window, as if . . ."

His sentence drifts off, like the supply boats and barges that move away from us in the distance. "As if he couldn't lie to my face."

"And why would the police be lying, Mr. Miles?"

He looks at me blankly. "Why have you been experiencing blindness as of late, Captain Angel?"

"I don't really know. No one knows."

"Exactly. I wish I could tell you that's where my story ends but it doesn't. A day after I spoke with Detective Carbone, I received a visit to my hotel from a representative of the US Embassy."

My heart sinks deeper.

"Was his name David Graham?"

He nods. "Yes. He asked me for a favor."

"A favor."

"He asked me to forgo interfering in Grace's disappearance. That it was a police matter now. He also told me if I continued to get involved, the Italian government might be forced to detain me for an unspecified amount of time." Pursing his lips, he said, "I'm sixty-two years old and I project-manage commercial construction jobs in a terrible market. I have barely enough vacation time as it is. Being detained for months or even weeks would cost me my job."

"I get it. I don't want you to lose your job."

He raises his right hand, sets it on my shoulder.

"Listen, Captain," he says, "during the war . . . my war . . . the army asked some of us to do things."

"What kinds of things?"

He exhales, bites down on his bottom lip. "Most of it has been made public by now. The army wanted to see how long a human being could go without sleep and still be able to fight. Pre-deprivation performance testing, they called it. Some of us volunteered for the program, took the drugs, drank the Kool-Aid, played the role of guinea pig to a bunch of white-lab-coated doctors. Anything to get off the line and back to the States for a while. I think, in the end, one of us made it a week before even the drugs wouldn't work and he collapsed from a coronary at nineteen or twenty years old. But the things they made us do while on those drugs . . . well, let's just say that a coronary was a more merciful way to go out."

. . . *Crawling through a culvert in the pitch-darkness . . . emerging from the opposite side into an open trench . . . The heat is oppressive . . . Music playing through a radio . . . Arabic music . . . Up above me, a café . . . Men drinking tea, smoking, talking . . . A bearded man wearing a uniform, surrounded by more uniformed men . . . a television mounted to the wall beside a fan . . . the sign reads,* Café Baghdad . . . *I crawl in the darkness . . . place the package under an empty table . . . crawl back into the pipe . . . await the shock of the explosion . . .* Dizziness. Headache. Nausea. I inhale, exhale.

"What's the point of all this, Miles? What's it got to do with my fiancée?"

"It has more to do with your eyes. Your temporary blindness. Listen, Captain, some of those men who volunteered for that experiment . . . the ones who made it through . . . their memories of the experiments were repressed for a long time, socked away in some kind of vault or file cabinet in the backs of their brains. Until one day, the file cabinet drawers started to open, one by one, and the memories started coming back. The results weren't always pleasant."

"And you? What about you?"

He shakes his head. "I see some of the things we did to one another in my dreams. Makes it hard to sleep sometimes. Insomnia, the docs call it. I call it the persistence of memory. Like that famous painting of the melting clocks." He smiles, but it's not a happy smile. He removes his hand. "My wife and I are leaving in a few hours. From here we head to Florence and Rome, and then back to Cleveland. I just want to wish you the best of luck in finding your fiancée."

"Thank you," I say.

"No need to thank me. I hope you find her. She loved you. I could see it in her eyes before she disappeared."

Chapter 48

I relay most of what Miles told me to Giovanni. The both of us standing at the bottom of the Rialto staircase, the tourists passing us in both directions.

The waiter mulls over what I've revealed, smiles, stuffs his hands inside his jacket pockets.

"I told you the police cannot be trusted. But then, perhaps your Grace could not be trusted, either."

Under normal circumstances, I might punch another man in the mouth after a comment like that. But staring into his smooth, almost childlike face, I can't help but believe he is absolutely right. Perhaps in the end, Grace did simply get up from the table and leave me. For good.

Just the thought of her doing something so drastic and so final, and performing it so coldly, makes my already-bruised heart feel like it's about to split down the center.

"Your shoulder," he says. "Did you also hurt it when you stumbled inside your apartment?"

Startled, I look down and pull my hand out of the collar of my button-down shirt. It didn't even dawn on me that I was rubbing the scar on my shoulder. Doing it without realizing it. I relive the flash of memory I experienced up on the bridge just moments ago. Crawling into a culvert, awaiting the blast. Feeling the blast. Crawling away to safety. Did I make that up? I'm an infantry soldier, for Christ sake, not a commando assassin.

"No," I say. "I cut my shoulder during the war."

"Which one?"

I close my eyes, see a fighting knife in my hand. And an identical one held tightly in another man's hand. But when I try to see his face, it is a featureless blank. Like a mannequin.

"Maybe you would like me to stay with you at the studio?" Giovanni asks. "It's not a problem."

The thought of walking back to the apartment alone is unsettling because my vision could cut out completely on the way. But what's the alternative?

For now, I trust no one.

I haven't yet taken a step in the direction of my temporary home when my cell phone rings.

Chapter 49

I answer the call from Anna Laiti, press the phone to my ear.

"What did you find out?"

"There are many prints on the ring, as would be expected, including yours and your fiancée's. Prints from overseas military personnel are easily accessed. Grace's prints were also in the system as your significant other. No doubt she has visited a base you've been assigned to back home."

"How is it possible that such a small surface area can reveal so many prints?"

"Allow me to correct myself. There are a lot of *partials* being picked up by the digital fingerprint scanning equipment. Naturally the dominant print will be Grace's. Maybe your prints would also be somewhat dominant."

"What about the overcoat man? Were his on there?"

"We have no way of knowing. But there is a third set of prints that might interest you."

My breathing grows shallow. "I'm listening."

"The prints belong to a man who works for Interpol."

I look out onto the canal, barely able to make out a gondola carrying a young couple under the bridge. As they pass beneath the bridge only a few feet away from me, they look at one another and smile longingly, then kiss. I see Grace and me sitting in their place, and it makes my heart grow as heavy as a stone. Makes it bleed. Right now, I wish I were blind.

"Interpol. We've had no contact with someone from Interpol."

"But apparently your fiancée has."

Turning, I eye the shiny black gondola, which has now passed under the Ponte di Rialto. Although my sight seems to be slowly retreating, I can make out the gondolier precariously perched on the impossibly narrow bow while the young lovers nestle together in their red velvet-covered seats. The Venice that surrounds them a romantic dream come true. In the back of my mind, I picture my Grace, lying at the bottom of the Grand Canal. It is an image I see with 20/20 vision, and it rattles my nerves.

"That's impossible," I explain. "She was with me the entire time."

"Let me ask you another question then. Who, prior to yourself, was the last man to touch the ring?"

I shift my eyes from the now-blurry gondola to Giovanni, who is standing on the edge of the canal bank, lighting a cigarette. If I didn't already know who he was, I would have no way of recognizing him from where I'm standing.

"I'll call you back in a few minutes," I say, cutting the connection.

Chapter 50

I shout to Giovanni.

He turns to me, smiling. Always smiling, while blue smoke oozes out the corners of his mouth and nostrils.

"Did you find out about the fingerprints?" he asks.

"Just mine and Grace's on the ring. Some other partial, unidentifiable ones, but that only makes sense. A thin ring isn't exactly an ideal surface for finding prints."

He nods, smokes.

"I'll go home now," I say. "No need to follow me. I feel like my eyesight is going to stay for a while."

His smile dissolves. "It is my duty and my pleasure to look after you, Captain."

He's peering into my eyes like he's not about to take no for an answer. Like he's *ordered* not to take no for an answer.

"Grazie," I say, but it spills out of my mouth sounding as cold and dirty as the canal water.

When we come to the big wood door that marks the entrance to my building, I turn and thank Giovanni.

"How long have you worked at the caffè?"

He smokes the last of his cigarette, tosses it down onto the cobbles instead of into the garbage-infested canal, which is only a few feet away.

"Why do you ask?" he says, the smoke gently escaping out his mouth and nose.

In my head I'm hearing Anna. *"Who, prior to yourself, was the last man to touch the ring?"*

"The owners are generous to you. They give you a lot of time off."

He cocks his head over his left shoulder. "They are very generous indeed. But this is Italy, Captain. Not America. We are not so obsessed with making money. Our rather corrupt government takes it all away from us in taxes anyway." He works up his now-familiar smile, which I characterize as decidedly false. "Therefore, we are more concerned with *la dolce vita.*"

"Of course," I say, the first signs of total gray, total blur, beginning to mask my vision. In a few moments I will be blind again. But in the blindness, I will begin to see things. Things having to do with my lost Grace.

"The good life," I add.

"Yes, the good life."

The kind of life I wished for Grace and myself . . .

I unlock the door, step inside, and close it behind me.

By the time I get upstairs my eyesight is coming and going. Mostly going.

I use what sight I have left to view the keypad on my mobile phone while calling Anna back.

"I'm home," I tell her. "How long will it take you to get here?"

"Not long," she says. "I understand the urgency of the situation. The gravity. You know what they used to say back in '39 during the Blitz."

"No, what did they say during the Blitz?"

"Keep calm and carry on."

"I'll try and hold it together."

"Hold what together exactly, Captain?"

"Me. My vision. My memories. My broken heart."

———

When Anna arrives, I am seeing only gray. The French doors are open and I can hear familiar sounds coming from the narrow alley below and the occasional motorboat that travels over the canal. Voices. Footsteps. Laughter. Not a single one of them Grace's.

Will she have coffee? Anna tells me she'll take care of making it for the both of us. No arguments from me. I just stand in the French doors, letting the sunlight soak my open eyes. The breeze blows in on me, and the smells from the water city fill my head.

"Interpol," I say after a time. "The last person to touch the ring besides myself was a man I know. His name is Giovanni. He works in the caffè where Grace was abducted. He helps me."

"How exactly does he help you, Captain?"

"He was the one who found Grace's ring. He was the one who alerted me to it and gave it back to me. He also acts as my seeing-eye dog. He even walks with me when the blindness isn't there, just in case it should suddenly come back."

She's standing by the kitchenette, filling the coffeepot, setting it on the stove, turning on the gas, lighting the flame, setting out the cups. I don't have to see her to picture her every movement.

"Do you know Giovanni's last name?"

"I've never asked."

"Maybe you should. Or perhaps we can go see him together. This afternoon."

"I'm not exactly seeing anyone right now." I laugh. But nothing's funny.

The sound of percolating coffee claims the studio space. She shuts off the gas, killing the burner. Anna pours the coffee and carries the cups over to the table, sets them down to cool. About a minute later, she places my cup in my hands.

"How long will your blindness last?" she asks.

"It could last a week. Or it could last a few minutes. I've come to learn that it usually means I need to rest. Sleep. Most times, when I wake up, I can see again. Sometimes I sleepwalk, and apparently I can see when I sleepwalk. But of course, I cannot remember what I've seen. The sleepwalking is brand new to me and pretty damned frightening. I'm a combat soldier. I prefer to be in total control of my fate."

"Sounds dangerous."

I recall waking up on the roof of this building. For a brief moment I think of telling her about it. But then I decide not to. I don't want her to think I'm crazy.

I set down the coffee cup. "Can I have the ring?"

She shuffles around in her pockets. Or that's what it sounds like she's doing, anyway. She takes hold of my hands, places the ring into the palm of my hand. I close my fingers around the ring, squeeze tight. It isn't until I feel a trail of wetness on one of my cheeks that I realize I'm weeping.

"What do you feel?" asks the journalist.

"I feel Grace," I say. "I feel her heart beating. Her lungs breathing. I feel Grace alive."

"You understand that if she has been abducted, she could be anything but alive, Captain."

Another tear slides down the opposite cheek. "I refuse to believe that. Just like I refuse to believe she has simply walked away from me."

"This man who gave you the ring . . . Giovanni. A waiter. You believe he could be with Interpol?"

"I'm not sure what to believe anymore. Maybe this whole thing is an elaborate dream. Maybe Grace isn't really missing. Maybe you're not real. Maybe I died on that hill in Afghanistan."

Maybe the little boy's bomb detonated and killed me . . . killed us all . . .

She shuffles around in her pockets once more. By the sound of it, I know she then unfolds a sheet of paper.

"I have an image of the Interpol man we identified by his print on the ring. But of course, you can't see it now."

"What's his name?"

"Heath Lowrance. Originally from New Jersey. Princeton undergraduate in criminal justice. Did his master's at Oxford before joining the military and earning the rank of captain in the Army Rangers. Fought in Operation Desert Storm. Strangely, however, his outfit and unit information are not available. The file does list him as decorated. He also fought in Iraq in the second Gulf War. Decorated. Fought in Afghanistan. Again decorated. Knows several languages fluently including Italian, his dialect decidedly Tuscan. More recently he'd been recruited by Interpol to work in both the war crimes and terrorism divisions."

His résumé sounds a little too similar to my own.

"Could be he waits tables in Piazza San Marco on the side."

"Could be that's his cover right now while he keeps an eye on you. That is, if Interpol and the US military feel the need to keep an eye on you."

In my head, I'm seeing the hill in Tajik country. I see the ancient village situated near the top of it. An ancient village bombed back to the Stone Age. I also see a battlefield from twenty years ago. A wide-open desert in Kuwait, littered with damaged tanks and vehicles, bodies burned beyond recognition. Oil wells on fire, thick black smoke rising up to the heavens.

"Captain," Anna says. "Is there something else that happened to you in Afghanistan? Something you have not told me?"

With full clarity, I see the sun reflecting off the A-10 Thunderbolt's tan, green, and yellow "splinter" color scheme as it screams across the valley. See it nosedive toward the hilltop. See the bursts of 30mm rounds from its nose-mounted rotary cannon and the rockets shooting out from under the wings. See them strike the village, the red-hot lightning explosions visible before I hear their back-to-back concussive bursts. In my head I climb the hill once more, see the wrecked stone and wood buildings, the burnt-out shells and the dead bodies. I see a small boy coming around the corner of a building. See the package strapped to his chest. I see him coming for me and my men as I shoulder my M4, plant a bead not on the bomb, but the only place I can without detonating it. His face. My finger on the trigger, I shout, "Don't do it. Don't you do it!"

Exhaling, I say, "Like I've already told you, I ordered an airstrike on a village. A Tajik village. A Taliban holdout. I ordered an airstrike and it killed people. Other things happened too."

"People die in war, Captain. What made this different from any other airstrike?"

"I'm not at liberty to discuss it."

"But if the bombing or what happened after the bombing stole your eyesight, perhaps you *should* talk about it."

Shaking my head. "I am not at liberty to discuss military affairs with the press. And you are not my shrink. In my time as a professional soldier, I bombed a lot of villages and saw a lot of people die. Men, women, children."

"Captain, your fiancée is missing. It's possible you are being monitored by Interpol's war crimes division. The police seem to be uncooperative and you are left alone to find out the truth in a foreign country with eyes that are no longer reliable. I wish you would speak to me."

"War crimes?" I say. "Maybe the president should spend a week in northern Afghanistan. Then he'll realize that fighting a war with both hands tied behind our backs is not the sure path to success." I close my eyes, lie down on the bed. "Please just let me rest for a moment," I say, exhaustion rinsing over me from head to toe. "It's possible my sight will return if only I can sleep for a few minutes."

Soon I feel a blanket being draped over me.

I hear the words "Rest. I'll be here when you wake up."

I want to tell Anna, "Thank you." But before I can get the words out, I'm already drifting off to sleep.

I'm riding with Karen in the passenger seat of her Volvo station wagon after she's picked me up from the bar. The look on her face is not a happy one. It's the same face I've been seeing day after day over the past few months. She pushes her long dark hair back behind her ear with her right hand, shakes her head. "If only you'd open up to me," she says. "If only you'd talk." I know what she wants, but also how impossible it is to make her happy. "I want a child," she says. "I want a child more than I want you. Do you understand me?" I say nothing. She drives onto the Patroon Island Bridge that spans the Hudson River. She turns to me again, her hands on the wheel. "I'm going to have a child with or without you!" She's screaming now, her eyes not on the road, but on me. Just up ahead, a road crew, a cement truck, a man standing there, a sign that says STOP gripped in one hand, while he waves his other hand frantically to capture our attention. "Karen!" I shout. "Stop!" She turns to face the road, screams, the car veering to the right. We burst through the barrier, the front end plummeting the twenty feet into the river. The car takes on water. Karen is stunned from the impact. I reach over, try to open her door, but the pressure of the water against it is too great. "Karen, we have to get out." But she just looks at me, smiles. "My baby," she says. "Our baby is already inside me." My window is open, the water rushing in as the car sinks. I manage to undo my seat belt, but Karen's is stuck. She just stares at me, like she wants to drown. The cold water overtakes us as the car becomes completely submerged. I try to pull her out with me, but I can't. My last vision of her before I escape out the open passenger window is her wide-open eyes and her hair swimming in the water . . .

Chapter 51

When I wake I'm shivering. I open my eyes, and although I am not entirely blinded, my vision is blurry at best. I am breathing. Hard. Heart pounds. There's a sharp pain behind my eyeballs as if someone were pressing their thumbs against them, only from the inside out.

It takes me a moment to realize Anna is holding my hand, tightly.

"You were having a terrible nightmare," she says from where she sits beside me on the couch. "You shouted, 'Karen, stop!'"

Pulling my hand away from hers, I yank off the blanket and sit up, my head aching from the battle of memories waged inside my brain. My head ringing like a bell. My brow moist with sweat.

"How long was I out?"

"Thirty minutes," she reveals. "Perhaps a few minutes more."

I rub the life back into my face with my ice-cold palms. Try to rub some sight back into my eyes. Rub out the soreness. But the world around me is still blurry and nondescript. My sight is returning again. But I have no idea how long the process can take. A few more seconds. Or hours. It's entirely up to God. Or is it?

"Tell me, Captain," Anna presses. "If you won't tell me what happened in Afghanistan after you bombed the village, then perhaps you can tell me the circumstances behind your wife's suicide."

The car is being pulled out of the river by a flatbed tow truck. I see myself standing on the edge of the riverbank, the bridge that spans the river from Albany to Troy only a few yards away. My clothing is damp . . .

Suicide . . . Was it ever a suicide? Or was that just something I wanted to believe? Detective Carbone's report said it was suicide, too. Are my memories exposing the lies of my past? Or am I lying to myself now?

"Why?" I say to Anna. "What does any of it have to do with Grace's disappearance?"

"It could have nothing to do with her. But then, my instincts say it could have everything to do with her."

Getting up, I fumble for my cell phone. I find it, but I still can't read it.

"Do you know if anyone has called?"

"It's been silent," she says, her tone apologetic.

"What time is it?"

"A little past noon."

"Are you busy right now?"

"Do I look it?"

"I'd like you to accompany me to Piazza San Marco," I say. "You will be my seeing-eye dog for a while. Together, we'll find out one important truth."

"What truth, Captain?"

"If Giovanni, the man who has been helping me, is in fact my enemy."

Chapter 52

Anna wraps her right arm around my left, as if we're lovers contemplatively strolling along the banks of the Grand Canal instead of a half-blind soldier with a big post-traumatic stress problem and a curious British journalist trying to negotiate the two flights of marble stairs to the bottom without tripping. We exit the front door of the building, proceed past the empty bookshop window, and make our way beyond the feeder canal toward the Grand Canal, where we take the Number 1 Vaporetto along the busy, winding, S-shaped canal to San Marco.

Anna's arm still wrapped around mine, we enter the piazza, make our way through the crowd to the caffè. Past the tour groups and the tour guides waving bright flags high above their heads so no one gets disconnected or, worse, lost. Past the flocks of pigeons and a brass band that strikes up a dramatic song that bounces off the stone floor and stone walls of the square and the cathedral.

By the time we come to the caffè situated along the basin, most of my eyesight has returned. Raising my head to a sky of clear blue accented with fluffy white marshmallow clouds, I then lower my gaze to the table where I last sat with Grace. The table is now occupied by a family. Mom, dad, and two teenagers on vacation. But to me, the table screams of emptiness. It's all I can do to hold back tears. But I'm not sure if I'd be crying for myself or for Grace.

"Let's go inside," the journalist suggests.

Together we head for the entrance. "Before we go in," I say, just outside the glass-and-wood doors, "I want to see the picture of the man from Interpol."

"Your eyes have recovered?" asks Anna, some of the thick strands of her short red hair moving with the breeze coming off the basin.

"As well as can be expected for the time being."

For the first time since we left my apartment, she releases my arm. She reaches into her bag and produces the folded sheet of standard copy stock. Unfolding it, she hands it to me.

I look at the face of the man. Look at it for almost a full minute. "Is it him?" she asks.

The man in the photo has brown eyes and thick black hair. He is clean shaven, his face round and smooth and pleasantly inviting. Lips not too thick, not too thin, his thick brows protecting his eyes with an expression of permanent curiosity and kindness.

The man in the photo is someone I've seen before. But not in Italy. He is a man I've seen in another life.

"Yes," I say, "I believe it is."

I hand her back the paper and open the door to the caffè with all the caution and anxiety of reentering a combat zone.

———

The caffè interior is as busy as its exterior seating area. Waiters of all shapes and sizes dressed in black and wearing long white aprons dart around the tables like hungry starlings around a couple dozen nests.

205

We stand in the doorway, my now-seeing eyes searching the gold-trimmed and gilded-mirrored interior for Giovanni. But he doesn't seem to be working.

"Do you see him?" Anna says.

"Not yet. He could be in the back office. He took me there on two separate occasions."

"You're sure the man in the photo is the man who works here?"

"I can't be one hundred percent sure," I explain. "Much of the time I am blind, or see only a blur, or at best, I have limited vision. But I think it's him."

Soon a waiter greets us at the door. He's an older man sporting a thick mustache and a large gut that makes his apron bulge out and away from his legs like a tent. Since he speaks no English, Italian-fluent Anna volunteers to be my translator. He speaks something and the journalist translates.

"If we wish to be seated," she says, "there is a wait of one half hour."

I peer at the waiter, his face deadpan and tired.

"We don't want to sit," I say, waiting for Anna's translation. "We're looking for someone who works here."

She tells the waiter what I said and he responds with a question.

"He wants to know who you are."

"My fiancée was abducted from this place just a few days ago," I say.

She translates. Afterward, the waiter's eyes peer into my own. Unblinking.

"How can I help you?" he asks via the reporter.

"A man who works here helped me out. His name is Giovanni. I would like to speak with him."

The heavyset waiter starts shaking his head. He speaks.

"He is very sorry," says Anna. "But he has no Giovanni in his employ at the moment. Are you sure you weren't mistaking him for someone else?"

"He must work here," I insist. "He was waiting on some tables just the other night when I returned. He found a ring that belonged to my fiancée, and he took me into the back room." Raising up my arm, I point to the rather obscure image of a door located all the way at the rear of the caffè. I've never actually laid eyes upon the door before, but even in my visually impaired state, I'm sure that must be it.

Anna reaches into her bag again and produces the paper. She unfolds it and shows the waiter the image of the man printed upon it. She then speaks something in Italian.

"I told him this is the man we are looking for," she says to me, waving the photo. "I told him he claims to be employed here."

The waiter continues to shake his head and speaks again.

She turns to me.

"He says he is the owner of this caffè and he can assure us that the man in the photograph does not work for him. Nor has he ever worked for him."

I gaze into his eyes. They are neither blinking rapidly, nor is he attempting to avert his gaze. My gut tells me he's telling the truth.

The caffè owner turns, makes a sweeping gesture with his thick left arm, and says something else. Anna nods and then shakes her head, disbelievingly.

"He says to take a look around, Nick. All the waiters he employs are currently on the floor. All of them. And something else. He claims there is no back office attached to this establishment. That the back door simply leads to an alley where they keep the trash receptacle."

My throat goes dry. I try swallowing, but I can't seem to work up the moisture. I step away from Anna and the caffè owner, make my way quickly across the floor, bumping into a table and then another one, a big man enjoying a meal with his family telling me to watch where I'm walking. I feel all the many sets of eyes upon me when I come to the door and open it. But there's no office located on the other side. There is only a dark alley. Set on the narrow cobblestoned alleyway maybe six or seven feet away is a blue dumpster. It smells of rotting food. I feel lightheaded and a bit dizzy. Before I close the door, a dark brown rat pokes its head out from under the plastic dumpster cover, slithers out, drops down to the cobbles, landing on all four claws, and scurries away. I close the door and recross the floor to the front of the caffè.

"The owner says he is sorry about your fiancée, Nick," offers Anna. "But we are upsetting his customers. So if there is nothing else, he must get back to work and we must leave.

"I'm sorry," she says, as soon as we're through the door. "Is it possible you have the wrong caffè?"

Stepping back, I take in the long building, and the doors and windows that belong to it.

"I suppose it's very possible I was led through another doorway instead of this one," I say. "I was blind, after all."

She nods, because it's the only valid explanation. Unless, that is, I'm entirely crazy and delusional.

"Nick," Anna says, taking hold of my forearm. "Are you okay?"

My eyes lock once more on the table where I last spoke with my fiancée. Where a strange man in an overcoat approached us and possibly . . . quite possibly . . . stole Grace.

"Let's go back to the police," I say.

She takes hold of my hand, squeezes it.

"Let's go now," she agrees.

Chapter 53

It takes us nearly an hour to get to the Venice police station. We walk over cobbles, through narrow alleys, over stone bridges, ride water taxis, all in a desperate search for a truth surrounded by beauty, history, and water.

Always the water.

Anna remains physically close to me the entire time, pressing up against me while we ride the crowded water bus, holding my hand with her warm, soft hand. I've only just met her, but when I look into her brown eyes I see more than a journalist who is trying to find the truth behind Grace's story. I see a woman who genuinely cares about its outcome as much as I do, or perhaps I see something more. Maybe what I'm seeing and feeling is a woman who might be falling for me. Stranger things have happened, and this is Venice, after all.

But I feel her hand in my hand, and all I can think about is Grace . . . finding Grace.

Inside the old police building, we are escorted to a waiting area by a uniformed officer and politely offered coffee. Anna and I decline. A few minutes later, Detective Carbone enters the room. He's smoking a cigarette.

"I see your sight has returned once more," he says in his warm, if not gentle voice. "You must be delighted."

"Positively chipper," I say. "Truth is, I'm fighting the blindness every step of the way. No peripherals whatsoever. It's like I'm surrounded by a fog bank. Unless you're right in front of me, I have a great chance of missing you. How are you coming with the investigation?"

He smokes, listens, exhales blue smoke.

Switching his gaze from me to Anna, he says, "And we have not had the pleasure of meeting."

She holds out her hand. Tells him her name. Her occupation. Who she works for.

He smokes.

"I am familiar with your work," he says. "I read your small report on the web about the Captain's unfortunate circumstance. I understand you spoke with one of my officers on the phone."

"They did not tell me much, Detective," Anna points out, her voice taking on a formal tone, her British accent more pronounced. "Only that you believe it's possible Grace left of her own accord." She looks up at me with her deep brown eyes. "Captain Angel begs to differ."

More smoking.

"Captain Angel," he says through a haze of secondhand smoke, "we have yet to find the true reason behind your fiancée's disappearance."

"But you know what happened," I say. "There was a man. He's been following us. He went after her in Piazza San Marco. He abducted her. What you don't know is that she pulled off her engagement ring and left it behind for me to find."

His brows rise. "Where is that ring?"

I dig it out of my pocket, hold it up to his face with my index finger and thumb, the square-cut diamond shimmering in the overhead light.

"May I?" he asks, holding out his free hand.

I set the ring in the palm of his hand.

"I would have it tested for prints if I didn't think it a waste of time. Such objects are difficult to work with."

"Funny you should say that, Detective," Anna interjects. "We already did have it tested for prints. Or I did, anyway."

My sight might be severely impaired, but that doesn't stop me from noticing Detective Carbone's face take on a red patina behind the salt-and-pepper beard.

"That might be construed as obstruction," he says.

"Obstruction of what exactly?" the journalist presses. "Sounds like your investigation is going nowhere. And, as it turns out, the ring proved a valuable resource for prints."

Nodding, the neatly dressed detective smokes the last of his cigarette. When he's done, he simply drops the spent butt to the tile floor and stamps it out with the tip of his shoe.

"I could demand to withhold this ring," he says to my face. "Instead, I will leave it up to you, Captain."

My return gaze says it all. I open up my right hand and he places the ring back on my palm. I shove the ring into my pants pocket.

"So then, what were the results of your print analysis?" he asks.

"There's a third set of prints on the ring besides Grace's and the Captain's," Anna says. "They belong to a man named Heath Lowrance. An American. A professional soldier turned Interpol war-crimes agent. He's befriended Captain Angel while under the guise of a waiter named Giovanni who works in the caffè where Grace went missing. He's been pretending to assist the captain while he goes in and out of blindness."

Vincent Zandri

"How do you know for certain this man is a fake?"

"We just stopped at his caffè. He's not employed there."

The detective works up a grin. "You are doing some excellent detective work for a man who has limited use of his eyes. I applaud you. It's possible you are becoming as adept at managing the dark world around you as a person born with blindness. That is, as long as you're careful not to blindly walk into one of the canals."

"Detective Carbone," Anna goes on, "why do you suppose an investigator from Interpol would be attaching himself to Captain Angel? And why would it happen concurrent with the disappearance of his fiancée?"

"That seems to be the major question, doesn't it, Ms. Laiti?"

Her left hand takes hold of my forearm. Squeezes it gently. Without her having to say it, I sense the purpose of the squeeze. It tells me the police are hiding something. Maybe she's sensed this all along, and maybe that's why she's invested herself in both the story and me.

Detective Carbone lights another cigarette.

"Captain Angel," he says, exhaling his initial drag of smoke, "might I have a word with you alone?"

I look over my shoulder at Anna.

She nods.

"I'll be outside the door," she says, slipping out, closing the door behind her.

I shove my right hand into my trouser pocket, feel Grace's engagement ring.

"What's happening here, Detective?" I say.

"Captain Angel," he says, "it's time you stopped looking for Grace."

Chapter 54

"I don't understand," I say after a stunned beat. "Why would I even consider such an option?"

The detective's face has become sullen and drained of blood. He appears oddly comfortable with this new visage, as if his more common happier demeanor were nothing more than a mask designed to hide the lies. Or hide the truth. And I must admit, it makes him appear far more believable to me. More trustworthy, perhaps.

He smokes, exhales, nervously flicks the growing tube of gray ash onto the floor.

"Your fiancée did not leave you of her own accord," he says. "You must forgive me for having to lie about it. But those have been my orders. I did not want to speak freely in front of the journalist."

The floor feels like it's shifting right out from under my feet. "The overcoat man."

He nods. "A few days ago when you first reported Grace missing, we had no leads to go on. You two had been reported as arguing in a caffè on the late afternoon before her disappearance. You were just returning from an extremely traumatic war experience. With no tangible leads and no witnesses coming forward to corroborate your story of abduction, we could only assume you might have had something to do with her sudden vanishing."

I recall my conversation with the American man this morning. He claimed to be a witness and to have personally spoken with Carbone. It's exactly what I tell him now.

"That man did come forward. But not until nearly forty-eight hours after the fact. And by then it was too late. I thanked him for his time and told him that if he should continue with interfering in a police matter he would be detained. The US Embassy told him the very same thing."

"I would never do anything to harm Grace."

"Of this I am now certain. But let me assure you, Captain, it's not all that unusual for a seemingly happy relationship to go violently wrong even in Venice. I've been in the position of investigating murders of passion before. Yours would not have been a unique situation had it turned out to be the case."

"Is that why Interpol is watching me?"

He shakes his head. Smokes. "Not exactly."

"Why, then?"

Behind me, a door opens. A door in a place where there seemed to be no door, but instead a wood-paneled wall. A secret door in a room that is no doubt equipped with audio/visual surveillance equipment, just like any other police interrogation room.

"I'll prefer that Agent Heath Lowrance answer that question himself, Captain."

Chapter 55

Agent Lowrance is the same man whom I've known as Giovanni for the past couple of days. Tall, thin, smooth shaven, round faced, thick black hair, brown eyes, a friendly smile, and young for his years. Only he is not an Italian caffè waiter. He is under the employ of Interpol. And he has been assigned to me.

He holds out his hand. I'm not sure if I should take it. I'm a soldier. I realize how futile it would be for me to fight these men. Combat should only come about as a last resort. But that doesn't mean I have to make it easy for them.

I stare down at the hand in my hand.

The *click* sounds in my brain. The hand. Its touch is familiar. It brings me back to a place where I'm standing on the precipice and looking out onto a great, dark unknown. A land full of shadow memories.

Deep night. Winter . . . Climbing a hill all alone . . . A dog chained at the collar, barking, growling . . . Use my knife to neutralize the animal, then enter a village that is fast asleep . . . I cut the sentry's neck, too, and when he drops, I pull the grenade from my belt, release the pin, wait three seconds, drop it through the open window of the target house . . .

He takes back his hand.

"Your eyes are being kind to you now," he says with his usual smile, but this time, without the Italian accent.

"You really interested in the condition of my eyes?" I say through gritted teeth. "Are you truly interested in Grace's welfare? Or are we getting in the way of Interpol's agenda, and yours?"

His smile dissolves. "My orders involve international security, Captain, which includes the well-being of your significant other. And yes, I do care about your eyesight, believe it or not."

Exhaling, I say, "I suspect the periods of blindness are becoming less and less frequent. The doctors told me that would happen. Sooner than later."

"I'm happy for you. And the doctors are right. You will recover."

"Why are you assigned to me?" I say, after a beat. "And what does it have to do with Grace's disappearance?"

"Captain, the village you ordered an airstrike on in northern Afghanistan . . . I am of the understanding that the difficulty there didn't end with the airstrike. That something else happened up on that hill. And that the event is perhaps the source of your emotional troubles . . . your temporary blindness."

In my head, I see the village, parts of it still burning and smoking in the moments following the strike. Wounded men and women crying, confused animals running around. A small boy with something strapped to his chest. A black vest filled with explosives. A suicide vest.

"Yes," I say, while wondering if Lowrance has followed me all the way from Frankfurt or even from New York's JFK International Airport. "There was some difficulty."

I see the boy as he came around the corner of the stone building, the bomb strapped to his chest. I never hesitated to plant a bead on him with my M4. I shouted, "Don't do it. Don't you do it!" Didn't matter if the boy understood English or not. When he continued approaching us, I aimed for the head and fired. Did it without hesitation. Did it because I was trained to kill without remorse.

"We believe the stranger you spoke of on the day of Grace's disappearance is a man who comes from that same village. He's somehow traced your movements and, in retaliation for what happened in the war, has kidnapped your fiancée and is now holding her hostage. You should have stayed in New York as originally ordered."

I feel the breath knocked out of me, the floor under my feet shifting. Behind my eyes I feel a kind of pressure building. I can see, but I sense the onset of blindness once more. If it's possible to hold it back, I will. But something is happening to me. Has been happening for days now. Weeks. A dam is breaking in my head.

"Captain Angel," Detective Carbone breaks in, while pointing to one of the wood chairs set in a far corner. "Would you like to sit down?"

I shake my head. "I'll remain standing, even if I am a bit dizzy. Is Grace still in Venice?" I ask Lowrance. "Or has this man smuggled her out of the country?"

"Thus far we have no reason to believe he's taken her anywhere. But that would most likely be the plan. That is, if she's still alive at all."

Grace, floating in the Grand Canal, her lovely hair swimming in waves like the talons on a jellyfish. Like Karen's hair when she died. I try to drown both images as quickly as possible.

"How can you be sure this . . . man took her?"

"We'd like to show you how we know," Lowrance says.

The door behind me opens again, and this time, David Graham of the US Embassy appears. For a brief moment, his face is hidden by the bright ceiling-mounted track lighting in the large room outside the office. But I know it's him by his clothing, his tall slim build, and his graceful demeanor. His presence is accompanied by yet another wave of déjà vu–like recollection.

217

"Hello, Captain," he says, in his chipper voice. A voice that makes me want to kick him in the gut. But is my fury because of Grace or because of something else not yet completely understood? "Would you care to follow me, please?" he asks.

I agree. But only under one condition. That Anna Laiti accompany me.

Graham gives Carbone a look.

Carbone shoots Graham a similar look. *Not a chance.*

Lowrance shoots Graham his version of the same *no fucking way* expression.

"How about I ask Laiti to write up a new report for CNN?" I say. "Don't hesitate to mention that after blaming me for my wife's disappearance it turns out that she's been abducted by the Taliban. That you assholes kept it a secret until now to save your own bureaucratic asses. That my fiancée could be dead now because of your inaction."

Graham holds up his right hand. "Hold on, Captain. Let's not get carried away. Despite the break in protocol, you may ask Ms. Laiti to join us. This is all bound to go public anyway."

Chapter 56

The five of us enter into an area through the secret door set into the wood panel. In contrast to the interview room, this space is outfitted in black acoustical wall and ceiling tiles, and black rubber-mat flooring laid upon a computer subflooring system. Just about every square foot of space is occupied with computer and surveillance equipment of one kind or another. Several flat-screened LED monitors are mounted to walls along with stacks of electronic equipment too complicated and high-tech for me to recognize, even as a professional soldier in the digital age.

Graham, Lowrance, and Carbone lead Anna and me to a laptop set up on a counter. Carbone sits down in a tall, black leather swivel chair before the computer, swiftly types in several commands, then sits back in the chair contemplatively. After a few seconds an image appears on both the computer screen and every wall-mounted digital monitor in the room.

It's a clear black-and-white shot of Piazza San Marco filmed from a couple dozen feet above the stone surface. Included in the picture is the caffè where Grace and I sat for our last lunch together. In the video, we are seated at the table.

"What you're viewing here," Carbone begins to explain, "is a surveillance video shot from five meters up on the north corner of the cathedral. It took us a couple of days to get our hands on it from the cathedral authorities and then some doing to sort through the video, but we eventually narrowed it down to the twenty or so minutes from your arrival at the caffè to Grace's disappearance."

Anna steps forward, her stocking-covered thighs pressing up against the counter.

"Detective Carbone," she says, "are we about to witness the kidnapping of Grace Blunt?"

"Just keep watching," Graham says, crossing lanky arms over his narrow chest.

On the monitor, Grace assists me with taking my seat at the table. She then makes her way around to the opposite side and sits. A waiter approaches us, takes our orders, and brings us our drinks. That waiter is not the man I would later come to know as Giovanni. It's then that Grace seems to become distracted. She's not looking at me, even though I am clearly speaking to her. She's instead looking over my left shoulder at someone who must be standing behind me.

The overcoat man.

"I'm going to speed things up a bit here to save time," Carbone says, hitting a key that makes the video fast forward. But he stops when a key figure enters into the scene.

"There's the man you spoke of, Captain. You can see him standing only a few feet behind you. He appears to be staring directly at Grace and he's getting away with it, too, because of the massive amount of people already crowding the caffè."

The detective is right. Despite hordes of people moving all around the caffè perimeter and even rudely walking in between the tables, the overcoat man seems to present a formidable figure. Tall, dark, bearded, wearing sunglasses, and slowly approaching our table. He eventually comes so close, Grace is visibly shaken and looks like she's about to scream in alarm.

"You can see the man approach the table," Carbone observes. "He doesn't stand behind you for more than a few seconds before making his move."

On the screen, the overcoat man scurries around the table and makes a threatening move toward Grace. But that's when he disappears. Rather, he doesn't disappear so much as his presence is blocked by a group of tourists who suddenly enter the frame.

"People," I say. "All I see is people."

"Yes, a Japanese tour group entered into the frame at exactly the wrong time," Carbone says. "Or, perhaps for the abductor, at exactly the right time."

"You can eventually make out the man and Grace as they move away from the table," Graham adds. "Watch."

On the screen it takes the tour group maybe five seconds to pass by our table. By then you can see the overcoat man, with his right arm wrapped around Grace. He's forcibly shoving her in the direction of the basin.

Carbone says, "A closer look shows that this man is pressing something into her ribs with his left hand. A gun perhaps. Or a sharp object like a knife."

He clicks a couple more keys and the scene appears far more enlarged but at the same time, far more grainy and distorted. But there is no doubt in my mind of what I'm witnessing. The kidnapping of Grace.

"From there," Graham adds, "we believe he boarded her onto a boat or a barge disguised as a supply vessel, and carted her away. Perhaps to one of the islands. Perhaps to one of the buildings on Murano or Torcello. We just don't know yet."

Carbone turns in his chair to face us.

"We are fairly certain Grace has not left the country. There are only two publicly accessible ways out of Venice other than by water, and that's by train or motor vehicle. Our eyes are constantly monitoring roads, water, and rails and thus far we've picked up no sign of their leaving."

"What about a chopper?" I suggest.

"We've not been alerted to helicopters operating in or around the area since Grace's abduction," Carbone answers.

"We'd know if someone did a hop-skip in and out of one of the islands," Lowrance adds. Then, shaking his head, "I only wish I'd been on the scene just two minutes earlier. I might have caught him in the act."

His words sucker punch me in the gut. "You were already watching me by the time Grace was taken. So you knew there was a possible assassin on the loose. Why didn't you warn us? You could have given us a heads-up. Protected us."

Lowrance nods. "I feel your frustration, Captain. But Interpol orders took precedence, and I was sworn to keep my distance from you and Grace. Other factors come into play also. For instance, you are not supposed to be here. Some army brass might have done you a favor, but you're here at your own risk. I was able to observe you but only from a distance, since, technically speaking, you aren't in Venice at all, but instead, back in New York recuperating."

Anna looks at me, then locks her eyes on Lowrance.

"What's all this mean, Agent Lowrance?" she says. "You used Grace and Nick as bait?"

His face goes tight. "I did what I was told. Observe and report. We'd spotted the man earlier but we still couldn't be sure what we were dealing with."

"Wait a minute," I say. "You knew this guy was coming after me even before I showed up? How is that possible? I mean, how the hell did a card-carrying member of the Taliban even get past customs?"

Lowrance shakes his head. "There are certain elements of the situation I'm not allowed to speak about. But to answer your question as directly as I can, we did not know someone was following you until you got here. If the abductor got into the country he did so illegally and perhaps even had help."

"So then, even though I'm 'technically not here'"—I make quotation marks with my fingers—"you knew I was here."

"Yes," Lowrance says. "We've been following you."

"You're spying on me, just like that Taliban creep."

"Yup," Lowrance says. "For your own good. And the US military's good, naturally."

"But you weren't watching us close enough to prevent Grace's abduction."

"Yup?" Laiti says wryly. "Did you just say 'yup'?"

"Listen, Captain," Graham chimes in. "You are government property and when you defy direct orders, regardless of who helped you out in DC and Frankfurt, a whole bunch of red flags are raised. And if you don't mind my saying so, you should be glad we've kept an eye on you, or you and Grace might be dead by now."

I chew on his words for a bit. He's right, of course; if these men hadn't been watching me they might never have caught sight of the overcoat man. Still, questions remain, not the least of which is . . .

"But you knew what you were dealing with when Grace was taken." Acid permeates my tone.

"Yes," Lowrance says. "Then we most definitely knew."

"But you kept your true identity from me."

"Again, orders are orders. And do I need to mention New York one more time?"

The room goes silent for a moment, its poisonous atmosphere so palpable I can feel it coat my skin like a mist. Maybe Lowrance is right. If I had stayed in New York, Grace wouldn't be missing. But then, if the overcoat man knew I was in Venice, he must have also known I was in New York. And if I stayed in New York, chances are he would have come after me there too. If he wanted to terrorize Grace and me that badly, he would have called on his own intelligence network to track me down no matter where I was. I could point this out to Lowrance and the others, but to what end?

"Perhaps we should concentrate on the present situation," Detective Carbone interjects, "rather than busy ourselves with pointing accusatory fingers."

"Like we have a choice, Detective," I say. "Let's get back to finding Grace. Before something worse happens to her."

Graham clears his throat. "We also have a solid theory as to why the abductor wouldn't want to cart Grace away from Venice," he says.

"And what would that be?" Anna asks.

"We believe he wants to eventually flush out the captain. They want him to find Grace and, once he does, he will kill them both."

"Christ, why not just kill us at the caffè?" I ask. "Why not shoot us in our sleep at our studio? Why go to all the trouble of abducting Grace just to flush me out when he could have taken a shot at me at any point?"

Lowrance and Graham exchange glances.

"It's possible that killing you would be simply too easy," Lowrance says. "Too unsatisfactory for him."

"He wants to prolong the terror," Graham adds. "Prolong the torture. He's testing your pain threshold, teasing you, playing with your temporary blindness like a demented child tortures an insect, tearing off a leg here, a wing there. The bug can still move. It will even live for a long while. But it will be seriously damaged. It will also come to realize how powerless it is."

"But why?" Anna asks, running both her hands through her hair. "Doesn't he realize that with every minute he spends tearing Nick's wings off, he stands the chance of being caught himself? Why risk it?"

"Retaliation," Graham says. "Revenge not only for the bombing of his village, but perhaps something far more personal."

"What could be more personal than the bombing of one's home?" she says.

"That's precisely what we'd like to find out."

Chapter 57

"What happens now?" I ask.

"We wait to make contact," Lowrance says. "He'll want to be heard. It's possible he'll crave the satisfaction of letting you know that he's responsible for the abduction and be only a relative phone call away. Most abduction cases, even military-related ones, involve a ransom. But in this case, the ransom is you, Nick. Doesn't make any difference, though, because we won't negotiate. What we will do instead is to try and get a fix on his location, and then send in a team to rescue your fiancée. Right now, we have no idea where he is." His eyes now locked on Anna. "And I trust we can keep our conversations under wraps for the time being? Is that a plausible request?"

She nods, but then pauses. "On the contrary, gentlemen. Perhaps news of this story is precisely what you need to make our man show his head—to be properly coerced."

Carbone stands, takes his place beside Graham. "She has a point. Time is of the essence. If his inevitable objective is to kill the captain out of revenge, we must attempt to trip him up, give up his position. Do it immediately."

"I agree," Graham says, biting down on his bottom lip. "Agent Lowrance. What about you?"

The Interpol agent crosses arms over chest.

"Maybe you're right. We're dealing with two human lives here, so I will defer to the captain."

"And if we do make contact with him, what precisely do you have in mind for extracting Grace?"

"Can't say until we know exactly what kind of hiding place we're dealing with," Lowrance says. "A building, a boat, a vehicle. You get the picture."

I plant my eyes back on Anna. "How long will it take you to write the piece and have it published?"

"I can get started right away, if you'll allow me the use of your apartment."

Adrenaline fills my battered brain. There's a distinct sound to it, like an orchestra about to reach a climactic crescendo. My already-fragile vision is beginning to fade, the sight flickering on and off. From light to gray to dark and back again.

"Let's go now," I say. "I fear I need some rest."

"Your eyes," Anna says.

"Yes, my eyes," I say. But then, I'm blinded in so many other ways, I want to tell her. Blind to the best way of rescuing my fiancée. Blind to the future.

Once more, she takes hold of my hand.

"I'll lead the way," she says.

Chapter 58

Anna and I arrive back at my apartment. While she sets up her laptop on the harvest table behind the couch, I swallow another sleeping pill. Lying down on the bed, I quickly fall into a deep sleep.

Grace is standing alone in the center of a gondola, her long hair draping her pale face and shoulders like an angel. She's wearing a black gown covered with sequins. The gown doesn't match the rich glossy black finish on the narrow boat so much as it blends into it, becomes one with it. Wrapped around her ring finger is her engagement ring. The diamond sparkles brilliantly in the daylight.

The canal is calm, the water as clean and clear as newly drawn bathwater.

Hers is the only boat on the water while the old buildings and stone canal banks are empty of people. Empty of life. Framing Grace is an arching stone bridge. She begins to float backward under it. I'm not in a boat. I am treading water. I'm floating calmly at first, but then desperately toward my fiancée, my hands outstretched like I'm trying to grab on to her.

But she's moving away from me far too fast, her boat sinking, fill-ing with the clear canal water, her black-gowned body being swallowed up by Venice.

I too am sinking, no matter how hard I try to stay afloat by kicking my feet and slapping at the water with my hands and arms. Then I am underwater and so is Grace. Only she's no longer Grace. She is Karen.

My wife and I lock eyes underneath the silent veil of water. Her expression hasn't changed since she began to sink and drown. She peers at me with wide brown eyes and a slightly open mouth.

The more I sink, the more my lungs constrict, and I feel the need to open my mouth, take a breath. But I know that if I do it, I will drown. I will die.

Karen stares at me. Into my eyes. She knows I'm about to die.

But then the dream shifts, and I am flat on my back on a table. I'm paralyzed. A man is standing over me. He's got a board shoved in my mouth and he's pouring water into it from a bucket.

"Breathe, Nick," comes Karen's calm voice. "Breathe."

"Do it," says Grace. "Do what Karen says."

I open my mouth. I breathe in the water.

And I die.

Chapter 59

Anna is sitting beside me on the bed, my hand gripped in hers, as if she fears I'll drift away into endless outer space unless she holds on to me.

"You were dreaming again," she says softly. "A nightmare."

She dries my forehead with a warm washcloth, presses the back of her hand against my face like she's taking my temperature.

"I saw Grace," I whisper.

"In your dream?"

"She was floating on the Grand Canal. In a gondola. I was swimming for her. We both sank under the surface. But that's when she turned into Karen. We all drowned."

She pats my forehead.

"It was just a dream," she says. "Just a dream."

I sit up, my face close to her face, her eyes looking into my own. For a brief moment, we are desperate figures caught up in a still life. I feel my hand in hers, until I pull it away, slowly, and stand.

"How are your eyes, Captain?"

"I needed rest," I say, looking out over the easel, out the open French doors and into the fading afternoon sunlight. "That's all. Rest and sleep."

My gaze shifts from the doors to the harvest table and her laptop. It's open, a sheet of notes set beside it, a pen sitting on top of the notes, her cell phone set beside the pen.

"And your article?" I ask.

"Finished. Submitted to my editor, and posted. Thank God for the digital age."

"Let me read it."

She stands, then sits down before her laptop and turns it in my direction.

"Please," she says.

I sit down, read the piece from off the CNN website.

It's not much of a piece. But that's not the point. It's the spin Anna has put on the piece that counts. To most people it will seem like a follow-up to the "American woman goes missing in Italy" story published yesterday; this short article states that after further investigation, it's been determined by the Venice police that Grace Blunt was indeed abducted from the caffè in the Piazza San Marco in broad daylight. While no one has claimed responsibility for the kidnapping, the police welcome open contact with the abductor or abductors in order to "consider their demands." The piece ends with the police phone number and website contact address.

I sit back in the chair, run my hands through my cropped hair. "Do you really believe this will work?"

"It's common knowledge the police always claim to never negotiate with terrorists or kidnappers. Publicly, that is. But I think if Grace was taken by a member of an angry Afghan faction or Taliban as payback for what you had to do to their village, then I believe they will want their demands to be heard. Even if that demand is simply one woman's or one man's life. Like any politician or religious fanatic, they crave the soapbox."

"But will we get some kind of proof of Grace's life?"

"We have to wait and see," she says, setting her hand on my shoulder.

She quickly removes it when the phone rings.

Chapter 60

I jump up from the chair. Run to the wall-mounted phone, grab the receiver. In my mind I know now that the only way this creep could have gotten this number, and even acquired a cell phone from some poor soul who lost it weeks ago, is that he has inside help. Taliban sympathizers living in northern Italy.

"*Pronto,*" I bark into the phone, aware the police will record the conversation.

"I see," says the gruff, almost indiscernible voice. "I see."

"Who is this?" I ask. "Do you have Grace?"

"I see," repeats the voice.

"What do you want? Do you want money?"

"I see."

"Please. Tell me. Do you have Grace?"

"Yes. Grace. Yes." It's the first thing he's said to me other than "I see," and what's remarkable is that his voice is without accent. While it's coming through the line shrouded in static, it could be the voice of an American if I didn't know better. But my gut tells me he is the one. He is the one who took my Grace away from me.

My legs turn to rubber. "Is she alive?"

"I see," the overcoat man repeats, before cutting the connection.

Chapter 61

My cell rings. I hang up the wall-mounted phone and go to it.

"Yes!"

"We have confirmation of the call, Captain," Detective Carbone says. "It's from the same cell as before, but this time we are more prepared to track its location. We are trying to trace the location now via GPS."

"Thought you weren't equipped with the Hollywood high-tech."

"Given enough time, we can perform a sophisticated maneuver or two. And you've seen our situation room firsthand. Not exactly a low-tech operation either."

"I'm waiting for the location," I say, my eyes locked on Anna's.

There's some commotion coming from the background. Police yelling at other police. Until Carbone comes back on the line.

"It's Venice, Captain," he confirms. "The call has come from inside Venice. And we have an address."

He pauses, then recites the address to me.

I nearly drop the phone, but manage to hang on.

"Captain," he says. "Captain, are you there?"

"I'm here, Detective. I'm sorry."

"You need to come to the station as quickly as possible, so that we will discuss how to handle our next move."

"On the contrary, Detective Carbone," I tell him. "Perhaps you should meet me here. The address is mine."

Chapter 62

The detective orders us to vacate the apartment, get ourselves to the station immediately. Anna packs up her computer. I grab my coat and my keys. As we leave the studio apartment and head out onto the stair landing, I resist the urge to grab a kitchen knife and begin making a search of the entire building. I know that would be foolish and dangerous. It could result in getting Grace killed, not to mention myself.

We make our way down the stairs to the first floor, all the time feeling as though we are being watched. And my guess is that we *are* being watched.

Detective Carbone is there to greet us as soon as we come through the wooden doors of the police station. He's smoking, which is par for the course, and he is clearly agitated.

"Something to show you," he states, while leading us through the vestibule, through the security doors, and into the heart of the operation. "Come . . . Now . . . Come."

We enter into his office, where Agent Lowrance is already standing before Carbone's big wood desk.

"New developments," the Interpol agent says. "Important developments."

"Not the least of which is this." Carbone comes around his desk, flips up the screen on his laptop.

He turns the laptop so that Anna, Lowrance, and I can clearly see the image. It's Grace. Still dressed in the same black sweater and skirt she was abducted in four days ago, her dark, almost black hair parted down the center of her forehead, her eyes bloodshot and exhausted, but very much alive. In her two hands she grips a newspaper. The *International Herald Tribune*. The date printed above the headline is today's.

"Grace is alive," I say.

"Alive," Anna repeats as if she too only now believes it.

"Did he send this?" I ask, my voice barely able to exit my mouth.

"The 'he,'" Anna interjects. "The 'he,' as in the man who just called you in your apartment? The overcoat man?"

"The overcoat man," says Carbone.

"He is Taliban," offers Lowrance. "He's calling himself Hakeemullah. No last name. Tajik resistance, most likely. From the village you bombed, Captain. As we suspected."

I shift my eyes to Lowrance. "You got all that from his last phone call just a few minutes ago?"

"And more. But not from the phone call. From this photo of your fiancée."

"He identified himself?"

"In transmitting proof of life, he also forwarded a statement. Interesting that it's written in English. Perfect English, like he went to school in the UK or maybe the United States."

Carbone removes a sheet of paper from a file on his desk. Hands it to me.

I am Hakeemullah. I have the infidel's wife. She is alive for now. But she will die for what the infidel has done to my village. For the death he brought to my Dear One.

I read the note and reread it several times over. Each time it says the same thing.

"What does he want?" I say. "Who or what is this Dear One?"

"He's taunting you for now. Dear One could be anything or anyone. Maybe his wife. His dog, his horse, his spirit. Who knows, Captain. You know what war is like. You, better than anyone standing in this room."

"Why so cryptic? Why no demands? Why stay here in Venice at all?"

"He's making you suffer. First he made you wait a few days before being flushed out by our intrepid reporter." He shoots a grin at Anna. "Now he's ready to communicate, but not ready to make specific demands. He took it as a compliment that we were willing to speak and perhaps negotiate with him. It offered him some kind of empowerment and feeling of being respected. He feels like the ball is in his court and he wants to play for a while. Taunt you. Give you nightmares."

"Why?"

"Punishment for what you did to his Dear One. For being an American. For being a capitalist pig, for being free . . . the usual story. But the good news is Grace is alive and close by and you are well enough to see her with unblinded eyes."

I look at her on the computer screen. Look at the copy of the *International Herald Tribune*. I see the fear in Grace's face. I see her hopelessness. If I could jump into the photo and steal her away I would. But I am just as helpless.

"Will he make specific demands eventually?" I ask.

"Almost certainly," Carbone answers. "And soon."

"Not soon enough," Anna murmurs.

"But we're not going to wait for not soon enough," adds Lowrance.

"You have an address," I say, recalling my brief cell phone conversation with Carbone not a half hour ago.

"We know where he is."

"In the building I've been living in for over a week," I say. "Sounds improbable."

"But not impossible," Carbone adds. "In the empty bookstore. On the first floor. Perhaps that's how he's been able to tap into your phone line."

That makes sense. Son of a bitch has been underfoot the entire time. No wonder my soldier's gut was on high alert as Anna and I exited the apartment only moments ago, the sensation of being watched draping me like a robe.

Carbone comes back around his desk.

"We're ready to begin our rescue operation now," he says. "With your permission, of course."

My mind spins; the thought of police raiding the building where Grace is being held hostage is not exactly settling. What if Hakeemullah decides to kill her at the first sign of a raid?

Shoving my hand into my pocket, I feel Grace's ring. There's something more—my soldier's gut, telling me this is way too quick, way too easy. That I'm not meant to come out of this unscathed. "Will it be safe, Detective?"

He nods, smokes. "We will take every precaution. Surprise is on our side." He heads for the door. "Let's move, people. Let's go get Grace."

I follow, my heart in my throat.

Chapter 63

A helmeted and flak-jacketed Anna Laiti and Agent Lowrance occupy the lead outboard-powered boat about five boats up ahead of us. Anna is filming the operation with a small handheld video camera. Behind them is a second boat filled with uniformed and heavily armed police. Another squad armed in ballistic armor and helmets converges on the old two-story stone and brick building on foot. Carbone and I stand in the aft of our boat while an officer drives and a second officer records the proceedings on a larger video camera.

Alarmed at our sudden presence, the boats, barges, and gondolas that traffic the Grand Canal make way for us as best they can. It doesn't take long for the train of police boats to arrive at the feeder canal that runs exactly perpendicular to the Grand Canal. Because it's so narrow, the boat train is forced to proceed one by one, with Anna and Lowrance's police boat taking the lead. We move slowly through the canal as I pray I do not lose my eyesight over the strain of knowing Grace might be in the line of fire should this thing get ugly.

As fast as Carbone's people have organized this raid, the boat train has now slowed to a crawl as the first craft reaches the canal side of the target building.

My building.

Grace's building.

Carbone and I are located so far back the detective suggests we get out and make the rest of the way on foot.

"We will, however, maintain a safe enough distance should the lead start flying, Captain," he adds, grabbing hold of the rungs on a rust-covered metal ladder bolted into the stacked stone canal bank.

Looking up, I spot my studio apartment, the open French doors, Grace's easel and paints set beside them. Over the radio comes some chatter in Italian. I'm having some trouble understanding what's being said. But, as a soldier, I can only imagine the police are announcing their intention to assume their respective positions around the perimeter of the building, and that they will wait for a final approval from Carbone before going in.

I'm about to follow the detective up the metal ladder when the explosion knocks me off my feet, slams me against the boat's floor.

Chapter 64

The explosion rips through the block, sending a shock wave across the feeder canal, loose brick and stone acting like shrapnel, shattering the boat's windshield, causing the two policemen to quickly duck for cover. Carbone drops down into the boat, his head and back colliding with my right side, bruising my ribs.

All breath is knocked out of me. But I shove Carbone away, and together we try to get back up on our feet while the boat bobs on the now-unstable canal. He pulls his service weapon from inside his jacket and goes for the metal ladder bolted to the canal's stone wall.

"You stay here!" he demands.

"Not on your life!" I shout, following him.

Chapter 65

The sounds of screams and moans from the wounded are entirely familiar to me. So is the smell of blasted granite, acrid smoke, and detonated C-4 explosive. A scent that's reminiscent of burnt motor oil. What's not so familiar is knowing that Grace most likely perished in the ground zero of the blast. As I run toward the building, I feel caught up in a nightmare where the stone is quickly turning to mud and my legs are sinking into it, slowing me, drowning me.

Sirens blare from every direction. They echo off the stone walls and inside my head. Police and innocent bystanders are shouting. Screaming. As I approach the building and the site of the explosion, I see the first of the dead lying on the narrow canal bank. I see several bodies floating on the water. One of the bodies is unmistakable. It's Anna. She is floating facedown in the canal, her red hair spread over the water's surface like a doll that's fallen into a bathtub. A policeman attempts to fish her out.

"Grace!" I scream. "Grace!"

I'm running, but I no longer feel like I'm running. The scene before me—smoking rubble, shattered glass, a sinking boat, and still-life bodies—isn't real. It's a made-up dream manufactured inside my head. I don't feel like a participant. I feel like a helpless observer looking in. I make it to within a few feet of the building when the pressure builds and grows behind my eyeballs. I can move no further. I can't move at all.

Once more I want to scream, "Grace!" I want to throw myself into the blast zone, grab hold of her hand, and carry her away from the destruction, but I can only fall to my knees. The pressure behind my eyes grows so intense that my vision begins to go gray and then black. Like steel curtains have come down and bolted shut. I fall forward, feeling the cool damp of the cobble-covered bank and the sharp shards of shattered glass and splintered brick that pierce the skin on my cheek.

Knowing all is lost, I fall into a deep, dark unconsciousness.

Chapter 66

Lying on my back, I slowly focus in on a white ceiling. Hospital white. It takes a moment or two for reality to sink in. For my skin to shed the sensation that I'm waking up from a long and vivid nightmare about Grace being abducted and killed. But when I feel the pinch of the intravenous line needled into the vein on my left forearm, and see a nervous Detective Carbone standing at the end of my bed, I know I have not been dreaming.

I have, in fact, been living this nightmare.

"Grace," I whisper, my voice physically peeling itself away from the back of my throat. "Grace. Is she alive?"

"Grace was not there," he says, his eyes peering into mine.

"She wasn't there," I repeat. "She wasn't in the building?"

"It was a trap. A—what do you say in America—a setup. Neither Grace nor Hakeemullah were inside the building when the explosive was detonated. That bookstore has been empty for some years now. The empty space made it all the easier for Hakeemullah to access it with no one knowing."

I feel at once relieved and at the same time horrified that a Taliban agent still has my fiancée, and has the means to set off IEDs in the middle of a tourist-filled heaven on earth like Venice.

"That bomb was meant for me."

Carbone nods. "Perhaps. But it killed three others instead."

"Anna," I whisper, remembering the feel of her small hand in mine.

"And Lowrance," Carbone says. "They were killed instantly when the bomb exploded only a few feet away from them."

I lie back on the pillow, feeling the weight of three more innocent deaths on my soul. My life seems measured in the number of casualties I cause. My life. A soldier's life.

"Hakeemullah," I say after a while. "Have you heard anything from him since the blast? Did he claim responsibility? Has he attempted to make contact?"

"He has thus far been silent. But we are scouring Venice for him without trying to alarm a daily stream of many thousands of visitors. The blast has of course made international headlines. Nothing like this has happened since a bomb was detonated outside the Uffizi in Firenze in ninety-one. Now the story of your missing fiancée is spreading all over the world. Also the story of your operation in Afghanistan."

An eye for an eye . . .

"Revenge," I say, sitting up, the needle in my left arm pinching my flesh. "This is why war never ends. Revenge."

"What happened in that village, Captain?" Carbone says. "What happened after the bombs were dropped?"

"I'm not at liberty to discuss what happened after the bombing."

"But it was bad, wasn't it?"

"Worse than you can imagine."

"I am old enough to recall your Vietnam. The things that happened there. To some of the villages. The people who lived in them. Women. Children."

247

"It's a hard thing to live in fear, Detective Carbone. And in war, you live in fear all the time."

"I have been to war. I have witnessed the things it can do to people like you."

"And now Grace."

"Yes. Now Grace."

Soon a nurse comes in. In Italian she apologizes for interrupting. Carbone nods politely in her direction, takes a step back as she checks the levels on my drip and then proceeds to take my temperature.

"I'm not sick," I mumble over the electronic thermometer.

But the nurse merely gazes up at me and smiles like she doesn't understand what I'm saying. Maybe she doesn't.

"I'm not sick," I repeat as she removes the thermometer. I say it directly to Carbone.

"You've been through a lot," he says. "You passed out. Your eyes. Your nerves. You are here to recover. But all you have found is turmoil, threats, attacks, and now death. Rest here while we figure out our next move, Captain."

The nurse reads the thermometer, makes a note on my chart, which hangs on the end of the bed by a metal hook. Then she exits the room.

"What's our next move, Detective?"

Carbone crosses arms over chest. I know he's jonesing for a cigarette right about now. But you can't smoke in the hospital. Not even in Italy.

"Another Interpol agent will no doubt be assigned to this case. Perhaps even a team now that the situation has escalated. I must also worry about what could be a network of terrorists. Plus copycat attacks."

"Meanwhile, Grace is still out there. With him."

"She is alive. That's what matters. Believe me, Captain, he will make contact with us again and it will be soon." He gathers his coat and his hat. "I will let you get some rest for now. In a little while I will come back to check on you and perhaps have a plan in place for finding Grace."

"Please," I say.

"No more bombs," he says, as he leaves the room.

"No one else dies," I say, closing my eyes.

Chapter 67

Maybe twenty feet separate me from the boy, but it's not hard to make out the tears that are falling from his big brown eyes. He weeps as he bears the burden of the package not in his arms but strapped to his chest.

That's when the reality of the situation washes over me like a wave. The package—the thick black vest strapped to his shoulders and chest—is an IED and the boy is the delivery mechanism. As he steps toward me, I see his hand reach for a cord that dangles from the bomb. There's a device attached to the end of the cord. A trigger mechanism.

Shouldering my M4. "Don't do it!" I scream. "Don't you do it!"

Pressure behind my eyeballs, beads of sweat coating my forehead, a brick lodged in my throat, adrenaline making my pulse pound in my temples. I don't hesitate to kill. It's an act as natural as breathing. I am conditioned to act and react. But this time, the reaction isn't as automatic.

I've never fired on a child before. But this child is a bomb. A living bomb.

The boy comes closer, the sound of his weeping audible.

"Don't you do it. Please, don't you do it."

His face is in the crosshairs; he is already dead.

My index finger depresses the trigger and I don't let go until the magazine is emptied out.

I wake up, startled, breathing heavily. This dream is worse than all the others. There's nothing surreal to pass off as the product of my subconscious. Only reality.

Memory.

The truth.

⌣

I fall back to sleep after a time, and when I wake up again, it is full night. The room is dark, the only visible light coming from the space between the wooden door and the tile floor and from the small square glass embedded into it at the top. My mouth is pasty dry, a profound thirst making me feel like I'm back in the arid Afghan badlands instead of inside a Venetian hospital.

I reach for the water cup on the table beside me, but I find I don't have the strength to lift my arm. It's then I realize I must be medicated. Sedated. Makes sense. I am already a casualty of war. The victim of severe PTSD. I suffer from an unexplainable temporary blindness. And now I have become the casualty of another kind of war.

The door opens.

Someone from the hospital support staff steps inside, closes the door behind him. Not all the way, but only partially, so as not to disturb my sleep by letting the hall light spill in. As he steps closer, I make out green scrubs, a matching green surgical mask covering his mouth, and a matching cap on his head. A gauze bandage covers his right eye. It's slightly skewed, held in place with white surgical tape.

He does not bother to see if I'm awake or not. He does not speak to me. He goes straight for the drip, unplugging it at the top and adding another clear vial to the line, and then reconnecting the line.

"Hey," I attempt to say. "Hey." But my mouth is parched. I only manage to utter a pathetic grunt.

His job completed, the man turns, goes for the door. Opening the door, he shoots me a look over his left shoulder. He smiles at me.

"I see," he whispers before disappearing from view.

Chapter 68

Black sky fills my eyes. Black sky filled with brilliant stars. I wonder if I have died and this is what traveling to heaven looks like. It's
precisely the way I imagined it as a child. Leaving my earthly body
and becoming an angel who soars through time and space on a pair
of wings made of white feathers.

But I am not traveling through space and I am not dead.

I am instead lying flat on my back, all one hundred eighty pounds
of my body pressed against the flat bottom of a wood boat powered
by what sounds like an outboard motor. Wrists duct taped together.
Ankles bound in the same manner. A duct-tape gag covering my
mouth.

I am the newest hostage of the man controlling this boat. Looking up at him, I see him plain enough in the dim, bow-mounted
red and green lights. He is tall and bearded, his right hand gripping a black steering wheel that looks like it's been yanked off an
old pickup truck. His black hair is cut close to the scalp. He wears
a long overcoat, which has become his trademark. Wears it in direct

defiance of the police who by now must have memorized his physical description.

He is the overcoat man.

His name is Hakeemullah.

I bombed his village and killed a boy who was trying to kill me and my men.

He took Grace.

Now, he has taken me.

⌣

The water beneath the boat is rough. Choppy.

I'm straining to get a bearing. But for the time being, all I see is night sky. I do my best to gather up some clues, make a logical determination as to my position relative to Venice. We seem to be riding on open water. Unsettled open water. The basin comes immediately to mind. Makes sense too. The overcoat man would want to drug me, sneak me out of the hospital under the apparent blind eyes of police security, then transport me off the main island as quickly and efficiently as possible.

Precisely which of the smaller islands he's taking me to is a mystery. Darkness surrounds me like a cool wet blanket. But after a few minutes, the darkness is interrupted by illumination. Forcing my head up off the boat floor barely half an inch, I'm able to see something in the near distance. It's the top of a tower made of brick. A tower that's lit with lamps from top to bottom.

The church tower of San Giorgio Maggiore.

For now anyway, I'm heading in that direction.

Toward an ancient island dedicated to a saint.

⌣

Still we proceed slowly for a while more, until the overcoat man drifts up to a dock, the water never still.

Two men are there to greet him.

One of them jumps down into the boat. He drapes a thick black cloth hood around my head so that I am once more blinded. He and the other man lift me out of the boat and set me down on a wood plank that serves as a crude stretcher. They quickly carry me the length of the dock and into an old island settlement that's made up of small wood and stone houses and shops. That is, if my memory serves me right. They do not speak, but I make out the thick soles on their boots slapping against cobbles. We travel like this for what seems an hour, but what must constitute only a few minutes.

The island is asleep at this hour. The only people awake will be the bums and the drunks. Even the fishermen will still be asleep.

We stop.

I recognize the sound of tumblers dropping, a mechanical bolt releasing, and the squeak of old hinges forced to survive in salty sea air and to bear the burden of a heavy wooden door. Quickly I am shoved through an opening so narrow both my arms rub up against the door frame.

As soon as I've cleared the opening, the door slams shut behind me.

For the first time, someone speaks.

I do not know what he is saying, but I recognize the language. It's Tajik. These are northern Afghans. Survivors from the hot village I was forced to neutralize, no doubt. I'm not aware of precisely how many of them survived the bombing run. But the Tajiks know how to hide underground. They know how to survive in tunnels and caves. They know how to survive the centuries of invaders.

Now, the sound of a padlock being unlocked, and a heavy chain being pulled out from steel rings. Next comes the squeal of more hinges. I'm moving again, this time at an incline. I'm being transported down a flight of stone stairs into a basement. A basement that immediately surrounds me with cold damp and the smell of mold. Most of Venice can't support basements because of the high water table and the constant flooding. But this island must offer some high ground, at least enough for this partial basement or crawl space.

When we come to the bottom of the stairs, I am carted another few feet into the interior of the musty room. I am dropped onto my back on a wet gravel floor. I collide with the packed earth so violently, it takes my breath away. A fist grabs hold of the top of my hood and it is suddenly yanked off. It takes a moment for my eyes to adjust and, for a brief few seconds, I'm convinced I'm about to once more lose my eyesight. But I don't lose my eyesight.

I see clearly.

The room is dimly lit with only a bare lightbulb dangling overhead by an exposed electrical wire. The two men who carried me down here work as a team, lifting the plank while setting a cinder block beneath it so that I am no longer parallel to the floor but instead set at an angle, my feet elevated and my head lowered, the blood rushing to my brain.

The two men strap me to the board tightly with more duct tape. Fast and efficiently, like they're no strangers to the process. I've been drugged and the result is paralysis. But now there's no chance of moving my limbs at all once the drug wears off.

Whispering a spattering of words to one another in Tajik, they pull a plastic supermarket bag over my head. Just as the men step away, the painful squeak of rusted hinges fills the room and sets an ominous tone for what's to come. The bag has blinded me, but it does not interfere with my sense of smell. When I make out the odor of incense, I know that the man who's come in the door is him. The overcoat man.

Hakeemullah.

I want to shout, "Grace!" But the tape gag silences me.

Words are spoken between the three men, and then comes the sound of water being poured from an open spigot, filling an aluminum bucket. This is what I'm picturing in my overheated brain.

My chest is heavy, like my lungs have been filled with concrete.

"Hello, Nick," speaks the voice I've come to recognize from the phone, from the hospital room. "We are not strangers, you and I. We knew one another in a former war. Now we can get to know one another even better in another land. In Venice."

He might be talking in riddles, but his English is nearly perfect, almost without accent. He's referring to me by my first name, like we're not strangers or enemies.

"I don't expect you to remember me from all those years ago," he says. "After all, the purpose of the program was that we forget everything, no matter how dreadful. Like waterboarding, for instance. Do you remember the first time you were waterboarded?"

Click . . . *On my back on a table in a basement . . . A tall, dark-eyed, dark-haired young man standing over me. A second man has shoved a board in my mouth, forcing it open. The second man is baby faced, brown eyed, and always smiling. They are both my friends. My friends pour the water into my open mouth . . .*

I sense something being lifted, held over my head. When several drops of water slap me on the forehead and chin, I know for certain it's the water bucket.

"Here's another question, Captain. Why did you bomb my village?"

A slight commotion follows.

The bucket being tipped.

When the water slaps me on the face, it doesn't simply pour off the plastic bag and onto the floor. Rather, the water feels as if it's penetrating the plastic, filling my mouth, running down my windpipe, entering into my lungs and stomach. I'm drowning. Lungs filling with filthy water.

My reflex is to gag violently. To convulse against the tape that binds me until one of two things happens: the tape splits or my bones break. Again, I'm screaming but no sound is coming out other than something horrible and guttural deep down inside of me.

"You were fucking killing us," I want to spit in answer to his question. "You were shooting us and mortaring us night after night. Killing us."

The flow of water stops, and I suddenly realize it hasn't violated my mouth and lungs but only given me the sensation that it has.

"Tell me again, Captain," Hakeemullah goes on, "what makes a man insult God by killing so many innocent souls inside a small village? Or perhaps God has nothing to do with it. Perhaps man wasn't formed in God's image at all, but something else. Something evil. Isn't that what we were taught all those years ago? What value was there in capturing my village? The hill it was situated on? What strategic value in destroying it?"

The water pours again and once more I'm drowning, my world going from light to dark to light again as consciousness begins to take its leave while my brain is fooled into believing it is being deprived of oxygen.

The water stops.

"You fucking tried to kill us first," I say against the tape. But no words can be heard.

I inhale through my nostrils. That's when I discover that the torture is not all psychological. Some of the water has breached the bag and penetrated my nostrils. Water has entered my lungs and stomach and I am now regurgitating it. Vomiting. But the gag is preventing the filth from leaving my system. I'm choking on my own vomit. If he doesn't remove the gag, I will die.

"Are you aware that waterboarding was invented in Italy during the time of the Renaissance? How interesting that the creators of such magnificent works of art and architecture could give us something so frightening and destructive."

Why the hell is he telling me about the origins of waterboarding? I've never waterboarded anyone in my twenty years as a soldier. Not once.

Or am I lying to myself?

The flash of memory invades my brain in brief, rapid snippets. *Me standing over a man strapped to a table. A man with dark eyes and dark hair. A tall young man who was my friend. It's the same table I was once strapped to. I'm pouring water into his open mouth and I have no guilt over my actions, no compassion for the pain he is enduring. I am following orders I've been conditioned to follow. If my friend dies, well then he dies . . .*

The bucket is lifted over my head once more. Tears fill my eyes, run in reverse down off my brow, collect inside the waterlogged plastic bag.

Son of a bitch . . . You Tajik son of a bitch . . . Why didn't I kill you when I had the chance?

"Why did you kill my dear one when you could have shot his legs out from under him?" he says. "Shot his shoulders? Why did you shoot his head off?"

The heavy stream of dirty water immediately follows. The flow never seems to stop and as I struggle for a breath through my nostrils, I only manage to swallow more water, like a boat that's sinking fast.

"Why did you kill my son, Captain Angel?" Hakeemullah screams as something inside my body snaps, and the hell I am living gives way to nothingness.

Chapter 69

I might be dead, if not for my dreams.

I'm lying on my back inside a hole that's been dug out of the ground. The hole is rectangular and maybe six feet deep. It only takes a second or two before I realize I'm lying inside my own grave. A number of people are standing along the edges of the grave, peering down at me. I look up into their faces. I see Detective Carbone and Heath Lowrance, and I see David Graham and Anna Laiti. I see men from my squad, all of them dressed for battle, M4 Carbines slung around their shoulders. I see Karen, her hair and clothing still wet from the river.

And three more people.

Hakeemullah. He's wearing his wool overcoat, his beard trimmed, his dark eyes wet and angry. Standing beside him is Grace. Cradled in her arms is a child. A toddler. A little boy whose face has been blown away so that it no longer resembles a face.

"Don't fight it," Grace whispers.

Tears pour out of Hakeemullah's eyes. But soon the tears turn to streams of water that are as powerful as a fireman's hoses. The water shoots down upon me in the grave. I begin to gag, choke, drown . . .

When I come to, I can still see. The two men who carried me from the boat into this building have removed my gag, and cut away the duct tape that bound me. Doesn't matter much, since I can hardly move a muscle. As they carry me into an adjoining room, I can only wonder how long I've been out.

Two minutes or two hours.

I've been transferred to a second basement room surrounded by old walls of stacked stone. Ancient stone. The room is as barren as an old woman's womb and just as cold. But it is not empty. Sitting up against the far wall, her knees pressed up against her chest, is Grace.

My Grace.

Dressed only in her underwear.

Duct tape covers her mouth and binds her wrists. She's awake, staring at me with wide eyes, her filthy hair draping her face like a veil. I can tell she's trying to say something to me. But she can't possibly speak through that gag. My stomach is still sickened, my lungs aching, my limbs feeling as if they weigh five hundred pounds apiece. My heart pounds, but not for me. It pounds because my Grace is alive.

Grace is alive.

Chapter 70

Footsteps. Coming from above. Pounding on the floorboards. Then, a door opening. Footsteps descending a second stone staircase into the basement.

It's him. Hakeemullah.

He's holding a long blade in his right hand. It's not exactly long enough to be a sword, but it's too long to be a knife. The blade is wide, shiny, and curved at the end in the shape of a crescent moon. The weapon of a horse-mounted warrior maybe. A mullah.

He allows the blade to brush his right leg, the sharp edge of the steel grazing against loose trousers. Looking up at him from where I'm lying on the dirt floor, I see that his eye is bandaged heavily, as if the eye has been knocked out of its socket, or cut out. There is a dark red, almost black bloodstain in the area where his eyeball should be. He's moving his mouth. He's saying something, but he's speaking it silently. Until the silence becomes a whisper.

"I see," he mumbles under his breath.

My eyes shift from his face to Grace's. She too is watching him, her chest bulging in and out in great heaves of breath. I know she's panicking. She sees the knife. She's watching it graze his leg. She's feeling the pain and the burn of the knife as if it were already entering into her flesh. I cannot see her like this. Not when I am so helpless.

"I see," he repeats, his voice growing louder.

Something begins to happen to my eyes then. They are suddenly losing their focus, as I knew they would. As I feared they would. I shift my gaze back to Hakeemullah. His eyes are focused on mine. Deep pools of black ink.

"I see," he says again, this time the "see" ending in a long drawn out "zzzzz." Like "seeeeezzzzzz."

My eyes cut out on me.

"I see," he repeats yet again.

Along with his voice, I make out the sound of water lapping up against stone walls. I hear muffled voices coming from the basement room attached to this one. Faint voices speaking in Tajik. I hear the very distant hint of a motorboat, and I swear, I hear the delicate voice of a songbird.

I hear something else, too.

I hear Hakeemullah's voice. But I no longer hear the words "I see." Perhaps I never heard the words "I see." Maybe I was deaf to the actual word he was speaking to me. Because if I concentrate . . . if I listen closely, I know for certain that he is not saying "I see."

No. He is saying something else entirely.

He is saying, "Aziz."

Chapter 71

"Aziz."

When you are undergoing bouts of temporary blindness for which there seems no cure, your hearing becomes acute. The words coming from the mouth of a man who appears to have kidnapped your fiancée will sound like "I see." But he is not saying "I see."

He is saying, "Aziz."

A part of my job in Afghanistan was not to fight with the rebels, but to speak with them, to negotiate with them, to try to make them understand the process of peace without terror or the trading and distribution of heroin. Like I've said many times before, combat should be waged only as a last resort. In doing so I was able to pick up some Tajik and some Arabic. Not a lot, but some words and phrases here and there.

One of these words was Aziz.

It means *Dear One*.

Boots shuffle on the gravel floor.

Just a couple of steps.

The steps move away from me, not toward me. When I hear the faint sounds of struggling and screaming through a duct-tape gag, I know Hakeemullah has approached Grace. I know he is doing something to her and that I can't possibly come to her rescue. I am helpless and useless.

I am blind. I can't move.

I close my eyes as if this will help shield me from what he is doing to her. I somehow see her gagged face, though I don't want to see it. I try to turn off all my senses, all of my abilities to see something without the use of my eyes. I want to be blind and deaf. I want my sense of smell and taste to disappear. I wish for my heart to stop and my brain to cease functioning. I want imagination to be erased and my ability to paint a vivid picture of what is happening to my Grace only a few feet away from me on this cold damp floor.

God in heaven, I want to die.

From where I lie on the floor on my side, I hear Grace thrashing about, her torso and legs slapping the hard-packed earth like she's a fish that's suffocating out of water. I try gathering up all my strength, use it to shove my body forward in her direction. But a boot heel connects with my shoulder, pushing me back. Tears pour out of my blind eyes. My lungs have become two overinflated balloons about to burst.

Until the room falls silent.

Chapter 72

The noises coming from Grace have suddenly stopped. No longer am I able to hear her body thrashing about. No longer can I hear her muffled screams and gasps. I no longer register anything other than stillness and calmness.

I can't help but think the worst: Hakeemullah has killed her.

He has cut her with that knife. Cut her neck. Perhaps even beheaded her. Did it while filming the act for the Internet with a digital video camera. Maybe even his smartphone. Will my decapitated Grace show up on YouTube for the world to see, much to their horror? To my horror?

God have mercy on our souls, for we know not what we do . . .

I try again to shimmy my body toward hers. But now, in the silence, I'm not even sure which direction to move.

I am a failure.

I am death.

I make out the cloth-against-gravel sound of a body shifting itself, then rising up off the floor.

Footsteps.

I smell a musty odor. A raw, organic scent. Like old clothes that have not been washed in ages. I breathe in the faint odor of incense and spices. Cooking spices. Then I sense a body lowering itself beside me. Not so close it touches me, but so close I can almost feel its heart beating.

"His name was Aziz," he whispers. "Dear One. And he was my son. My only son. You ordered an airstrike on my village. You killed our elders. You killed our animals and destroyed our homes. You killed our women. And you killed my little Aziz. My Dear One. You took his life and you broke my heart."

I see what's left of the face of the boy I killed. Bits of flesh mixed with a mash of blood, brains, shattered bone, and black hair. But I also see him carrying a bomb meant to kill me and my men. See the detonator gripped in his hand, his thumb only a half second from depressing the trigger. This man is his father. But the father is a hypocrite. Because he must have wanted the boy to die. And now he has killed Grace in revenge for doing what I needed to do to prevent my men from dying.

"My Dear One is an angel now," he goes on. "He resides in a paradise you cannot begin to understand. I wanted you to know that. I wanted you to know how it feels to lose something so precious, Nick."

I feel the *click* in my brain.

Karen . . . her car being dragged out of the river, her body still strapped to the driver's seat . . . Karen, pregnant with our child . . .

Tears push up against the backs of my eyeballs. The fury, building up inside my soul, like a boiler fire being stoked. I want to kill this man. Tear him apart with my hands.

I say, "I'm no stranger to death . . . the death of someone you love with all your heart. And you are no better than me. You strapped a bomb to your son. You killed him. Not me."

"It wasn't me. It was the elders who insisted upon it. They had to hold me back while they strapped that bomb to his chest. I kept praying to God that the bomb wouldn't work, or that you and your men might arrest him before it was detonated. Instead you shot him . . . You fucking shot him in the face."

"His thumb was triggering the device. I was almost as close to him as you are to me now."

"And you shot him dead." He's crying now. "You stole the life from my Dear One. And you know what? You know what makes it even more tragic? I would have done the same thing. It's what we were trained to do. But that didn't make me hate you any less. So when I had the chance to make you suffer, I took it."

He falls silent for a moment while I begin to make out his panted breaths. From down on the floor, I can practically smell the salt in his tears. But then he says, "Ask yourself this question, Captain Nick Angel: Why am I not dead yet?"

Grace . . . I thrust myself forward, reaching out for her. But he stiff-arms me in the sternum, shoves me back. I feel the blade tip suddenly pressed up against the underside of my neck.

My head spinning, heart beating, breaking. "Okay, I'll play the game, asshole. Why am I not dead yet?"

"You don't remember me, do you? It's okay, you're not supposed to. Rather, you're not supposed to remember much. None of us are. Even I still don't recall most of what happened, most of the past. But then, that's the way the program was designed. So that none of us remembered a thing. But what they didn't bank on was that one day, the memories would begin to return. One day, we would slowly but surely start to remember everything. And when that happened, we would begin to talk. We would become liabilities."

"What the hell are you talking about?"

The blade tip presses harder, breaking the skin, drawing blood.

"You'll know exactly what I'm talking about once you remember. But then, you've already been remembering things, haven't you? Something goes snap inside your brain and a little bit of memory emerges. It's not a pleasant experience. More like one black hornet after the other landing on your forehead, stabbing you with their stingers. Only with each painful sting comes a new memory. Déjà vu, triggered by another person's touch, or his voice, or his smell. Even your blindness is a symptom of what can happen when the memories begin to return after so many years."

"Go fuck yourself," I bark.

But he pushes that blade against my neck. The pain is sharp and breathtaking. At the same time, something is happening to me . . . the shadows once again revealing themselves. *Lying on a gurney in a brightly lit room, a strange uniformed woman doing something unspeakable to my sex, while white lab-coated men look on . . . Bare chested outside in a gravel-covered yard that looks like it belongs to a max security prison. I grip a fighting knife in my right hand. So does my opponent, who lunges at me, plunges the blade into my shoulder . . . Lying in fetal position on a padded floor, the cacophony of battle piped in so loud my eardrums bleed . . . A baby-faced man strapped to a table, as a board is shoved in his mouth, and I pour water from a bucket down his throat. Do it with a smile on my face . . .*

Three soldiers, one of them me, trapped inside a basement surrounded by concrete walls. We're naked from the waist up, strapped to chairs, electrodes hooked up to our skin, bright lights shining in our eyes, loud heavy-metal music blaring, the lab-coated men standing behind a thick glass embedded in the wall, monitoring us . . .

I sense now . . . no, that's not right . . . I *know* these flashes of memory are not imagined. They are not delusions. They are not lifted from a movie or a book. They are not the hallucinatory product of the PTSD. They are the cause of the PTSD. They happened to me.

The shadows are real.

"We were friends once. Don't you remember? We served together, along with Heath Lowrance in Operation Desert Storm. Third Battalion, Seventy-fifth Ranger Regiment. We were good soldiers. Good fighters. Better than good. Perhaps even fearless. You remember, don't you, Nick? I was the Afghanistan-born young man who'd moved to the States as a teenager and now, I was a US citizen who took up arms in the battle for freedom. My name was not Hakeemullah then. It was Benjamin Sobieck, a name adopted by my parents, who wished for us to be as Western and American as possible."

It's coming back to me now. Fast. As if his words are the catalyst I've needed all along. *A tall, wiry man of dark complexion. He's wearing the uniform of an American soldier. An Army Ranger. He's smiling, holding his hand out for me. Another man, also tall. He's got black hair, and big brown eyes, and although a scraggly beard covers his face, he has a boyishness about him that is infectious. Lowrance. The three of us sitting in a Kuwaiti bar not long after combat, cheering our victories.*

Then ten years later. It's only days after two airliners were used like ICBMs and deliberately crashed into the Twin Towers. I see us being choppered to a secret site, where we meet with a man inside a trailer. He's tall, groomed impeccably, and always smiling the smile not of a happy man, but that of a diplomat. But he is no diplomat. He is a CIA agent who wishes to recruit the three of us for a project that is so top secret, there is no record of it anywhere to be found. That man is David Graham.

"Project MKUltra," I whisper, my Adam's apple bobbing up and down against the blade tip, my stomach doing flips, knowing that not only is my past coming back to me, but it might be indirectly responsible for Grace's death. "I remember now. They resurrected Project MKUltra in the wake of 9/11. The things they made us do to one another. To test us. Our resolve, our guilt . . . our memories. Waterboarding, hand-to-hand combat, electrical torture, sleep deprivations . . . fucking electroconvulsive shock therapy."

"They transformed us into something every army wants, Nick. Modern, twenty-first-century assassins with an almost superhuman ability to dish out death and to withstand torture."

Downtown Baghdad, behind enemy lines. Dressed all in black, gripping a fighting knife. I'm coming up on a man from behind, plunging the blade into his side, muting his mouth with my free hand. When he's down on the ground, I slice his throat. From ear to ear...

I see a dozen killings just like this one.

Breaking into a residence in Ramadi, slicing the throat of a man and his wife while they sit at the dinner table, stealing a satchel of documents, stepping over a crying child as I make my escape into the night... Five Saddam loyalists down on their knees outside a junkyard up in Kurdish country. I pull the trigger on each one of them, without hesitation, without prejudice, without feeling... Setting fire to a hilltop barn doubling as a weapons depot in northern Afghanistan, my 9mm gripped in my shooting hand. Shooting each robed man as he exits the structure. Head shots, all of them... A nighttime raid on a Taliban hideout, a single grenade taking out a dozen leaders... A village I am ordered to bomb by command. The village houses a little boy who is turned into a bomb. I neutralize the boy with a head shot...

That's why I have never missed a conflict in more than two decades of near constant war. I'm an assassin. I am conditioned for war. Conditioned to kill. Conditioned not to feel any of it. Until I killed Aziz. Until I killed Hakeemullah's boy.

He smiles. "Amazing how the floodgates of memory burst wide open when those big, impenetrable doors are given just the slightest nudge," he says. "You see, the CIA knew that the wars we would face in the coming years and decades would not only be extremely difficult, they would be never ending. They would take a special brand of soldier. Because, after all, what better way to fight a fanatical fighter who embraces his own death than with another fanatical fighter. Which is why they developed a soldier who could kill without prejudice and guilt, who could withstand torture without breaking, could employ torture without compassion. You see, it's the humanity in us that makes us poor killers. It's the revulsion, the guilt."

The pressure of the knife blade against my neck relaxes just a little.

"A soldier who would be immune from the dreaded PTS fucking D," I say.

"Operation Perfect Concussion. It was a secret revival of MKUltra after that program became illegal in the 1980s. It utilized sub-aural frequency blasts to erase memory. Sensory deprivation, drugs, isolation in order to achieve selective amnesia. They worked on altering our personalities so that we would become attracted to war and battle rather than repelled and crippled by it over sustained periods of time . . . even decades. We became perfect killers with the ability to engage in military activities without memory of them, so that in the event of capture and interrogation, the events could not possibly be recalled. But what it resulted in, in the long term, was delusional disorder and acute psychological repression."

"They tried to make us inhuman."

"We tortured one another in that hellhole down inside the tombs of that secret site. Did unspeakable things." He grins. "That scar on your shoulder. We were made to fight one another. With our bare hands, our teeth . . . with knives. I stabbed you out in that hot yard, and you fell. I could have run the blade across your neck and killed you off then. I would have thought nothing of it. Perhaps if I'd succeeded then, my village would be whole, and Aziz would still be alive."

"I went back to war again and again. After my first wife died."

"Each time we were subjected to the violence, the torture, the conditioning, we were whitewashed of our memories. Then, when it was all over and we were physically recovered, we were made to go our separate ways. You went back to war. Lowrance entered into the Special Forces. I became a double agent of sorts."

"You went back to Afghanistan." A question.

"Not as a traitor, but to infiltrate the Taliban. In turn, I would deliver crucial information back to the CIA. I was still following orders. But after a time, I chose to break away from my keepers and fight for my Tajik people. I changed my name, renounced my US citizenship, and fought the new enemy. The same US military who had trained me to be a killer without remorse."

"Are you telling me we met on a battlefield as big as northern Afghanistan by chance?"

"I'm telling you that it's possible you were sent to kill me. After all, what strategic relevance did my little village on the hill in the middle of nowhere hold for you? Now that our memories were returning, it's possible the CIA decided to eradicate us, one by one."

"And you," I say. "Did you recognize me on the day I shot your boy in the village? Did you know that was me when we visited the afternoon before, and tried to speak with you about giving up your weapons?"

"I recognized you," he says, nodding.

"Why didn't you just kill me then?"

"Let's go back to my original question of why I haven't killed you yet."

I shake my head. "I don't know. Maybe you want to kill me out of a personal revenge for your son, but then you don't want to kill me because we were friends once. Brothers in arms. That sounds awfully sentimental. But if you've harmed Grace, I won't be so sentimental. I'll blow your fucking brains out."

"Spoken like a true modern assassin. But I can tell you this, for as many chances as I've had to kill you, I did not arrange that explosion under your apartment. That bookstore was my safe house, the place where I would meet up with Graham. He was angry that I stole

Grace. It wasn't supposed to play out like that. But then, how else could I avenge what you did to my son? An eye for an eye. That's the way I thought it through. But I never had any intention of killing her. Just scaring her. Scaring you."

"But Lowrance died. Was that intentional?"

"Lowrance had no idea who Graham was," he says. "The memories had yet to come back to him. I led Graham to believe I had no idea who he was either. He worked with me because he knew I wanted to get to you. That I wanted revenge. He wanted me to kill you, even made arrangements so I could kill you."

"But you didn't. You simply stole Grace."

"And all three of us combat brothers were nearly killed in that explosion." He exhales. "We have something in common now, Captain, besides being trained assassins. I am partially blinded for life."

The knifepoint presses against my neck once more, a droplet of blood running down my neck.

"Are you going to kill me now? Did you kill my Grace?"

It's only the pain I fear. The first few slices of the neck. Until the jugular is severed. Nothing more. I want to die now. If he has cut Grace and allowed her life to bleed out, then I too want to die. What more can he do to me, now that Grace is dead?

"I know now there is no bringing my son back to me, Captain. There is no way to replace him, any more than we can rebuild the old stone walls of the houses in my village, any more than we can return the blood to the bodies of my people and your soldiers. Any more than we can forget about Operation Perfect Concussion. It is over now. All I want to do is return to my country to live out my days."

Maybe I deserve to die for what I did to him. To his little boy. I prepare for the sharp slice, to feel the warm blood running down my neck, but instead, he pulls the knife from my flesh and I hear him shuffling across the room.

"I will tell you what I will do on behalf of my Aziz," he says. "I am going to enact the rule of law from your own Christian Bible. I am going to take an eye for an eye. When Grace's eyes are plucked from her head, and your blind eyes are plucked from yours, you will both see the light of God."

I scream as I listen to him grab hold of Grace. She struggles, and although she is gagged I can make out her terrified shrieks. There is a violent pounding, like he has picked her up and tossed her on her back.

"Be still," he says, like a father trying to put an agitated child down to bed. "Be still, please, be still."

In my head I see the tip of that blade entering her eye socket, and like St. Lucy centuries before, the first of her two eyes being plucked out. Rage courses through my veins. Rage and adrenaline. The life returns to my limbs. Forcing myself up onto my knees, I launch myself at his body, thrust him onto his back. I can't see in which hand he holds the blade, but I manage to grab both his wrists, which I slam against the gravel-packed floor while head butting him in the face. The blade comes free of his grip, and I feel his lips explode, his nose break, and his front teeth scar my forehead before they break inside his mouth. He screams something from deep within his black soul.

"Aziz!" he screams, the word mixing with the soup of blood and mucus that now surely fills his mouth. "Aziz!"

Then, the sound of footsteps, heavy and rapid. Two or three bodies descending the stairs. The door slams open, as if it's been punched by a battering ram.

Men enter the room.

Soldiers. Police. I know them without having to see them.

The sound of hobnailed boots slapping against stone and hard-packed dirt floor.

Orders shouted. Assault rifles shouldered. Rounds chambered. Suddenly a bright white light shines in my face. I sense the light in my open eyes despite the blindness. It's so bright it makes me want to close them. I release Hakeemullah and thrust myself backward. I know without having to see him that, despite his wounds, he's once more snatched up his blade.

Three sharp shots ring out, reverberate against the stone walls.

Blood spatter slaps my face.

His body drops like a heavy sack of rags and bones.

I kneel motionless while someone approaches me and, in perfect English, asks me if I've been hurt. Another soldier shouts out the same words. "Are you hurt?" But they are not directed at me. They are meant for Grace.

"Grace," I say, the word barely coming out. "Grace . . . Grace."

"She is okay, Captain. Do you understand me? She is alive and unhurt." I know the voice. It's spoken with a heavy Italian accent. Detective Carbone.

I feel a great wave of something wash over me then. It engulfs me and fills my veins with a relief so profound, I'm not sure I can speak another word. I drop onto my side, open my eyes wide, and wish only to see Grace again.

And then it comes back to me, like a light switch turned on inside my brain. My vision. Blinking my eyes rapidly, I see Grace, see that she's alive. I see Carbone, standing in the center of the room, a semiautomatic gripped in his hand. I see two more soldiers outfitted with black ballistic gear and gripping automatic rifles. I see Hakeemullah lying on his back, the hole in his forehead bleeding crimson arterial blood.

I also see one more man.

David Graham.

Chapter 73

Graham has switched up his diplomatic suit and tie for military greens, over which he wears a military-style, multi-pocketed utility vest. A mode of dress he is not entirely unfamiliar with, it turns out. I pull myself up off the floor, one eye on Carbone, and the other on Graham.

"You're not a diplomat," I say. "And you never worked at the embassy."

"Captain Angel," Carbone interjects, "perhaps I should explain something—"

"Shut up," I say, my eyes shifting to Grace, who peers at me from behind the two nameless soldiers. "You don't have to explain. Graham here is running the show and always did run the show. Isn't that right, Agent Graham?"

Graham takes on one of his smiles.

"Captain Angel," he says. "Look on the bright side. You have your fiancée back. You have life and what's even better is you have your memory back. How wonderful is that?"

"That bookstore was my safe house, the place where I would meet up with Graham. He was angry that I stole Grace. It wasn't supposed to play out like that."

"I have my life because you fucked up. When I didn't kill Hakeemullah in his village, you made it possible for him to follow me. What you didn't plan on was his refusal to assassinate me right away. It's true, he made me suffer, but I think in the end, he might never have killed me or Grace. He was still a killer, but he'd also become a human being again, just like I was becoming human. Just like Lowrance would one day become human again, had he been allowed to live."

"This is quite the crazy plot you've cooked up here, Captain." He laughs. "Clearly you need rest. You're suffering from acute PTSD. You need immediate hospitalization."

"Really? I'm crazy? How did Hakeemullah get that cell phone? How did he get the number to the apartment? How is it he had a key and always knew where to find me? How is it I even managed to get to Venice? You worked it out so that he would get to me no matter what. You've been pulling the strings all along because you need to erase your past. Your illegal CIA operation. The best way to do that was to get all three of us to kill one another, and when that didn't work, you set the bomb."

"This is absurd. The words of a crazy man. Arrest him before he does damage to himself and others."

When Carbone makes no move, Graham turns to him.

Carbone looks at me, then at Grace. Finally, he says, "Arrest him on what grounds, Mr. Graham?"

"Because you know what can happen should you disobey my directive."

In my head, I'm picturing the detective and Graham arguing in Carbone's first-floor office days before. Now I know why. Graham has something on the detective that might destroy his career. Or something worse.

Carbone nods.

"Okay," he says, "I've accepted a few bribes in my long career. Maybe it will mean the abrupt end of my work, but I tell you this, Mr. Graham, this man and his fiancée have been through hell. I will not arrest him."

Graham turns toward the two soldiers. "Apprehend this man!" he shouts. "That is a direct order."

But the soldiers do nothing.

Reaching inside his jacket, Graham pulls out his sidearm. He aims the barrel at my face.

"Nick!" Grace screams.

"Put the gun down, Graham," Carbone says. "You have no right."

"No right?" Graham says. "Captain Angel is US government property. In the event that the property becomes a danger to himself and others, it's my duty to neutralize him."

He thumbs the hammer back, takes a step forward so that the barrel is almost pressed up against my forehead.

"Graham!" Carbone shouts.

"No, Nick, no!" Grace shrieks.

The two soldiers lunge forward at the same time the trigger is pulled.

Chapter 74

I'm down on my back again before I realize the trigger that was pulled was not Graham's, but Carbone's. He stands beside the faux diplomat, shaking his head, a nearly invisible trail of smoke rising up from the barrel on his gun.

Graham has dropped his semiautomatic, and now his hands are raised up over his head, so high they nearly touch the low ceiling of timbers and heavy wood planks. I'd like to think Carbone's warning shot put the fear of God into Graham, but you'd have to be human for fear to have any effect on you in the first place. Graham simply dropped his piece because that's the way he chose to play it. The Venice police wouldn't be arresting an American CIA agent. And as for the explosion that killed Lowrance? That was still going to go down as a terrorist attack.

Graham lowers his hands, looks me in the eyes. "Once you're in, there's only one way out. That's the way it works. That's what you signed on for."

Turning, he heads for the exit.

"I was retired yesterday, Graham," I call out. "Today, I'm even more retired."

But he takes the stairs without saying another word, as if he hasn't heard me.

Grace rushes to me, and as I get back up on my feet I take her in my arms and hold her so tightly, I feel I might break her.

"You're okay, my love," I say. "You're going to be okay."

She sobs, her tears running down my cheeks and hers.

"How could I ever die on you?" she says. "I'm your state of Grace, after all."

We hold one another for a long moment, until we turn to Carbone as he bends at the knees, retrieves Graham's weapon.

"In all my years of police work," he says in his rich raspy voice, "I never once shot a man. Not . . . once." Standing, he slips the automatic into his jacket pocket. "I'm happy that my streak continues."

"Killing is a terrible business," I say. "Take it from one who knows."

"It's too bad that it has to be a business," he says.

"Let's get out of here," I say.

He pulls his eyes away from the body, nods, and pats the pockets on his suit jacket.

"Damn," he says. "Out of cigarettes once again."

"Come on," I say, "I'll buy you a pack back in Venice."

We head for the stairs. But before I take them, I turn to gaze once more at Hakeemullah. The look on his face is not pain. It is not sadness, nor surprise. It is peace. Perhaps what they say about heaven is true and he is now back with his boy. Like life, nothing in death is guaranteed. But it helps to believe that one day, men like Hakeemullah and me will be forgiven.

Chapter 75

Grace and I have been transferred to the same Venice hospital where Hakeemullah snatched me up four days ago. Now that many of my memories have finally come out from behind the shadows, I don't seem to be having any more problems with the hysterical blindness. But then, not all of the memories have revealed themselves, and only time will tell when it comes to regaining 20/20 vision 24/7.

Grace shares the bed beside me and she continues to sleep off the effects of her prolonged nightmare. Other than the frightening situation Hakeemullah put her through, she's unhurt and unwounded. But she does bear the scars of her emotional struggle. In the end, what happened in Venice was not motivated by war, or the bombing of a village, or even the CIA's illegal Operation Perfect Concussion. It was motivated by the loss of Hakeemullah's child. In the end, my old friend lost his life and perhaps that's the way he wanted it. To lose his earthly life and spend eternity in paradise with his beloved Aziz.

———

"Feel this one," my fiancée tells me a week later. Her voice is insistent yet light and happy. I make out the sounds of many voices, the clatter of plates on the metal tables, the clinking of wineglasses, the unhurried laughs of the lovers and friends who come to this caffè to fall in love, or fall in love again.

I hold out my hand, palm up. Grace sets something inside it.

"Now, don't cheat," she insists.

My eyes are already closed. But I try to shut them tighter. As if it's possible for my lids to come down any harder than they already have. I close up the fingers on my hand, make a fist around the object.

"Well," Grace says, "let's have it."

I feel a solid metal band. It's cold in my warm palm. There's no stone attached to it. It's just a plain ring.

"Couldn't you come up with something harder than this, Gracie?" I say, not without a laugh.

"Really see it," she says.

"I see."

"No, you don't see. How can you? Your eyes are closed."

"That they are. But you wouldn't believe what I see when my eyes are closed."

"What do you see?"

"You, me, in bed. The windows open, the breeze blowing on our pale skin."

"You can open them now, Romeo. Or should I say, Casanova?"

I do it. I also open my hand and reveal a gold band. A wedding band. My eyes fill.

"Go ahead," Grace whispers, her voice choking. "Read the inscription."

I hold the ring up to my face so that I can read what's been inscribed in the band's interior. I see, *My Love. My Life. My Heart.*

"It's too early to wear this."

Grace reaches across the table, takes hold of my free hand, squeezes it.

"You've earned the right. We. Us. We've earned the right to be married before a priest or a judge tells us it's so. Screw the rules."

"I guess we've always been married. Even when we were apart."

Grace exhales a breath, and once more paints a smile on her face. This smile is different. It carries with it a different message.

"Now *feel* this, Captain," she says, once more reaching out for my hand. "Gently," she adds, placing my hand on her flat belly. "What do you feel?"

Blood fills my face. Warm blood. I feel Grace and what might someday grow inside my Grace.

"I'm home, Gracie," I whisper. "I'm finally home and healing."

We sit like that for a while. In silence. Not needing to speak. Needing only to feel one another's hands. One another's presence. One another's heartbeats. We don't dare release our hold on one another. Not even to steal a drink of our wine.

"Are you ever going to open the envelope Detective Carbone gave you yesterday after he took our final statements?"

It begins to rain.

"Methinks soon . . . But not yet, me lady."

I can hear the sound of the raindrops falling on the canvas awning above us, and against the stone cobbles of the square. I imagine the heavy raindrops making thousands of small splashes and explosions in the water that's collected in the stone fountain across the way.

"You were with her, weren't you?" Grace says after a time. "When Karen died."

Inhale. Exhale. "Yes."

"Why did it take you so long to tell the truth about it?"

"I've always been telling the truth about it. I just haven't been telling the whole story. It's possible I just didn't want to remember everything. Remember what happened that day when our car ran off the bridge."

"Was it really a suicide?"

"I think she could have gotten out. But she didn't even try. When I tried to save her, she wouldn't move. She just kept staring at me, like that was what she wanted. But there was only so much air, only so much time. In the end, I saved myself. I put it all out of my mind for a long, long time. Now I remember everything."

"Do you think if you hadn't become a part of that CIA project soon after, you would have remembered everything?"

"Forget the bad. That's part of what the project was all about. Selective amnesia. For a long time, I packed up the memory of Karen's death, stuffed it inside a drawer."

Grace gives my hand a little squeeze, stares down at the table.

"And you forgive me? For what happened with Andrew?"

"Some things are better off forgotten."

Another squeeze. She looks up again.

"Tell me now," she says. "Are you or are you not going back?"

Flashing inside my brain, the image of a hill in a valley surrounded by crystal-clear blue sky. The sound of screaming jet engines breaking the silence. Then two explosions that rattle the earth. I see myself climbing the hill only to come upon a little boy. If I had my way, I would erase it from my memory bank forever. But I can't. It's impossible to erase all the memories. Erase them forever. You can only create new memories while trying to put the old ones behind you.

"I'm making my own separate peace now," I say after a slow beat. "My wars are over. I can give you that. I want to give you that, Grace. I want to give our own Dear One that. When the time comes."

285

I stare into her green eyes, take in her black hair, her thick lips, her slightly blushed cheeks. I see tears begin to slowly fall down those cheeks and I want to swallow them. Swim in them.

Behind us, a boy has begun to kick a soccer ball in the square. He's kicking the ball against the fountain, in the rain. Some of the people who occupy the surrounding tables take notice of him, and they begin to laugh and smile.

Grace turns and eyes the boy. He's dressed in a button-down shirt, a blue crewneck sweater with a small square patch with the name of his school embossed in its center over his heart, short pants, and black shoes over ankle socks the color of red wine. A boy who's just gotten out of school for the day and who now wants to play in the rain.

Grace turns back to me.

"Well," she says, "shall we?"

I toss a twenty-euro note onto the table and together we stand, head out from under the awning and into the rainy square. As if anticipating us, the little boy kicks the ball to me and I kick it to Grace. She laughs and kicks the ball back to the boy and the rain begins to soak her hair. It begins to soak my leather coat and pelt the cropped hair on my head. I look up at the sky and I see the clouds and the raindrops falling from them. Every one of them is for Grace and for me. I let the rain soak my face. Let the raindrops fall into my open eyes.

I see now. See with full clarity. See the meaning of it all.

I see my life flash before my eyes like a lightning strike off in a distant horizon. I am haunted by its fleeting essence, tremble at the thought of losing this moment forever. But then, it is already gone.

Grace continues to kick the ball back and forth with the little boy. I reach into my pocket then, pull out a plain envelope with my name scrawled on it in blue ballpoint. I tear open the envelope and pull out its contents. It's a small photograph. A handwritten note is attached to the photo with a paper clip. It reads, "Graham asked me to pass this on to you." The note is signed "Carbone." I stare down at the photo as the raindrops pelt it. I see a much younger version of myself standing beside three men. Heath Lowrance, Ben Sobieck, and Dave Graham. We're dressed in our desert combat gear, M4s slung over our shoulders, helmets stuffed under our arms, thick heads of hair disheveled, week-long beards sprouted on our fresh faces. Behind us is the never-ending desert and there's a plume of black smoke rising up from the burning oil fields in the distance. But the smiles on our faces are unmistakable. Victory smiles. Turning the photo over, I see another note written in a different script. It says, *Brothers in arms, Kuwait, 1991.*

Standing together in the rain in the square, I lock eyes with Grace. She smiles and so do I. We're learning how to love one another again. We're learning to love. We're making progress. Seeing one another for the very first time.

Going to her, I hold out my free hand. She takes it in hers as she bids the now-drenched little boy a heartfelt good-bye. Together, we head out across the square toward the stony banks of the canal that will lead us back to our hotel. I feel her hand in mine and I hold it tight. I hold on to my state of Grace like she is the last breath in my lungs and just as dear.

Over my shoulder, just beyond the corner of a crumbling brick building, the Grand Canal appears for us. The boats and gondolas bob in a thick green wake that never sleeps. The water flows in from the sea through channels and feeder canals like blood through arteries and veins. It splashes up against the stone walls and wooden piers and it seems to speak to me. I toss the photograph in and watch it float away on a ripple that blends in with a thousand other ripples just like it. The water destroys the memories and it cleanses, makes things new again.

It belongs to me, to Grace.

And it is eternal.

Author's Note

The CIA's selective amnesia project, Perfect Concussion, also known as Subproject 54, is said to have been canceled and therefore, never carried out. However, detailed information on the psychotronic weapon development program has been systematically erased by the editors of Wikipedia as well as numerous other online information sources over the course of several years.

Acknowledgments

It might come as a surprise that *When Shadows Come* started out as a short story called "Portrait," which I wrote prior to entering the MFA in Writing program at Vermont College back in the mid-1990s. Apart from being my most anthologized piece to this day, one of my then writing professors suggested I consider fleshing it out for a novel. Something that seemed logical to me at the time, but also a frightening task of gargantuan proportions. After all, when a writing prof suggests a project, you know it's going to be not easy, but impossibly hard.

That said, I wrote nineteen novels before I was able to take on the task of "fleshing out" the short story. But in the end, I'm glad I took up the challenge, as exhausting as it was. And as for that encouraging professor, wherever you are, a long-overdue thank-you!

But I also owe a whole bunch of deserving literary pros a profound thank-you as well, not the least of whom is my T&M developmental editor, Caitlin Alexander, whose guidance and vision allowed me to shape this novel into something extraordinary and hopefully, timeless. Along editorial lines, I'd also like to extend heartfelt thanks to Kjersti Egerdahl for being the first person to recognize the possibilities of this book. Also Alan Turkus, for encouraging me to raise the bar higher with each attempt at one of these Hitchcock-inspired psychological literary thrillers. Also JoVon Sotak, my new editor, friend, and cheerleader. The title *When Shadows Come* did not arrive easily, but it was honed from the brilliant mind of my publicist and bud, Jacque Ben-Zekry. No surprise there. I also owe a shout-out to development editor Holly Lorincz, agents Chip MacGregor and

David Hale Smith, my boyos, Jack and Harrison, and my favorite daughter, Ava.

Lastly, thanks to everyone who has supported me over the past twenty years and twenty novels, be it in the form of encouragement, food, drinks, cold hard cash, or all of the above. I couldn't have broken through without you. Here's to the next twenty books.

Cheers,
Vince
November 13, 2015
Florence, Italy

About the Author

Photo © 2013 Jessica Painter

Winner of both the 2015 ITW Thriller Award for Best Paperback Original and the 2015 PWA Shamus Award for Best Paperback PI Original, Vincent Zandri is the *New York Times* and *USA Today* bestselling author of more than twenty novels, including *Everything Burns, The Innocent, The Remains, Orchard Grove,* and *The Shroud Key*. He is also the author of the Dick Moonlight PI series and the Chase Baker Thriller series. A freelance photojournalist and solo traveler, he is the founder of the blog *The Vincent Zandri Vox*. He lives in New York. For more, go to http://www.vincentzandri.com/.